BOOK TWO
OF THE
ST. EDMUNDSBURY
MYSTERIES

PENITENT'S SWORD

ANNE-MARIE AMIEL

HEADLIGHT FLUID PRESS

PENITENT'S SWORD

Copyright © 2022 by Anne-Marie Amiel

This is a work of fiction. With the exception of those characters whose lives and conduct have been recorded in historical works, any resemblance to persons living or dead is coincidental. The Crusades and the locations in which the action of this book take place did exist, and every effort has been made to portray known history as accurately as possible at this distance in time.

Editing: Elizabeth Patrick, Headlight Fluid Press
Cover: Cathy Helms, Avalon Graphics
Formatting: AuthorTree

FIRST EDITION
Printed in the United States of America
ISBN: 978-1-956992-02-1

https://annemarieamiel.com

Dedicated to my mother, Eileen Mary Amiel, who sacrificed much and loved more.

ACKNOWLEDGMENTS

As always, there are more people than I could possibly name whose words or deeds have contributed to this book. I would like to single out just a few to thank for their particular contributions to this instalment in the St. Edmundsbury Mysteries.

First of all, there would be little enjoyment of this work of fiction had I not a great editor. Libby Patrick finds all the knots and nonsense that needs fixing, and I'm deeply grateful to her for her hard work and great skill.

I would also like to thank the owners and staff of The Dillard House Inn in Georgia. When I need somewhere quiet to write, somewhere that inspires me to write well, and somewhere where the phone and the day-to-day stresses of work do not interfere with my efforts, I go to this beautiful place in the Georgia mountains. A fair bit of this book was written by the window of Eddie's Cottage in Dillard.

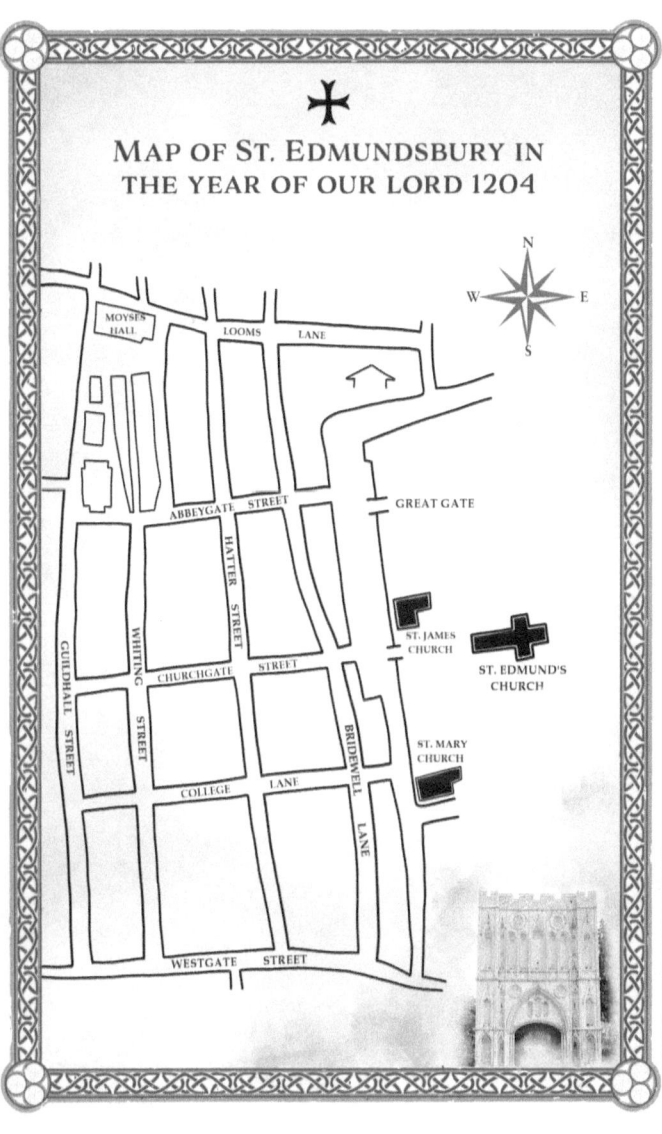

MAP OF ST. EDMUNDSBURY IN THE YEAR OF OUR LORD 1204

N
W · E
S

MOYSES HALL

LOOMS LANE

GREAT GATE

ABBEYGATE STREET

HATTER STREET

WHITING STREET

GUILDHALL STREET

CHURCHGATE STREET

ST. JAMES CHURCH

ST. EDMUND'S CHURCH

BRIDEWELL LANE

ST. MARY CHURCH

COLLEGE LANE

WESTGATE STREET

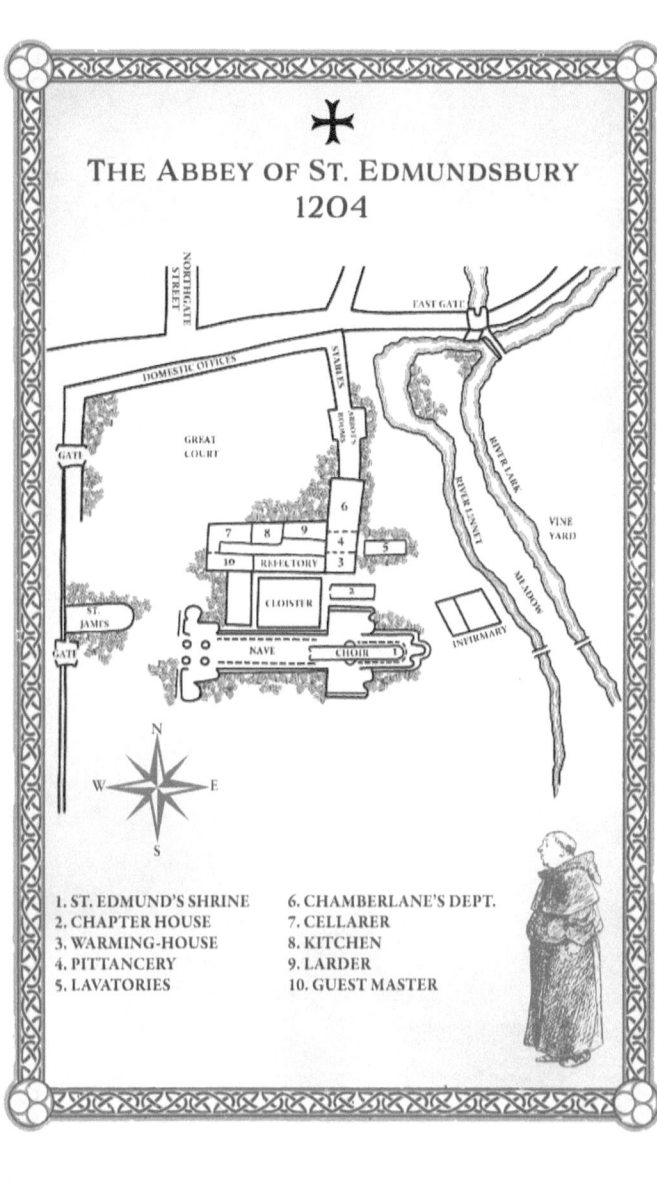

THE ABBEY OF ST. EDMUNDSBURY
1204

1. ST. EDMUND'S SHRINE
2. CHAPTER HOUSE
3. WARMING-HOUSE
4. PITTANCERY
5. LAVATORIES
6. CHAMBERLANE'S DEPT.
7. CELLARER
8. KITCHEN
9. LARDER
10. GUEST MASTER

Historical Note

The Abbey and town of Bury St. Edmunds are real, and Abbot Samson, Brother Jocelin and the reeve really lived. Bury St. Edmunds was founded about 600 years before the time of this story and was originally called Beodericsworth. The name was changed to St. Edmund's Bury in the 10th or 11th century, the word "bury" coming from the Germanic/Norse word for a fortress. Eventually the town became known as Bury St. Edmunds, and so it remains today.

Bury is still a market town, although the Abbey was destroyed in the time of King Henry VIII and little remains today except for ruins. You can see the ruins if you pay a visit to the Abbey Gardens, which lie behind the only gate of the Abbey still standing. The streets along which the characters in this book walk are also still there, as is the market square (which still functions as an open-air market on certain days of the week).

Much of what we know about Bury St. Edmunds at the beginning of the 13th century comes from the journal of a monk of the Abbey named Jocelin of Brakelond, who recorded the daily events in the area from 1173-1202. Brother Jocelin was the Guest Master of the Abbey for periods of time during his life, and I have made him so in this story, although we do not know anything of his history after the end of his chronicle in 1202.

While Sir Gilbert de Cley and Sir Thomas Warren are fictional characters, the de Warenne family is not fictional. The first Earl of Surrey fought with William the Conqueror at the Battle of Hastings and was greatly rewarded as a result. He and his wife later went to Rome and, having visited a Cluniac monastery in the course of that journey, founded a Cluniac priory on their own lands once they returned to England.

The Via Francigena, also known as the Chemin des Anglois, was a pilgrim route for those who wished to visit Rome and the tombs of the apostles Peter and Paul. It made its way from Canterbury through France and Switzerland, and then on to Italy. It was not one road, but rather a choice of routes that changed over time with the vicissitudes of trade, politics, and pilgrimages. There were several routes over the Alps, Pontarlier being one of the last stops before one of those crossings on the way to Rome.

Churches in the early Middle Ages did not have pews. Until the early 13th century members of the congregation all stood. Even when seating began to be provided it was only sporadic, and it consisted mostly of hard seating around the walls of the church. In this story there is some limited seating at the front of the church, provided for the nobles in attendance.

In this book there is mention of a Mystery Play. These plays were among the earliest style of play performed in medieval Europe. The plays could be presented over as much as a three-day period and focused on presenting Bible stories as tableaux with accompanying religious chant. Gradually, prose in the local language was added, and civilian actors began to take on the roles of the Biblical characters. Popular subjects for the plays were stories of the creation, Adam and Eve, the murder of Abel by Cain and the Last Judgment.

Several swords, and the legends surrounding them, appear in this book. The legend concerning the finding of Charlemagne's saber in the tomb is one that was often repeated in medieval times. The sword that is the centerpiece of this story is taken from a sword discovered in the Great Ouse River some years ago. It was in very good shape except for a large hole in the blade just below the guard. It was dated to between 950-1000. The sword had iron inlay and the word "CONSTAININUS" on one side of the blade, and "+INOMINEDOMINI+" on the other. The original can be seen on display in the Museum of Archaeology and Ethnology in Cambridge, England.

A similar sword that was found in Fornham, near Bury St. Edmunds, can be found on display in Moyses Hall Museum in Bury itself. As readers of this series will know, both Fornham and Moyses Hall were well known to Aileen and Robert.

The Emperor Constantine was converted to Christianity in 312 A.D. on the eve of battle. He alleged saw a vision of a cross of light in the sky with an inscription saying, "In this sign thou shalt conquer." Although the emperor's conversion may have been as political as it was religious, the Roman Empire became Christian from that day forward.

All chapter heading quotes are taken from the King James version of the Bible.

Glossary Of Medieval Terms

Some words and descriptions that were in common use in 1204 may not be known to you. They include:

Abbey School: Abbot Samson established a school for poor scholars during the time he was abbot. Tuition was free, and the opportunity was given to boys of free men of the town.

Clodpoll: Clodpoll (or clodpole) is an archaic word used to call someone an idiot or a fool.

Different as Chalk and Cheese: This expression originated in the 12th century in England. It was first used in connection with a shopkeeper who swapped chalk for cheese in order to make a profit.

Grin and Bear It: This expression may well have been in use at the time of this story. It comes from the Old English for "show one's teeth in pain or anger." In this case bearing it means to endure.

Hair/Wimpole: In the Middle Ages, married women were expected to keep their hair hidden by their wimples. It was only unmarried girls or women of "low" character who would be seen with uncovered heads.

Liberty: The Liberty of St. Edmund was the term for all the land under the control of the Abbot. He effectively stood in the king's shoes, levying taxes and acting as the judge in civil and criminal cases.

Marshal: In medieval times the marshal was a senior official in a lord's household. He had charge of the fighting men and reported to the lord. Within the household he was second only to the steward.

Niello: Niello is a mixture generally made into a paste, used as an inlay on engraved or etched metal. It is made from combining sulphur, copper, silver, and lead.

Rag and Bone Man: Also known as bone-grubbers, rag-gatherers and several other similar titles, these itinerants were present in medieval England, although they were probably far more common in later centuries. They would travel on foot or by horse and cart, gathering any old rags and bones they could. The bones were sold on to merchants who would make glue and fertilizer. Rags were purchased at a price dependent on the quality of the fabric and would then be torn into strips and woven into yarn which was then made into cloth called "shoddy."

Reeve: In most towns, the Reeve was the man who did the police work for the nobleman appointed Sheriff of the whole district. In Bury St. Edmunds, though, there was no civilian sheriff, and the Reeve had less power. He reported directly to the officials at the Abbey.

Small Ale: This drink, which contained very little alcohol, was also known as small beer. Often more like porridge than pure liquid, it was commonly drunk in the Middle Ages because the water supply was often polluted, and true beers and wines were too expensive for most people to drink on a daily basis.

South Sea: This was the name given to the English Channel in Anglo-Saxon times, and it remained so until later in the Middle Ages.

Steward: The steward was probably the most powerful official within a noble household in the Middle Ages. He managed the lord's estates and frequently was in charge when his lord was away.

Villein: Medieval society was very hierarchical. Locally, the lord of the manor was top of the heap. Bottom of the heap was the serf. A villein was not exactly free, but he had more rights than did the serf. A villein was a tenant farmer who was subject to the lord's will. He owed dues and services in exchange for the land he was permitted to farm.

1. Chapter One

For the word of God is quick, and powerful, and sharper than any two-edged sword, piercing even to the dividing asunder of soul and spirit, and of the joints and marrow, and is a discerner of the thoughts and intents of the heart.

Hebrew 4:12

"It was the dead man's sword!"

Sitting on the banks of the River Lark as the sun's falling rays glided over the smooth water, Aileen and Robert looked with surprise at the boy who had burst out with such a statement. Friends from childhood, the trio made a striking picture against such a backdrop: Aileen, a willowy young woman with laughing grey eyes and curly brown hair sitting close by Robert, a gangling young man only a year older than herself, the possessor of piercing blue eyes and a smiling face. Hugh, a few years younger, seemed to diminish into the background in comparison to the lively pair. His slight frame, coupled with his ash blond hair, soft blue eyes, and quiet voice, made his words all the more startling.

"What dead man?" asked Aileen.

"What sword?" asked Robert at the same time.

Hugh looked from one to the other, his breaths coming quick and shallow and his face as white as paper.

Seeing his distress, Aileen leaned over and took his hand. He grasped it as though he were a drowning man offered a rope.

"It's all right, Hugh," she said. "Take a deep breath and then just tell us what has happened and why you asked Robert and I to meet you this evening. You know we will do anything we can to help."

Hugh's grip on Aileen's hand became less painful, and his breathing began to slow. Thus encouraged, Aileen continued calmly: "We have scarce seen you since you became a scholar at the Abbey School, Hugh. We were glad to hear you were doing well. Surely nothing has happened at the school to so concern you?"

"No," responded Hugh. "I have worked hard to reward the faith the Abbot had in me to take me as a scholarship pupil. Not many sons of blacksmiths are so honored, and I know that my father and mother are proud of their younger son."

"Then what is this about a dead man and a sword?" Aileen urged the boy as he paused.

"It's so hard to explain," said Hugh.

"There is still time before we must leave," said Aileen. "Just start at the beginning and tell us what has happened."

"Yes, and start with the sword," instructed Robert. Aileen shot him a warning look.

"The sword really is the beginning of the tale," said Hugh.

Settling more comfortably on the grass, Hugh began to talk. "Last Thursday, a pilgrim brought father a sword to repair. He said he had been sent by his lord to offer the sword as a gift at the Shrine of St. Edmund but that the pommel was damaged, and his master did not want to offer the saint anything but a perfect gift."

Hugh paused, turning a blade of grass between his fingers, and then continued.

"Father examined the sword carefully. He told us that night that the sword was old, but he did not think it as old as the pilgrim believed it to be."

"Did he say that to the pilgrim?" Robert asked.

"No," said Hugh. "He would never say anything that would offend a customer."

"Of course not," said Aileen, again shooting a look at Robert.

I had probably better keep my mouth shut, thought Robert to himself. I seem to be doing nothing but saying the wrong thing.

"So did he repair the sword?" asked Aileen.

"Yes," Hugh said. "He had thought that the pilgrim would return Saturday or, if he could not come before the Sabbath, today. The man had told my father that he would not tarry in St. Edmundsbury for more than the time it took to offer the restored gift at the shrine."

"But the pilgrim did not return?" Aileen said.

"No," responded Hugh. "And today my father realized why he had not come."

Aileen and Robert said nothing, but they leaned closer in joint anticipation.

"This morning, my father learned of a man who had been discovered murdered on the Sabbath morn," said Hugh, his voice rising a little.

"John Fuller came in early this morning with a broken plough he needed my father to repair. He could do little but talk about the pilgrim found dead in the ditch by the vineyard on Sunday morning."

"That is so sad," said Aileen. "I had not heard of such a death. I did see Mistress Palmer, the robemaker, talking to one of her friends in the Great Court at the Abbey this morning. They looked shocked about something, but they stopped talking when I approached. Perhaps it was about this poor man."

"Mayhap it was," said Robert. "Go on, Hugh," he continued, impatient to hear more of the tale of the sword and the dead pilgrim.

"My father is, as you know, little inclined to gossip," Hugh said. "But something the farmer said made him pay attention."

"What was it the farmer said?" asked Aileen.

"My father told us that John Fuller said the pilgrim was found without a cloak but with his purse intact. The purse hung from a very fine belt with a silver buckle in the shape of a boar's head."

"Most thieves would take anything of value," Robert said. "Are they certain the man was murdered and did not die of natural disease?"

"Not with a knife wound in his chest," said Hugh.

"Certain murder then," said Aileen. "But what was it that concerned your father?"

"The man who brought him the sword to repair had such a belt," said Hugh. "My father noticed it particularly because the buckle was so fine. The man, whose name he gave as Aylwin, said it was one he had from his father."

"It would seem then that this Aylwin must be the murdered man," Robert said. "But surely there is nothing about this to concern you or your family."

"It would seem that there is some mystery about the deed itself, though," said Aileen. "Is that what troubles your father, Hugh?"

"Yes." Hugh said.

"But I don't understand," said Robert. "Your father is a blacksmith of renown. Many people bring him work. Some are from the Liberty, some are strangers. Why does this death so touch your father?"

"You know my father to be a man of few words," said Hugh. Aileen and Robert nodded.

"His words are always direct and plain, but to those of us who know him, his stern appearance does little to hide his true feelings." Hugh paused to collect his thoughts.

"When father told us he realized who it was who had been murdered, it was clear he was disturbed," the boy continued. "He told us Aylwin was a man after his own heart. He was a Saxon and a plain-spoken man. Yet he was fiercely loyal to this Norman lord whom he served. My father liked what he saw, and thus he was saddened to hear of his violent death."

"So must all men be by such news," said Robert. "But still, I do not understand why you sought us out."

"The taking of a man's life by a desperate thief is not, I fear, uncommon," said Hugh. "But father was disturbed by the mystery of this failure to steal the victim's valuables."

"Mayhap the killer was disturbed in the course of his deed," offered Aileen.

"That is what my mother said," responded Hugh. "But father said if that were the case, then the alarm would have been sounded during the night, not the following morning, for surely whoever disturbed the murderer would have found the poor man lying where he fell."

"This is a mystery indeed," said Robert thoughtfully.

"Your father thought about this much, did he not?" said Aileen.

"Yes," Hugh said. "He became uneasy about the sword and began to wonder if that had anything to do with the killing."

"Is it so unusual a weapon then?" asked Robert.

"Father did not describe it to us," said Hugh. "All he would say is that the sword to him did not seem in keeping with the tale woven around it. Aylwin did tell him that the sword had been made for a Christian hero, but more than that he would not say. In the end, my father decided he would take the sword to the reeve for safekeeping and tell him about Aylwin's visit."

"And did he do so?" Aileen asked.

"Yes, he took the sword to Master Durand today," said Hugh.

"What did the reeve say when he heard your father's account?" asked Aileen.

"He thanked my father for bringing the weapon to him but said that he did not think that there could be much motive for anyone to wish to kill a man for such an old sword."

"Was that all he had to say?" Robert sounded almost indignant.

"No," said Hugh. "Durand said that if it was a good weapon the murderer wanted, then there were many finer swords to be seen in the town on any day. Yet Master Durand did acknowledge that if the story of the sword having belonged to a Christian hero was true, then there might have been some value if the killer were to sell it."

"That is true," exclaimed Robert. "Mayhap the murderer had heard tell of Aylwin's sword and thought to steal it and fatten his purse."

Hugh shook his head. "The reeve went on to say that he did doubt that this was what happened. He told my father that if the murderer had heard tell of the sword, then even the most desperate of men would know that others would hear of it as well. He would have to leave the Liberty in order to make his bargain in safety, and that is a journey of two days or more. Most thieves would not risk the roads for such an uncertain prize."

"Master Durand then did dismiss the idea of the murder having been committed by a thief desiring the sword?" asked Aileen.

"Not completely," Hugh said. "He said one who heard the tale and coveted the sword for himself might have dared to commit foul murder for the sake of the weapon."

"Master Durand does seem to have tested each possible

theory that would join the murder with the sword, does he not?" asked Aileen softly.

Robert was following his own train of thought. "But if the reeve had not heard tell of the sword, then how can he say the thief would have done so," he said, thinking that this was getting very confusing.

"My father asked much the same question," said Hugh. "But the reeve, although he reports to Abbot Samson, is not daily in the company of visitors to the abbey. Those who seek to profit from such visitors are more likely to hear accounts of their tales and their deeds."

"I can see that may be truth," said Aileen. "But Hugh, if your father has delivered the sword into the hands of the reeve, surely he has done his part to help find the murderer of the pilgrim. Why then did you seek out Robert and myself?"

"My father is still troubled," said Hugh. "He does not think this is a simple murder. I can see he does not want his family to be at any risk merely because he repaired a sword brought to him by a murdered man."

"It would not seem to be a great danger," said Robert.

"No," replied Hugh. "But I do not like to see my father so troubled. I thought...I thought..."

"You thought what?" asked Aileen, gently.

"Well," Hugh burst out. "It is well known that you and Robert were of great help to the abbot and the reeve in finding out who stole the holy relic last month. You always were good at puzzles, even when we were children. I thought..."

"You thought that Robert and I might solve this puzzle?" Aileen was taken aback.

Robert just looked at Hugh, his eyes wide.

"Could you? Would you?" asked Hugh.

"Hugh," said Aileen. "I thank you for your confidence in us, but we sought only to help find the truth when the relic was stolen. We were afraid for our friends who were suspected."

"I know that," said Hugh. "You were brave to defend them so. That was one thing that made me believe you could help my family now."

"It was God's blessing that we were able to aid in finding the thief," Aileen said. "But I doubt not that our 'help' in this matter would be little appreciated by those who are responsible for solving this crime."

"You did not allow that to stop you from doing what was right last time," Hugh said simply.

"He has a point," said Robert, trying hard not to laugh.

Aileen scowled at her companion. He is not helping, she thought, and now I have to find some way of telling Hugh that we cannot solve every mystery that may arise in the Liberty of St. Edmundsbury.

As though he could read the thoughts running through her head, Hugh said: "I do not ask for your help out of selfish reasons," he leaned forward as though to emphasize his words. "If my father is afeared, then so are we all. Is this not a matter of justice, just as was the search for the holy relic? This Saxon was a good man. Does he not also deserve justice? Must we remain in fear of a knife in the dark of night? Master Durand is a good reeve, but my mind would be more at ease were I to know that my friends are turning their skill to solving this puzzle."

Neither Robert nor Aileen had ever heard such a long

speech from their friend. They remembered a small boy, quick at his lessons, but silent unless pressed to speak.

This matter weighs heavily on him, though Aileen. Surely there is little for the blacksmith to fear, but Hugh is our friend. He is right that the bonds of friendship require that we do all we can to provide assistance when a friend is in need. Mayhap Robert and I could do something, however little, to put Hugh's mind at ease.

Aileen looked across at Robert, who returned her gaze with a slight nod.

"Hugh," she said. "I do not know what we can do, and indeed I am not sure that anything need be done." Putting her hand up as Hugh was about to protest, she went on. "But what we can do, we will."

"Thank you," Hugh said, drawing in a deep breath of relief. "Thank you both."

Hugh reached over and gave Aileen a hug. Robert avoided the same fate by the simple means of standing up and saying heartily, "We had better all go home now. I do not know what we can do to help, Hugh, but Aileen and I will certainly ask some questions and see what we can find out."

"Fare thee well," said Hugh. "Thank you once again."

Hugh ran toward his home quickly, leaving Aileen and Robert to walk together more slowly.

"I pray it will not be too difficult a task to set Hugh's mind at ease," said Aileen.

"There is a mystery to solve in this sad death," said Robert. "But I do not see how the blacksmith or his family can be at risk. How do you think we should set about this?"

"I think we should go and talk to the reeve tomorrow,"

responded Aileen. "He will not be happy if he thinks we are looking into the crime, but I believe he will answer our questions if we tell him we are doing this only to quieten our friend's concern."

"As always, Aileen, you have the best ideas," said Robert in a solemn voice. Aileen laughed, playfully punching Robert in the arm.

"We shall do as you suggest," Robert said. "I doubt not that by tomorrow evening we will be able to give Hugh some answers to his questions. That will be a most satisfactory end to our quest."

2. CHAPTER TWO

Take the helmet of salvation, and the sword of the Spirit,
which is the word of God.

Ephesians 6:17

Aileen woke to the warm scent of herbs permeating the house. It must be Tuesday, she thought. She turned over in the feather bed she shared with her younger sister Mabel only to find she was alone.

Time was mother would get me up before dawn on Tuesdays to help her collect the herbs needed to dye the fine cloth father sells. Now that I am grown and working on the abbey's embroidered linens, it is Mabel who must take my place. Mayhap I can take just a few more minutes before I must get out of this nice warm bed.

"Aileen!" Anne Arundel's voice came drifting up the stairs.

I think mother must sense when I am awake, Aileen thought. Resignedly, she pushed back the coverlet and quickly splashed cold water over her face before donning her clothes. Running downstairs, she kissed her father and mother, ignored Mabel pulling a face at her, and ruffled the hair of her young brothers, Richard and Henry.

"You had better hurry, Aileen," said her father Jude. "Remember you have to take that linen cloth to Mistress Butler on your way to the Abbey this morning. She needs it for shirts that have been ordered."

"Your pardon, father," said Aileen. "I had forgotten." Gulping down her goat milk, Aileen picked up the cloth, waved a farewell to her family, and hurried out the door.

If I hadn't been so focused on Hugh, I would not have forgotten that I had promised father I would carry this cloth to the tailor this morning, Aileen thought. Walking quickly up Abbeygate Street, she almost missed seeing the reeve as he passed her, walking down the hill toward the abbey grounds.

"Master Durand," Aileen called, turning to catch up with the official.

"Mistress Aileen," said the reeve. "It would seem that we are both intent on our tasks this morning. My regrets that I did not greet you as we drew close along the way."

"Your pardon, sir," said Aileen. "I did not mean to be so forward as to interrupt your thoughts. Given this chance encounter, though, may I ask a favor of you?"

Durand's eyebrows rose. "What is it you would ask of me?"

Aileen felt the blush rise in her cheeks. There is no need

to be embarrassed, she admonished herself. Just tell him what you want!

"Master Reeve," she said aloud. "Hugh Short is a friend of Robert and myself. He came to us last night distraught about the recent death of the pilgrim."

Durand was surprised. "I see no reason why he should be concerned. His father had but the briefest meeting with the murdered man. The blacksmith brought to me the sword that had been taken to him for repair, and I cannot think that there is any other connection between the Saxon steward and the blacksmith."

"He was a steward?" asked Aileen, thrilled to have so soon obtained information about the victim. "Is his master the lord of a great manor?"

Durand eyed Aileen with more than a little suspicion.

"Mistress Aileen," he said. "It is true that you were of no little assistance to me in the matter of the holy relic. That does not mean that I believe it appropriate for either you or Master Robert Palgrave to concern yourselves in every mystery that arises within the Liberty."

At least the reeve acknowledges that there is a mystery, thought Aileen.

"Please be at ease, Master Durand," said Aileen. "Neither Robert nor I wish to interfere with your search for the truth."

The reeve stood silent, waiting for Aileen to continue.

"It is only that Hugh told us of his concern for his father. He said that Master Short felt that there was something that did not fit in the story of the sword. Robert and I merely wish to calm Hugh's mind. We ask only that, when you have some little time, you would allow us to talk to you. Then we can return to our friend and explain to him why there is no need for continued concern."

The reeve looked hard at the young woman before him. He knew she had boundless curiosity, but she had been raised to be an honest woman. Hugh Short was a clever boy, but he had always been a delicate child and was perhaps given to fears and imaginings. It could do no harm to help his friends lift some of the burden of those thoughts.

"If this is all you ask, then I see no reason why I should not help you," said the reeve.

"Thank you," Aileen said sincerely. He is a good man, she thought. Not all men would have offered time to help them.

"Come to see me before it is time for the evening meal, and we will talk."

So saying, Durand took his way once again toward the Abbey. Aileen hastened to deliver the cloth to Mistress Butler and then ran all the way to the Abbey so that she should not be late to her work.

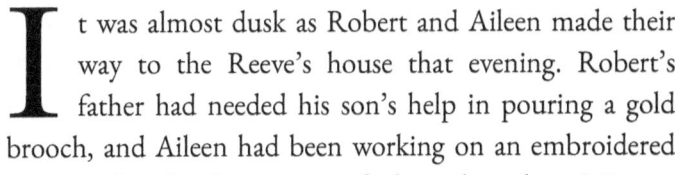

I t was almost dusk as Robert and Aileen made their way to the Reeve's house that evening. Robert's father had needed his son's help in pouring a gold brooch, and Aileen had been working on an embroidered cope under the keen eyes of the robemaker, Mistress

Palmer. Only when the light started to dim inside the work room did that good woman allow Aileen to put down her task and take her leave.

The reeve opened the door to their knock. "I had begun to believe you were not coming," he said.

"Your pardon, sir," said Robert. "Is the hour too late for us to talk?"

"No," Durand responded. "There is yet a little time before my evening meal."

The reeve motioned Aileen and Robert to sit. Following suit, he regarded the pair thoughtfully.

"Mistress Aileen tells me that you wish merely to put at ease the worries of Master Hugh Short."

"Yes, sir," confirmed Robert. "That is, Hugh would like us to do more, but we did tell him that we doubted there was anything we could do but ask some questions of those more highly placed than us."

Seeing the reeve frown, Aileen hastened to reassure him. "We ask only for some details of the sword and this pilgrim that you are able to provide," she said. "Mayhap that will be sufficient to calm our friend's discomfort."

"Very well," said Durand. "My knowledge of this Saxon steward is not great, but I have sent a rider to tell his lord of his death. Mayhap I will learn more of the man when that rider returns."

Durand rose from his chair and went over to a cupboard set against the wall. Opening the door, he took out something wrapped in sackcloth. Resuming his seat, he unwrapped the bundle to disclose a sword.

"Is that his sword?" asked Aileen, thinking that this weapon did not look to be of any great worth. It did not seem to her that this sword was quite as long as those she had seen at the side of those knights who visited St. Edmundsbury, and it looked as though it had been well used. There were some words inlaid into the blade, but she could not read them from where she sat.

"May I hold it, sir?" asked Robert.

Durand smiled and held it out for Robert to take from his hands.

"I do not know much about swords," Robert said, swinging the weapon from side to side and then balancing it in both hands. "But it feels good in my hand, and I do not think it would be difficult to wield."

"Yes," said the reeve. "The sword is well balanced. I too do not carry a sword very often, but it did seem to me to be well forged. The blacksmith did tell me that the weight of the sword was not too far forward and therefore any knight who carried it would not tire in the heat of battle."

Robert put the sword on the table, and he and Aileen both examined it carefully. The words Aileen had seen when Durand first produced the sword were to be found on both sides of the blade. They were inlaid in iron, as far as she could tell, and some of the letters were faint.

"Master Durand," she said. "I have my letters but some of these are hard to see in this light. What is it that is written on this blade?"

"On one side is written 'INOMINEDOMINI'," responded the reeve. "On the other is the word 'CONSTAININUS'."

"Constaininus," said Robert. "I too have my letters, but this word is strange to me."

"If the sword is indeed very old, it may be a word in a

language we do not understand, or it is even possible that this may be the name of the man for whom the sword was forged," said the reeve. "I cannot tell."

"Mayhap you will learn the answer to this question when your messenger returns," said Aileen. "If this lord sends for his steward's belongings, then you may learn more of the history of the sword."

"Mayhap I will," said Durand. "Aylwin served a great lord from the south. He brought the sword to our town as an offering from his lord to the blessed St. Edmund. His brief account given to Master Short that the sword belonged to a Christian hero contains few clues as to its origin. Mayhap his lord is powerful enough to have come into possession of a sword of renown. I do not know."

"The words on the other side of the blade are a blessing, are they not?" Aileen said. "I hear the priest use those words in the mass."

"Yes," said Durand. "They mean 'In the name of the Lord' so there does not seem to be any doubt that this weapon was carried by someone of our faith."

The three gazed upon the sword a few moments longer, then Durand roused himself. Whatever the meaning of the sword and its relevance to the murder of the good steward, I see no further role for the blacksmith or his family. Master Short brought me the sword for safekeeping until such time as I can return it to Aylwin's lord or his emissary. Master Short has no further role to play in this drama."

"Thank you, sir," Robert said. "We are glad to have had the chance to talk to you and see the sword."

"Yes," said Aileen. "We will tell Hugh all that you have

told us. When he understands that his father has no knowledge beyond the common rumor and has nothing else of Aylwin's to hold, mayhap his fears will be eased."

The pair said their farewells to the reeve and took their way home.

3. Chapter Three

The wicked have drawn out the sword, and have bent their bow, to cast down the poor and needy, and to slay such as be of upright conversation.

Psalm 37:14

As she walked across the Great Court of the abbey the following morning, Aileen heard running footsteps behind her. She turned to find Hugh Short skidding to a halt in front of her, red in the face and gasping for breath.

"Hugh, what is it?" Aileen asked. "What has happened?"

"My father was attacked last night," Hugh cried.

"Attacked?" Aileen gasped. "How fares your father? Is he injured? Where was he attacked, and by whom?"

Hugh put up his hand to stop the questions.

"I cannot say by whom, but he was attacked in the forge," he said.

"Truly?" said Aileen. "That your father should be assaulted within his own forge at night does seem uncommon strange."

"I told you there was danger," said the blacksmith's son a little more bluntly than was usual for him. The boy colored in embarrassment at his outburst.

"Your pardon, Aileen," he said. "I did not mean to be so rude. You and Robert are only trying to help."

"I took no offense, Hugh," Aileen said gently. "It must have a frightening experience for your whole family."

"It was," breathed Hugh.

Aileen drew Hugh over to the side of the court so that they could talk without curious looks from those passing by them.

"Robert and I have not forgotten the task you gave us," Aileen said. "We were planning to tell you what we had found out this evening. But now we need to take into consideration this news of yours. Pray, tell me what you know."

"It was close to the darkest hour when mother heard a sound from the forge," said Hugh. "She wakened father, and he rose and went down the stairs. My mother was afeared when he did not return, so she roused my older brother Adam and I."

"You had not heard the noise from the forge as had your father?" asked Aileen.

"To my shame, I fear I was hard asleep and did hear nothing." Hugh flushed and hung his head.

"Never mind, Hugh," Aileen said softly. "I doubt not you were sleeping the sleep of the just."

Hugh smiled tentatively, and Aileen signed for him to continue.

"Adam picked up a pot as he passed through the kitchen ahead of me," said Hugh. "He pushed open the door of the forge but found he could not open it all the way."

"Why not?" asked Aileen.

"Adam squeezed round the door," Hugh said. "As soon as he did, he saw father lying face down on the ground, unconscious."

"No!" exclaimed Aileen.

Hugh nodded. "Mother had followed us to the forge," he said. "Adam called to her to bring a cool cloth for father's head, for it was plain to see that he had been hit with something hard. As mother returned, to our great relief father started to stir. He was much embarrassed to find his entire family gathered around him, as you can imagine."

"Is he now recovered?" Aileen asked.

"Mother insisted that he rest," said Hugh. "His head is sore, as is his temper, but mother would not be denied."

"Was he able to tell you what happened?"

"Father said that when he opened the door to the forge, he saw a cloaked man on the far side bending over the finished work," Hugh said. "Before he was able to cry out or see more, he was hit over the head and knew no more until he regained his senses to see all of us looking down at him."

"His attacker was behind the door then," said Aileen.

"It would seem so," Hugh responded.

"But that means that there must have been at least two

of them," said Robert. "I have heard tell of robbers joining forces to waylay innocent travelers, but surely it is rare for two men to come together to break into a craftsman's home at night."

"It seems strange to me that a group of men would seek to steal from a blacksmith's forge at all," Aileen said.

"That is the most puzzling thing of all," said Hugh. "Nothing was stolen."

Aileen stared at him. "Nothing?"

"No," said Hugh. "Adam searched the forge after he had helped father to his bed. It was clear that the forge had been thoroughly gone through, for much was disturbed, but he could find nothing missing."

"That is indeed passing strange," Aileen said. "Perhaps your father disturbed the thieves before they could take anything, and they were too afeared after striking him down to stay and search more."

"Aileen," Hugh cried. "Think you not that this must confirm my fears are warranted?"

Robert and I were so certain of our way forward, thought Aileen, unsure how she could now comfort Hugh. They could not have predicted the assault on Master Short, and she did not know how this would fit into the tale.

"Hugh," she said. "I do not think we should assume that the murder of the steward and the attack on your father are connected." She put her up hand to forestall the comment Hugh was about to make. "The two events may not be connected," she continued. "Yet it is possible that they are. Two such violent attacks within a couple of days of each other is very unusual."

Aileen thought for a moment.

"Hugh, if it will not disturb your father, may Robert and I visit this evening?" she asked. "We can tell you what we have discovered to this point, and then mayhap your father will be able to give a greater account of last night's events."

"I am certain my mother and father would be glad of your visit," said Hugh. "They do not know that I did ask for your help, but you know how well regarded your family is in our house. Mother will be pleased to see you."

"It is arranged then," said Aileen.

With that farewell, Aileen returned to her work and Hugh to his studies.

4. Chapter Four

Every man hath his sword upon his thigh because of fear in the night.

Song of Solomon 3:8

I t was twilight that Tuesday evening as Aileen and Robert arrived at the blacksmith's home. Hugh answered their knock immediately, and it was clear he had been waiting for them.

"Aileen, Robert, pray do come in," said Mistress Short, welcoming them with a big smile as she dusted her hands on her apron. Abigail Short was a petite, blue-eyed blonde who never seemed to stay still for more than a minute at a time. Her family was her life, but she always had time to help those around her. In this she was much like Aileen's mother, which went a long way in explaining their friendship.

"Mistress Short," Aileen said. "I hope we do not intrude."

"Not at all," responded Abigail. "I am always glad to see you. And you too, Master Robert," she continued, turning to the young man.

Robert returned the greeting and then, seeing Adam come into the room from the forge, went over to talk to him.

"How fares your family?" Mistress Short said to Aileen. "I have scarce had time to talk to your mother in a week."

"I thank you," said Aileen. "We all fare well. My mother has sent you a gift of rose, lavender, and sage in hopes that they will be of help in reducing Master Short's head pain."

"How kind," Mistress Short said. "I will prepare it now."

"Mother," asked Hugh. "May I take Robert and Aileen to see father now?"

"Yes," his mother said. "Make sure you do not tire him too much, however. He must rest well tonight if he is to return to the forge tomorrow."

With that admonishment, the three of them climbed the stairs to Master Short's bedchamber. There they found Hugh's father lying in bed, his face grey with pain and a bandage wrapped around his head.

"Sir," said Aileen, a little shocked at the sight of the blacksmith, "I hope we do not trouble you. We can return another time."

"No indeed," responded Master Short, struggling into a sitting position. "I am glad of the interruption. I am not used to such idleness, but my good wife would have nothing else but that I allow her to rule me for the day." He smiled away any bad humor the words might seem to demonstrate.

"My mother and father send their greetings and wishes for a return to health," said Aileen.

"My father and mother also tasked me with their greetings," Robert said.

"Please thank your parents for me."

"Father," Hugh said, not quite sure how to broach the subject. "I hope you will not mind, but I have told my friends about the events of the past few days." The blacksmith's eyebrows rose, and he gave his son a hard look.

"I was concerned," said Hugh. "It did seem to me that Robert and Aileen might be able to find a solution to the puzzle of the sword. After all, it is known by many that they were of great help to the reeve in solving the theft of the holy relic."

"I do not see that there is any great puzzle to solve here," said his father. "My son should not have so troubled you," Master Short went on, turning to Aileen and Robert. "It is true that I was disturbed by the death of the steward, but my private musings about this sad event were only those that might be expected of any man."

Hugh hung his head in embarrassment.

Oh dear, thought Aileen, we have caused offense and made trouble for our friend.

If Master Short is unhappy now, thought Robert, he is going to be even more unhappy after we leave unless Aileen can help him understand Hugh was only trying to help.

"Master Short," said Aileen. "Pray do not be angry at Hugh. He knows that the reeve has been more often in our company than his and that mayhap Master Durand would therefore speak to us of the sword or the man who brought it to St. Edmundsbury."

"Yes, father," added Hugh eagerly, "I did not mean to offer any offense by speaking to Robert and Aileen. I did think only that we might learn more to put our minds at ease."

Well done, Aileen, Robert thought. I doubt I could have spoken as eloquently in defense of Hugh.

Guy Short looked at the three of them and sighed.

"Very well," he said. "But I know not how the events of last night could be related to the death of this worthy man."

"Would it be possible for you to tell us about the day the steward brought you the sword to repair?" asked Robert. "Mayhap there is some small detail that you had not before thought important that could provide a clue to the reason for the attack on you last night."

"I cannot see how that could be," Guy Short said. "I will gladly tell you about the sword and the man who carried it, however."

Signing to Hugh to hand him a tankard that was by his bedside, he drank deeply.

"Pray be seated," he said to Robert and Aileen, indicating the low stools beside the bed. "What is it that you have to ask of me?"

"Sir," began Robert, "Hugh told us that you believed there was something strange about the sword."

"It is not that the sword itself was strange," said the blacksmith. "It struck me that the tale that was told about it was not much in keeping with its design."

"Last night, Robert and I talked with Master Durand," Aileen said. "He showed us the sword. We could see that it was old and that there were Christian words inlaid in the blade. We cannot tell more than that without some guidance from an expert such as you."

Guy Short smiled at the compliment. "Hardly an expert in the swords of history," he said. "I do not know if I can tell you exactly why I did not feel that the sword matched the tale. All I can say for certain is that, if this indeed was a sword of a Christian born many centuries ago, it must have been repaired in the time since."

Robert looked a little puzzled. "Is that because of the words on the blade?" he asked.

"It is a little more than that," responded Master Short. "It is the design of the sword itself." He paused to collect himself before proceeding. "Master Aylwin told me that the sword was ancient and that it had belonged to a Christian hero. He did not tell me more. It was my own thought that there must be more to this than was being told."

"Did you believe that this steward was hiding something from you, sir?" asked Aileen.

"Not at all," Master Short said. "I think my son must have told you that I was impressed by Master Aylwin." Aileen and Robert nodded. "I had no reason then and have none now to doubt anything he told me. It may be that he was told the same history of the blade."

Taking another drink from the tankard, Master Short continued. "It was of no great matter to me if

the sword were that of a hero or of a mere foot soldier. I did not think it seemly to further question the man who brought me the weapon to repair."

"I am sorry if my question did seem to offer offense to

the memory of the steward," said Aileen, hearing the stern tone of the blacksmith.

"And I regret it if my tone suggested such offense," said Guy. "My head is sore, and my pride is offended by the attack upon my person." He smiled at Aileen.

"Let me explain," he went on. "I had doubt about the age of the weapon, but I had none about the man himself. He told me he was steward to a great lord in Sussex and that it was at his lord's command that he had brought the sword to offer at the shrine of our blessed saint. Until he was foully murdered, I had no reason to be concerned about the tale or the sword. Now I must needs wonder if there were others in the town who heard the tale and thought only that such a sword must be very valuable."

"You thought then that it was possible Master Aylwin was attacked because his murderer thought to find the sword upon his person?" asked Robert.

"It was possible," confirmed the blacksmith. "I know that Master Durand has doubts about that theory, but mayhap the thief who committed this terrible deed did not think his venture through to the end. Or possibly the desire to possess such a weapon was itself sufficient to lead to murder."

"I understand," Robert said. "In either case, murder was done."

"Yes, it was," Aileen said thoughtfully. "But it would seem that, whatever the motive for the deed, the killer is likely still to be within the town."

Surprised, Robert turned to his friend. "But why would you say that?" he asked. "Is it not more likely that the murderer would have left St. Edmundsbury at his first opportunity, taking any evidence of his deed with him?"

"Think about this, Robert," Aileen said eagerly. "Murder was done in the early hours of Sunday morning. Few who come to our town travel on a Sunday, and there are many who would note those who leave on the holy day. Before we did talk to him, Master Durand would have known if such passage had been reported."

"You are right, Aileen," said Robert, impressed by his friend's reasoning.

"I knew you would be able to think of something that would help," Hugh said, clapping his hands in excitement.

"It is but a small thought," said Aileen, a flush creeping across her cheeks. "But if we can be sure that the murderer is still within the town walls, there is hope that Master Durand may be able to find him."

"It is a good thought," said Master Short. "But could the felon not have left the town yesterday, for none remark the passage through the gates of those who leave on the day after the Sabbath."

Robert was not far behind his friend in his reasoning. "It is unlikely, sir," he said. "By Monday, the murder of Master Aylwin was known to all. The murderer might consider it too great a risk to leave St. Edmundsbury as soon as the gates opened on Monday morning. He needs must wait a day or more if he wishes to cause no comment."

"I agree," Aileen said. "But it now draws near the end of Tuesday. He will not wait much longer. We need more than this thought to ensure that the murderer is taken."

"What more is there that the reeve will not already have

considered?" Master Short asked, intrigued in spite of himself.

"I am not sure," replied Aileen. "We still do not fully understand whether there is any connection between the visit of the steward to your forge last week and the attack upon you last night."

"I see none," the blacksmith said bluntly.

"Such happenings are not common in St. Edmundsbury," said Robert. "It would seem passing strange that you should be attacked only two nights after Master Aylwin's death."

Robert is correct, thought Aileen. "Master Short," she said. "Can you think of nothing else that has occurred that is out of the ordinary?"

"No," he answered. "I did have a visit from two knights yesterday who asked me the cost of a new bit for a horse. That is not unusual, however. There are many pilgrims to the blessed shrine of St. Edmund who bring coin to the merchants and craftsmen of this town."

"It is true," said Aileen. "Yet I think we should consider every event of the past few days as something that may be of importance. If you are not too tired to continue, Master Short, pray tell us about these knights."

"I am not too tired, Mistress Aileen," he said. "Your visit has indeed quite revived my spirits."

Aileen smiled with relief and settled a little more comfortably on her stool.

"It was a little before the midday break," the blacksmith said. "I had just finished tempering a knife when the two knights entered the forge. They were strangers to me but were richly clothed. I deemed them to be pilgrims to the blessed shrine."

"Did they tell you so?" asked Robert.

"No, but they talked of traveling far to reach the abbey and of a long journey home within the next week. It was the journey to be made that prompted the fair knight to consider the purchase of a new bit. He said that his old one was worn, and thus he was considering the purchase while in St. Edmundsbury."

"You said one knight was fair," Aileen said. "Was the other one then dark?"

"No," responded Guy. "His hair too was brown as a chestnut, but his eyes were the most noticeable thing about him for they were of different colors. The second knight said little but looked with interest at all within the forge."

This is promising, thought Aileen. Two knights visit the forge for the business of but one, and the other one spends his time looking around.

"Did the knights give you their names or tell you anything more?" asked Robert.

"No, and of course it is not my part to ask more questions than may be necessary to properly carry out the commission," said Master Short. "The knight brought me the old bit to examine and measure. I did not think it so worn that it need be replaced immediately, but I would be a fool to turn away a good commission based on that opinion."

"Then the fair knight did order the bit," Robert said.

"Yes, he did," said the blacksmith. "He returns on Saturday to see it completed."

"Did the knights talk of anything other than the purchase of the bit?" asked Aileen.

Master Short hesitated for a moment. "Briefly." He then said, "I realize that is another reason I was so sure they were pilgrims. They mentioned the steward who was murdered."

This was news indeed, thought Aileen. She and Robert exchanged startled looks and sat forward on their stools, leaning in toward the blacksmith.

"What did they say, sir?" asked Aileen, trying hard not to appear too eager.

"As I examined the old bit, the fair knight mentioned that they rested in the abbey's guest hall while in St. Edmundsbury. He said it was sad that a fellow guest should have suffered such an end in our town."

"What did you reply, father?" said Hugh, taking the words out of Robert's mouth.

"What could I say but to agree?" Master Short said.

"Did the knights talk more about the steward?" asked Aileen.

"I confess I was already thinking about the bit to be made," said the blacksmith. "I remember the darker one coming forward and asking me if there was any talk among the people of the Liberty about what may be behind Master Aylwin's death, but of course all I could answer was that there were few in the town who had even seen the steward and certainly none who could know enough to give help to those who were seeking his killer."

At that moment, Mistress Short came in and shooed her son downstairs, telling him he had chores to do afore bedtime and that he had better do them now if he was to get any sleep that night.

"As for you two," she said to Robert and Aileen. "It is gratitude I must send to your mother for the herbs, Aileen, but it is time you left."

Turning to her husband, Mistress Short fluffed his pillow and then gently pushed him back down on the bed. "Here is a poultice for your head," she said. "Mistress Arundel sent it with her good wishes, and I believe you will heal the faster for taking your rest."

As they descended the stairs, Aileen and Robert could hear Master Short protesting that he was no little child. Smiling at each other, they wended their way home, agreeing that on the morrow they would have to see if they could find out more about the events of the past few days.

5. CHAPTER FIVE

Happy art thou, O Israel: who is like unto thee, O people saved by the Lord, the shield of thy help, and who is the sword of thy excellency!

Deuteronomy 33:29

s Aileen walked to the abbey the next morning, her mind was filled with all the information she had gleaned the day before. Not only did she have the blacksmith's tale to consider, but upon her return home last evening, her account of the discussion she and Robert had had with Master Short prompted her father to contribute something more.

"The murdered man was from Sussex?" Jude said upon hearing of the blacksmith's words. "I had not realized this could be the same man."

"What man, father?" asked Aileen.

"It was on the day before the Sabbath that a man came into the shop to purchase a length of fine cloth," said her father. "He was a courteous man, clad in plain but good clothes, and asked to see cloth that was suitable for wrapping an offering to be made at the shrine of St. Edmund on behalf of his lord. He said he was from a great manor in Sussex."

"That must have been Aylwin, father," said Aileen. "Did he say more?"

"We did not have a conversation about swords and tales of old, if that is what you are asking, Aileen," her father said with a slight smile.

"No, father, I understand. But you are from Arundel, and I wondered if mayhap his lord's manor is nearby."

Relenting, her father went on: "I did recognize the Sussex accent as soon as he offered me fair greeting," he said. "So we did talk a little. Master Aylwin asked me where my home was, for he too recognized that my accent was from the same region. I told him Arundel, and that led to us having a conversation about places we had both visited and customs that might not be familiar to the good folk of Suffolk."

"So Master Aylwin was from the same area as your family," said Aileen.

"His lord's manor is east of Arundel, close by the land of the great De Warenne family. Our conversation was not a long one for his purpose in visiting my shop was to purchase the cloth."

"It is yet more than we knew before, father," said Aileen quietly. "Master Short said the steward was a good man. He did seem to like him."

"I can understand that," Jude responded. "Master Aylwin purchased a fine linen cloth with strands of gold woven through it. I believe him to have been a devout man who spared nothing for the sake of the blessed saint and his lord."

Now, as Aileen entered the great courtyard of the abbey, she determined that the murderer of this man of Sussex would not go unpunished if there was anything she could do to prevent it.

I know Robert will feel the same way, Aileen thought, entering the linen room and settling down to work. I will talk to Brother Jocelin, the Guest Master, at the midday break. I am certain that Robert and I can do something to help the reeve. Master Aylwin must be avenged.

"Aileen!" Mistress Palmer's voice cut through Aileen's thoughts. "Stop woolgathering and get on with your work. Your needle has hovered over that one piece of cloth for too long!"

Thus chastised, Aileen turned her attention to the vestment she was embroidering and stopped only when the robemaker allowed that her ladies could take their midday break.

Making her way over to the guest hall Aileen found Brother Jocelin chivvying the lay servants to hurry up and prepare the midday meal for those guests of the abbey within the walls. Waiting patiently until the Guest Master appeared satisfied, Aileen greeted him as he returned to his room close by the entrance to the hall.

"Good morrow, Brother Jocelin," she said. "You are busy today it seems."

"Good morrow, Mistress Aileen," the monk said. "Yes,

praise be to God and His saints, our abbey fair bustles with pilgrims to the shrine of our blessed St. Edmund."

The monk settled on his stool and, moving a pile of parchment to his writing table from another stool, signed that Aileen also should sit.

"It is a pleasure for me to sit with you once again," said Brother Jocelin. "Yet I doubt not that there is a purpose for your visit."

A little abashed, Aileen blushed and lowered her eyes. I hate it when my face turns red, she thought, and now Brother Jocelin will think that I only come to talk with him when I want something.

"Come now, Mistress Aileen," Brother Jocelin said, laughing. "Do not distress yourself. It is a pleasure for an old monk to be able to rest from his daily tasks for a short time."

"I thank you, brother," Aileen said. "I would not offend you by being less than truthful. I must confess that I did come to ask you about one of your guests."

"I did think as much," returned the monk. "You do understand that I would not share with you anything that might seem to intrude upon the right of my guests to keep their own counsel?"

"Yes, brother," Aileen said. "I would not ask that you break a confidence. That would be wrong."

Smiling, Jocelin asked of whom they were speaking.

"Brother, I would ask if you could tell me anything about the poor steward who was so foully done to death last week."

The monk's face creased in sorrow. "Master Aylwin," he said. "He was, I believe, a good and devout man. It greatly distressed me that he should suffer such a fate in our town."

Aileen waited as Brother Jocelin crossed himself and bowed his head in silent prayer.

"But why do you ask me about this man of Sussex?" the Guest Master said. "Surely the death of Master Aylwin is a matter for the reeve. You had not met the steward?"

"No, brother," Aileen said. "My father did talk to him briefly, but I never met him."

"Then I do not understand why you ask me about him," said the monk. "When you asked me about my guests after the holy relic was stolen, it was because you were afraid for your friends. Surely that is not so now?"

"No, brother," Aileen confirmed. "But the son of the blacksmith is one of my friends as well, and he is worried about his father."

"I confess I do not see the connection," said Brother Jocelin.

"Forgive me, brother," said Aileen. "I am not making myself clear. Master Aylwin took the sword he brought with him as an offering to the blacksmith for repair. That was two days before he was murdered."

"Go on," encouraged Jocelin as Aileen paused.

"On Monday night, Master Short was attacked in the forge and rendered unconscious."

"That is shocking indeed," said the monk. "I pray that he has recovered his wits?"

"Yes, brother, I thank you," Aileen said.

"His son, Hugh, is afraid that there is some connection between the sword and the attack on Master Short," she said. "In order to put his fears to rest, my friend Robert and

I promised Hugh that we would find out more about the steward and the sword itself."

That is not exactly how it began, thought Aileen, but it does seem to be where we have found ourselves to be now.

"I see," said Jocelin. "And you believe that I may be able to help you discover more about Master Aylwin."

"Yes, brother," said Aileen.

The monk leaned back, knocking against some of the parchments he had moved from the stool upon which Aileen was sitting. Jocelin seized them as they slid off the desk toward the floor, and then having restored them to a safe place atop another pile of parchment, turned back to Aileen and composed his face into its usual kindly expression. "I see no harm in telling you what I observed of this good man," he said.

"Brother," Aileen said. "It seems that all those who talked with the steward say he was a 'good' man. May I ask why you believe that to be a just description?"

"I am not certain I can say exactly why I should describe him thus," replied the Guest Master. "It is an impression that I gained from the few times I spoke with him, and mayhap it had more to do with the way in which he held himself than any one word or deed.

"Let me tell you what I saw and heard of Master Aylwin," Jocelin went on. "You may understand better the impression he made upon me, and it seems on others, once I complete my tale."

"Pray continue, brother," said Aileen.

The Guest Master, once again grabbing at some sliding parchments and deciding placing them on the floor was the safest course of action for now, composed his face and turned back to his visitor.

"I am sure you know that important men oft require others to be attendant upon them when they travel," said the monk. "If I were a man of the world and not a lowly brother of the abbey, I might be tempted to think that such men bring many others with them on their pilgrimages in order to demonstrate their importance." Jocelin stopped suddenly and frowned at his own words.

Aileen tried hard not to smile.

Brother Jocelin cleared his throat and then continued: "I think that perhaps this was one of the reasons I was impressed by the steward from the moment of his arrival."

"His arrival was not what you would have expected?" Aileen asked.

"It was not," said the Guest Master. "I was in the courtyard when Master Aylwin arrived. He came without any other to keep him company or watch over him. At first I took him for a simple pilgrim come to plead for the blessings of our saint, but when I saw him hand over his fine horse to the stable lad, I took more note of the man himself."

"He was then so unusual a sight?" Aileen asked.

"Not unusual in that way," said Brother Jocelin. "But his horse was equipped with silver and good leather, while the man himself was little adorned. When I studied his appearance more closely, I saw that the cloth of his cloak was fine, as was the leather of his boots. I even saw the glint of a silver belt buckle as he strode toward me, but there was nothing about him that spoke of high position or wealth."

"And when he spoke to you?" Aileen prompted as the monk fell silent.

"When he spoke, his words were soft and courteous," said Jocelin. "He requested that he be permitted to sleep in the guest hall. He did not demand accommodation. He asked me for directions to the shrine of the blessed St. Edmund, but he did not order me to provide them. He stood aside to allow an old woman entrance to the guest hall. He did not push his way past those in his way. He spoke kindly to a lame man begging for alms and dropped a coin into the man's hand."

"I think I understand now why you and those others with whom I have talked were so impressed by Master Aylwin," said Aileen.

"He was a good man," said Jocelin sadly, bowing his head. "I was grieved to hear of his death and have prayed daily for his eternal soul."

"The steward of a great lord's manor is a man of power," said Aileen. "This steward would seem to have been of a gentle nature and not one who wielded his power with a heavy hand."

"I agree," said the monk. "I did not talk to him often in the three days he was within the abbey walls, but I know that he spoke to all kindly and was a quiet and undemanding guest. Would that the same could be said of his friends."

"His friends!" said Aileen. "I had not heard that he had friends in St. Edmundsbury."

"Mayhap 'friends' is not the way in which I should describe the knights," said Brother Jocelin. "Two young knights arrived at the abbey the day after Master Aylwin.

They were young and proud and were known to the steward."

I wonder if these two young knights are the same men Master Short told us about last night, thought Aileen.

"Did it seem that Master Aylwin had expected their arrival?" asked Aileen.

The Guest Master wrinkled his brow in thought. "I think not," said the monk after a moment. "He seemed a little surprised to see them. The steward and the knights were cordial enough, but it did seem to me that Master Aylwin was not entirely satisfied that the two young men had decided upon a pilgrimage to the shrine of St. Edmund at a time when he was here upon the request of his lord."

"Whether they were friends or no, the knights must have been distressed to learn of the death of the steward," said Aileen.

"I know not," Brother Jocelin said. "I know little of their time in our great town other than that some of their fellow guests have complained that the two young men have returned to the guest hall late at night and in their cups. I have tried to calm the tempers of those visitors who believe that pilgrims to the shrine within our walls should have more respect for our saint than to drink too deeply of the vine and offer offense to maids or men."

"The knights do seem to be of a different character from the steward," said Aileen. "Yet if they were acquainted, it may be that they also rode from Sussex."

"I believe that to be so," responded Brother Jocelin. "They did refer to Master Aylwin as 'Master Steward,' but beyond that I cannot tell you much."

"Can you tell me whether they are still within these walls?" asked Aileen.

"Oh, bless me, yes," said the Guest Master. "I confess to looking forward to the day Sir Walter de Nantes and Sir Edward Strode return to their homes, for they are unlike any other pilgrims I have tended as Guest Master. For the moment, the good Lord is testing my patience, and I pray that I may be equal to the test."

I have always liked Brother Jocelin, thought Aileen. He seems so like any other man, and so unlike the vision of a monk I had from childhood.

"Thank you, brother," she said. "You have helped me understand the steward, and I pray that this knowledge may help me ease the fears of my friend."

"Bless you, child," said Brother Jocelin. "The Lord keep you and grant you peace and health."

Aileen ran back to her work, the midday break having come to an end, excited at the thought of seeing Robert that evening and being able to tell him all that she had learned.

6. Chapter Six

By thy sword shalt thou live, and shalt serve thy brother.

Genesis 27:40

While Aileen was talking with Brother Jocelin, Robert was working hard at demonstrating to his father how well he had taken instruction on the making of the niello paste to be used to inlay a design on the fine gold plate Master Palgrave was making for the abbey. When his father was satisfied that Robert had the ratio of silver, copper, and lead just right, he told his son that he might take the afternoon hours to do as he pleased.

Such an unexpected gift should not be wasted, thought Robert, as he headed toward the merchants' shops on Churchgate Street. It is certain that some in the town must have seen the steward in those days before his death.

Mayhap someone will remember something that may serve to help us solve this puzzle.

"Good morrow, Master Robert," called Mistress Clay, the potmaker's wife. "How fares your mother today?"

"Very well, thank you," responded Robert, stopping to look at the wares displayed in front of the pottery. "I trust that you and your family are in good health as well?"

Mistress Clay laughed out loud, her cheeks puffing out like two rosy apples. "Thanks be to God that my brood is filled with health."

Robert smiled. It was indeed true that the potter's children were known in the town for being not only healthy and filled with loud energy but also as good-natured as their mother. This was perhaps just as well since there were eight of them, and it was sometimes hard to imagine such a boisterous family fitting within the walls of their small house.

"Mistress Clay," said Robert. "You have heard of the sad death of the pilgrim from Sussex?"

The smile faded from the good woman's face. Making the sign of the cross, she said: "Yes, indeed. Such a nice man and such a terrible end."

"You talked with him then," Robert said, thinking to have struck gold so early in his wanderings.

"Yes," replied Mistress Clay. "He stopped before me and seemed to be looking at the pots."

"'Seemed to be?'" said Robert, struck by the woman's hesitant tone.

Mistress Clay blushed. "I did not mean to sound unkind," she said. "He spoke courteously to me and asked questions about the decorations on the pots. Yet he oft looked over his shoulder, and it did seem to me that he was looking to see if mayhap someone was following behind him."

"Did he say anything that might have explained his behavior?" Robert asked.

"No," responded the potmaker's wife. "He spoke only of how beautiful was the shrine of St. Edmund and about preparing for his journey home. Yet as he moved on, having bidden me fare well, I saw him once again look back and study those coming up the street behind him."

"Did it seem that he studied anyone in particular?" asked Robert.

"Nay, not that I could see," replied Mistress Clay. "It did seem to me that there was nothing remarkable about the people coming up the street. There was the usual crowd of traders and shoppers, children running around and mothers calling to them to behave themselves. Pilgrims I saw, both rich and poor. There was no one who stood out that I could tell."

As she finished, a man came up to the table to ask something of the woman.

Realizing that he would learn nothing more from Mistress Clay, Robert bid her farewell and walked on.

In the course of the next couple of hours, Robert spoke to several tradesmen, some of whom remembered the steward well.

"He purchased cheese from me for his journey home," said the cheesemaker. "And yes, since you ask, he did seem nervous. Very courteous in his manner, but he left in haste after looking behind him. He seemed almost to duck around the corner."

"For such a gentleman," said one stall keeper in the

market, "he was almost abrupt in his leaving. He bought some lovely apples from me and agreed with me that the fruit in this part of the country is among the best to be found. Then, of a sudden, he said he must leave. Afore I could say another word, he was gone!"

"Why do you think he behaved so?" asked Robert.

"I cannot be sure," said the merchant thoughtfully. "In the midst of our conversation he looked to his left, and his face paled. If I were a man given to fancies, I would say he saw something to be feared."

"Could you see anything to give rise to such a reaction?" asked Robert.

"I confess, I did look to see if I could tell why he reacted so," said the man. "But I could see nothing unusual in the midst of the crowd. It may simply have been that something came to the steward's mind that he had forgotten to do." The trader laughed. "My wife is always complaining that I will walk away when she is in the middle of the sentence just because I have remembered something. Mayhap it was the same with this steward."

Something. Or someone, thought Robert. Leaving the merchant to turn to the next customer, Robert walked on.

By the time the afternoon was drawing to a close, Robert had gained a general impression of a courteous man trying to go about his business of preparing for his journey home but who nevertheless seemed concerned that he was being followed. Why that might be Robert knew not, but, since Aylwin had died that very night, it was clear that the steward had cause to be afeared.

"Master Robert!"

Robert started, hearing his name called from across the

street. Turning, he saw one of his father's suppliers, Henry Goode, smiling at him. Crossing the street, he greeted the man courteously, asking after his family and his business.

"All is well," said Master Goode. "My family prospers, as does my business.

"But you, Master Robert," he went on. "You were standing in the middle of the street scarce noticing those who jostled past you. What was it that you were thinking about that took you so far from where you stood?"

Robert laughed. "You are correct. I was very deep in thought."

Master Goode cocked an eyebrow and waited.

"I have been hearing from many people this afternoon about the steward who was murdered last Saturday night. He seems to have been a kindly man, and so I was wondering why anyone would wish to kill such a man in our town."

Master Goode sobered at Robert's words. "It was indeed a foul deed and does no credit to our burgh," he said. "I do confess that, ever since I heard about the murder, I have been worried that mayhap I could have done something to prevent it and yet did nothing."

"Why would you think so?" asked Robert, surprised at the man's words.

"It is my habit to go to the tavern on the Sabbath's eve," said Master Goode. "I do not drink to excess, you understand?"

Robert smiled away the man's concern that he might appear to be a drunkard. "Of course," he said. "A draught of good ale after a long week's work is for many men a just reward."

"Just so," said Master Goode. "Well," he went on. "As I was crossing the street to enter the tavern, I saw a man running fast across the end of the street. He turned his head to look back as he ran, so it seemed almost as though he might be in a chase."

"Did you see anyone else?" Robert asked.

"No, and I heard nothing either. Of course, it was a little distant to hear the sound of boots on the cobbles, had there been others to hear."

"Do you think the man you saw could have been Master Aylwin?" asked Robert.

"I do not know," replied the man. "I could not see the face of the man who was running. "It was full dark by then and a little chilly. I did not tarry to see more."

The man was a little shamefaced, probably guessing Robert realized his main goal that evening was his tankard of ale.

"There was no reason for you to suspect anything was wrong," said Robert, trying to make Master Goode feel better. "But you may want to tell your story to the reeve, just in case it may help to catch the killer."

"That is a good suggestion," said Master Goode. "I will do so tomorrow."

With that, the two parted, Master Goode with a spring in his step and Robert once again deep in thought.

Walking back toward Abbeygate, Robert came across another of his acquaintance. John Thetford was the elder brother of one of Robert's childhood playmates. He had protested mightily at being forced by his mother to spend time watching over his younger sibling at ten-years-old, but now, at twent-two, he was fast gaining a reputation as his farmer father's righthand man. He even appeared glad to see Robert.

"Robert Palgrave!" he exclaimed. "I haven't had a chance to talk to you in many months. How does your family fare?"

"We are all well," replied Robert. "I thank you."

Before he could go on to ask after John's family, the young man continued. "I never thought that we would see two such great mysteries in St. Edmundsbury in such a short space of time."

He must know that Aileen and myself were involved in the mystery of the holy relic, thought Robert. I wonder if that is why he is so eager to talk to me.

As if he had read Robert's mind, John Thetford said: "Has our worthy reeve once again sought your counsel in the matter of this poor pilgrim's death?"

"I do not think that Master Durand is oft in the way of consulting apprentices on such matters." Robert said severely, a little offended by John's tone.

"Do not be so prickly," John said, laughing. "Have you forgot how much I like to tease my brother's friends?"

Yes, I remember, thought Robert. I scarce thought at the time it could be called "teasing," though. Had I known the word at my age, I would have said John was being sarcastic. But times change, and now I will take his words at face value.

Robert laughed off any offense. "I remember something of the kind," he said. "But it was mere chance that Aileen and I were able to offer some information to the reeve in the matter of the holy relic."

"So say you," said John, laughing in turn. "But now, in

this matter of the murdered man from Sussex, I think perhaps you are not so involved?"

Avoiding having to answer the question, Robert took a more indirect approach. "I do hear the gossips say that Master Aylwin was much troubled on the day of his death. Have you heard such?"

"I have had little time to hear of anything since the Sabbath," replied John. "It is a busy time for farmers."

I feared as much, thought Robert. Never mind, I have gleaned some information to share with Aileen later this evening.

"I did have one strange experience on Saturday night, though," said John Thetford before Robert could say his farewells.

"You met the steward?" asked Robert.

"No, not that," John said. "I drank a tankard of ale as is my wont on the Sabbath's eve. As I was making my way home afterward, I came across Mad Meg."

It is some time since I heard tell of Mad Meg, Robert thought. The poor old woman was rumored to be out of her mind though harmless. I used to see her around the gates of the abbey begging for alms. I did hear tell that the abbot told her she could only enter the gates on feast days and barred her from entry at other times. Mayhap she now begs in less holy places.

"I did not realize Mad Meg was still within the burgh," said Robert.

"She can usually be found begging near the market at the end of the day or close by the taverns at night," said John. "When I saw her, she was coming out of an alley babbling about the devil taking on the guise of good men to smite the meek. When I spoke kindly to her and offered her a coin, she backed away from me as though I were myself the devil and muttered something about disturbing the sleep of the good with cries and shouting."

"That was indeed strange," said Robert. "Was this very late then?"

"I fear it was," said John. "I had perhaps stayed a little long in the tavern. Had I left to go home at my usual time, I doubt not that I would have avoided the encounter with the madwoman." So saying, John bid Robert farewell and continued on his way.

It was not to be that Robert should make much progress toward his home yet. He had taken but a few steps when he heard a whiny voice behind him.

"Methinks you ask more questions than be good for you," said the voice.

Spinning around, Robert found himself looking into the eyes of a bent old man with a wizened face and shabby clothes.

"Master Hadric," Robert said nervously. "I did not know that you were in St. Edmundsbury."

The man's rheumy eyes looked at Robert. His face was set in a gap-toothed smile. "Aye," he said. "The life of a rag and bone man is never easy, and I have had poor pickings of late. I thought mayhap the good folk of the Liberty would be more generous."

"And were they?" Robert was uncertain how generous any were toward the man who stood before him. Hadric traveled all over the Liberty and beyond, begging for old rags and bones. He made his precarious living selling those unwanted items to merchants who would turn the rags into yarn and the bones into glue.

Hadric glared at the young man. "Nay," he said. "The folks in the shadow of this great abbey gave me no more than the peasants in the poorest of villages. All they would give me was enough to drink a tankard of ale at the tavern last Sabbath eve, but not enough to keep me in more than bread and sops along the way."

Robert's interest sparked at the man's words. Hadric had a well-deserved reputation for being unpleasant to all, but in spite of his desire to get away from the man, Robert felt he had to tarry for at least as long as it took to find out a little more. "You were here last Sabbath eve?" he asked Hadric.

"Aye," he said. "What is that to you?"

Hadric took a step closer to Robert, who instinctively backed away. The man laughed and pointed a finger at the young man. "I heard you asking that Henry Goode questions," said Hadric. "Goode may be his name, but I've found no good in him when my travels bring me to St. Edmundsbury." The rag and bone man laughed at his own joke.

Robert was becoming a little uneasy. I did not realize there was anyone listening, he thought. I should be more careful if I do not want to stir up any trouble for myself or Aileen.

"Master Goode and I merely had some friendly conversation," said Robert, standing up straight.

Hadric laughed again. How can a laugh sound so sinister? thought Robert. Hadric really is a disagreeable man.

"Methinks you are more interested in getting information than in having a conversation," said the rag and bone man. "You asked just as many questions of that farmer's boy."

"Have you been following me?" demanded Robert, hoping his voice did not convey how nervous he was at this unexpected turn of events.

Hadric lowered his voice to little more than a hiss. "I know what happened last Sabbath's eve," he said. "But I ken not why it should be of such interest to you."

"You know what happened last Sabbath's eve?" Robert said, startled.

"Aye, of course I know," said Hadric. "Nought else has been talked of since that Saxon was murdered. I ain't deaf, and I ain't daft!"

Calm down, Robert, the young man thought. I will be of no use to Aileen or Hugh if I jump at every step or word. After all, we are standing in the middle of the street with people walking all around us.

Taking a deep breath, Robert looked Hadric straight in the eyes. "If that is so, why should my conversation be of such interest to you," Robert said.

That's better, he thought. Turn the tables on him and see how Hadric deals with that!

The rag and bone man looked a little surprised, but then he leant in close and said in a whining voice, "It did seem to me that mayhap I might be able to tell you something you do not know."

"I do not know if I much care," said Robert, gaining more confidence by the minute. The only way to get much out of this man, he thought, is to pretend indifference. In any event, I doubt much he knows anything that we do not already know.

"Oh, you don't much care," mimicked the bone-grubber. "What if I told you I saw the dead man the night he was killed?"

"Where?" Robert asked directly.

"Think you not information such as that is worth the price of an ale?" said Hadric.

Robert was taken aback. "You want me to pay you for a piece of gossip?" he said. "It is of no matter to me whether you know something more than do all the rest of the people of the Liberty, but if you do, then you should talk to the reeve. He it is who is investigating the crime." Robert was quite pleased with himself at how indifferent he sounded.

Hadric did not expect such a response, and his face showed it clearly. He stepped back and took a long look at the young man standing in front of him. "Are you certain sure you do not wish to hear what I have to say?" he said, trying one last time to get something out of Robert.

"I do not believe you know anything anyway," said Robert, making as though he was about to walk away.

"That is where you are wrong," said the rag and bone man indignantly. "You are like all the other proud people of the Liberty. You think I'm not worth any of your time. Well, you are wrong!"

"You mistake me if you believe I think the less of you for being a bone-grubber," said Robert. "I merely have no interest in paying to hear what you have to say about this foul murder. If you wish to talk to me about it as I have talked to others, then I will of course listen, for we are all concerned that the crime be solved. Otherwise I must needs go home."

I pray that he will not walk away from me now, Robert thought. I would like to hear what he thinks he knows.

Hadric pulled at his ear, thinking. "Well then," he said. "I will tell you. I ain't no liar. Methinks you will be sorry you did disbelieve me when you hear what I have to say."

Robert drew the man over to the side of the road so as not to be in the way of those walking down the street. "I want to hear what you have to say, Master Hadric," he said.

"I ain't no liar," the old man repeated. "I told you I was here the night the steward was killed, and I was."

Robert nodded, encouraging Hadric to continue.

"It's dry work going around day after day trying to make a living," Hadric said petulantly. "Most of the time, people just turn me away, and even when they have something for me, it's often nasty stuff."

"I am sure it is hard work," Robert said in a sympathetic tone.

"Aye, well, I had a need of a drink that night, so I headed for the tavern," said Hadric.

"It were a cold night, and those that were abroad did not tarry."

"That's understandable," said Robert, wondering if the man was ever going to get to the point.

"As I walked up Abbeygate, I spied a man ahead of me," the rag and bone man went on. "He were looking all around him as if he feared being seen."

That has to be Aylwin, Robert thought, trying hard not to look as interested as he now felt.

Hadric's eyes took on a faraway look as he thought back to that night. "I thought to follow him to see if...to see if there might be something I could do for him," the man continued.

I am sure that is why he followed the steward, Robert thought as he tried to keep his face from showing his skepticism.

"Anyways, it weren't long before I spied another man on the other side of the street," said Hadric. "He were keeping in the shadows, but he was for certain following the first man."

"What did the second man look like?" asked Robert, unable to keep silent any longer.

"Aye, I got you now, ain't I?" Hadric said, wheezing with laughter.

"I will not deny what you are saying is interesting," said Robert. "But unless you can say more than that you saw two men walking on the night of the steward's death, then you really have not told me anything that is not already common knowledge."

Hadric looked offended.

I hope I have not angered him, thought Robert. I really want to hear more. But he need not have worried.

"Why don't we get out of the cold and go have a tankard of ale in that tavern there?" wheedled Hadric. "I remember more when I'm not cold and my throat isn't as dry as dust."

"It is not that cold today," said Robert. "Mayhap if you finish your tale, I might feel more like satisfying your thirst."

With that, the old man had to be satisfied, although his

face showed how he felt about Robert's words. "Be it as you please," said Hadric.

"So, what did the second man look like?" Robert repeated his earlier question.

"It was dark," protested Hadric. "He was in the shadows. I cannot tell you the color of his hair or his eyes."

Robert sighed. "What can you tell me about him, then?"

"Only that he was passing tall, and I suspect he was thin," said Hadric. "His cloak did not bulge around a big stomach."

That description covers a large percentage of the population of the Liberty, thought Robert. Yet at least it may be something.

"What happened next?" he asked Hadric.

The question seemed to disconcert the bone-grubber. He hesitated before going on with his tale. "I kept my eye on both of them," he said finally. "All of a sudden, the first man stopped walking and looked back. Then he started to run."

"Had he seen you?" asked Robert.

"Nay, I am not a fool," Hadric said. "I kept out of sight of both of 'em."

"Then he either heard footsteps or saw the other man," Robert said.

"Aye, I suppose so," said Hadric.

"Go on," said Robert. "What did you do then?"

Again, the man hesitated. "I saw the second man begin to walk faster and then run," he said. "I did follow for a little way as the men turned into one alley and then another, but after a while, I tired of the game and went on to the tavern to have my ale."

Why the sudden end to the story? thought Robert. He was stretching out his moment of being important. Then he just stopped.

"You just lost interest?" asked Robert. "That does not seem like you."

"What do you mean by that?" said Hadric. "Do you think I have nothing better to do with my time than chase after two grown men running in the night?" Hadric's face was screwed into an expression of dismay.

Is he merely concerned that I do not believe him, thought Robert, or does he think I might suspect him of knowing more about what happened? Mayhap he followed them longer and still has hopes of obtaining some kind of financial gain for his knowledge.

"I am certain you do," said Robert. "You are a busy man. Yet I do wonder you had so little curiosity that you did not want to see whether the second man ever caught up with the first. Mayhap you wish to save some information for the reeve?"

Hadric's eyes shifted. "Mayhap I do," he said.

"You promised me an ale if I told you my story," Hadric said after a moment, seeing that Robert was not going to say anything.

Realizing that he was not going to get any more information out of the rag and bone man, Robert decided to earn some goodwill for possible future conversations.

"Here is the price of a tankard of good ale," he said, handing some coins to the other man. "I thank you for the information and bid you fare well."

Hadric mumbled something in return and then headed for the tavern. Robert once again headed for his home, thinking that so many people seem to have been abroad on the night of the steward's murder. The information I have gleaned may not add much to our knowledge of the events of that night, he thought, but mayhap Master Durand has found others with even more information. I pray that the murderer may be found out and suffer the fate of such evil men.

7. CHAPTER SEVEN

*There is that speaketh like the piercings of a sword: but the
tongue of the wise is health.*

Proverbs 12:18

"Father Abbot," said the reeve, "I doubt not that
this steward served a fierce and powerful lord, but
surely there is no need for concern."

The two men were seated on either side of the hearth in
the abbot's office, feet toward the fire and anxiety etched on
their brows.

"I had no great concern beyond that which you would
expect when first I learned of this unfortunate man's
death," replied Abbot Samson. "But now you tell me that
the lord whom Master Aylwin served was Sir Gilbert de
Cley, I must consider how to respond should this lord cast
any blame upon our Liberty."

"Foul murder is to be found in any burgh in the land," said Master Durand. "I see not how this lord could argue that the Liberty of St. Edmundsbury should be free of the evil side of Man's nature."

"You may be right," said the abbot. "But I must plan a proper reception and response when this lord or his emissary arrives and craves audience. If, as you tell me, you expect word of their arrival within the next day, then my preparations must commence immediately."

"I know only the name of this lord, Father Abbot," the reeve said. "Can you tell me what we may expect so that I too may prepare an appropriate response?"

"I have not met Sir Gilbert," responded the abbot. "I know only his reputation as a great and loyal warrior. His forebear fought with the Conqueror in the Battle of Hastings. He holds large lands from the King, and his family is closely allied with that of William de Warenne. I am sure you must have heard tell of that family?"

The reeve nodded. "Yes, Father Abbot," he said. "In the early days of the reign of the Conqueror, the de Warenne family was one of the most powerful in the land. Though their influence has waxed and waned in the centuries since, they remain very influential. I see now why you are concerned that our Liberty should present a good account of itself before such an important lord."

The two men gazed into the fire for a moment, each with their own thoughts.

"Master Durand," the abbot spoke into the silence. "You tell me that there may be some connection between the gift the steward brought to present at the shrine of our blessed St. Edmund and this murderous deed?"

"Yes, Father Abbot," said the reeve. "I cannot state with certainty that such is the case, but there seems little clear motive for such a murder when the man's belt and purse were not taken, and all said he was a man of quiet and generous nature."

"May I see the sword?" asked the abbot.

"Of course," responded the reeve, standing to pick it up off the table where he had laid it upon his arrival. "I made sure to bring it with me in case you wished to see it."

Unwrapping the sword, Durand handed it to Abbot Samson. The monk weighed it in his hands then, and, grasping the hilt, swung it from side to side a couple of times.

"The balance is good," he said. "Yet the sword is old and damaged. I do not think that it has seen battle in recent times."

Taking the blade closer to the fire, he peered at the writing on the blade in the flickering light.

"You tell me the blacksmith did say that Master Aylwin told him this weapon had belonged to a Christian hero, Master Durand?"

"Yes, Father," said the reeve. "Master Short gained the impression that the steward thought the sword to be very old, but the smith was not certain that the age was as great as the tale would suggest."

The abbot nodded but continued to stare at the sword with a puzzled expression.

"Father Abbot?" the reeve prompted after the silence had stretched out perhaps a little too long.

Starting, the abbot turned to the reeve. "Did the

steward say anything more to the smith about the origins of the sword?"

"No, Father," said Durand. "Is there something wrong?"

"No," the abbot said slowly. "It is simply that..."

This time the reeve stayed silent, waiting for the monk to continue.

"I would that we had a little more information," the abbot finally said. "There is something about the sword that seems familiar, yet I cannot put my finger on exactly what that may be."

The abbot continued to stare at the sword for a moment, and then, frustration written clear on his face, he sighed heavily and placed the sword back on the table.

"My lord," said the reeve. "You have traveled far and seen much. Do you think this sword reminds you of something you saw on those travels?"

"I know not," said the abbot. "It bothers my mind, but mayhap it is nothing. That this weapon may be connected to such a terrible deed may be enough to make me imagine more than there is to see in fact. All that is certain is that we desire to see justice for this murdered man."

"Indeed, Father Abbot," responded the reeve.

"So, Master Reeve," said the abbot, shaking off his mood. "Do you have any news for me that concerns more than the identity of the man who Master Aylwin served?"

"I fear I have little more to tell, Father Abbot," said the reeve. "My men have questioned all those we could find who were abroad that night as well as those who claimed to have seen the steward the day he died. We heard many accounts of Master Aylwin appearing to be nervous and constantly looking behind him as if he feared someone was following him. None of those we interviewed could speak of any one person who could be identified as following the steward."

"'Any one person,'" the abbot interposed. "You mean different people were identified by various townsfolk?"

"Not exactly, Father Abbot," responded the reeve. "You can imagine that, when faced with questions about dead men who seemed to be running away from some unknown enemy, some people make much of small things and others offer descriptions that owe more to their imaginations than their eyes."

The abbot nodded in acknowledgement of the truth of the reeve's words and signed for him to continue.

"Mistress Agnew spoke of a small dark man with an evil glint in his eye who stalked the poor gentleman," Master Durand said. "The potter's wife made certain sure that a fair young man wrapped in a rich cloak had crept behind the steward, making sure to keep others between them. Master Watkins saw a juggler with shifty eyes acting suspiciously right after Master Aylwin had passed up the street."

"In what way was he acting suspiciously?" asked the abbot, curious in spite of himself.

"He was walking up the street and stopping every few minutes to juggle balls and beg for coin from those who passed by," the reeve said dryly.

"I see," said the abbot, smiling. "It is indeed true that people will make great stories out of small facts."

The two men talked for a few minutes longer, and then the reeve rose to take his leave. Before he could retrieve the sword from the table, a knock came at the door. "Enter," commanded the abbot.

A young novice entered the room. He was clearly out of breath and nervous.

"What is it, Brother Junius?" said Abbot Samson, not unkindly.

"Father Abbot," the young man began. "Brother Jocelin sent me to say that a great lord and his party has arrived from Sussex. The lord is loathe to rest until he has had audience with you and begs that you will see him tonight."

"Sir Gilbert de Cley," the reeve exclaimed. "He must have ridden hard from Sussex if he has arrived so far ahead of his expected time."

"Indeed," responded the abbot. Turning to the novice to tell him the requested audience was granted, he was interrupted by an energetic knock on the door. Swiftly following upon the knock, a large knight clad in dusty traveling clothes swept into the room.

The knight came to a halt in the middle of the room, surveyed those present, and then, unerringly determining who was in charge, looked straight into the eyes of the abbot. "Was my friend killed for the sword?"

8. Chapter Eight

Gird thy sword upon thy thigh, O most mighty, with thy glory and thy majesty.

Psalm 45:3

The linen room was a hive of activity. The upcoming Feast of St. Luke meant a lot of repairing and decorating of vestments, and Mistress Taylor was not one for leaving any stain unremoved or any stitch undone. All her ladies were hard at work, eager to avoid the eagle eye and sharp tongue of the robemaker.

Aileen was uncertain whether she would even be able to leave the room for her midday meal. I really need to be able to ask Brother Jocelin some more questions about Aylwin's manner on the day of his death, she thought to herself, but I dare not risk Mistress Taylor's wrath.

At last the robemaker was satisfied that her embroiderers were far enough on with their tasks to permit a short break. Relieved, Aileen headed for the guest hall, but was delayed in reaching her goal by the arrival of a great party of riders. Initially frustrated by this further setback to her plans, she soon realized that observing the party from the other side of the courtyard was actually not a bad thing. She saw a group of perhaps a dozen men, weary and travel-stained from a long, hard ride. Some were clad in the plain garb of servants, but some rode richly adorned horses and were wrapped in cloaks of fine cloth and fur.

Scanning the party, Aileen saw, at the head of the column of riders, a tall man on a black horse. The man must be over six feet tall, thought Aileen. And his pure white hair, piercing blue eyes, and square jaw must be daunting to those who cross him.

The man dismounted and, seeing Brother Jocelin come out of the guest hall to greet the newcomers, strode over to him at once. Aileen could not hear their conversation, but it was clear that the tall knight was asking questions of the Guest Master. Brother Jocelin waved his arm in the direction of the abbot's lodgings and, nodding in reply, the knight turned and headed in the direction indicated. Brother Jocelin swiftly spoke to a young novice standing close to him. The novice immediately turned on his heel, grasped his habit in one hand, and ran toward the abbot's lodgings.

Aileen turned her attention to the rest of the party. Two young men who had ridden in behind the leader of the party caught her attention. At least one of them may be a son, thought Aileen. He's just as tall as the first man, although less solidly built. His hair was as thick, but brown in color. He looked around the courtyard with angry grey eyes, and his expression showed contempt for all he saw.

The man who rode beside him could well be his brother, although he was not quite as tall. He had the same brown hair though. He looked around the courtyard with quiet interest, his blue eyes seeming to take in the sights and sounds that imbued life into the abbey's precincts.

I doubt not that these three men are father and sons, Aileen thought. If so, this must be the lord of the manor whom Aylwin served. The steward must have been held in high esteem if his lord would come with such haste and bring his sons with him.

The sound of a man loudly telling a groom to hurry up and take care of the horses drew Aileen's attention. The source of the voice was a big man whose very bulk gave him an air of authority. His eyes and hair were as black as his temper seemed. Pity the poor servant who angers him, said Aileen to herself.

As the horses were led away Aileen saw two young men approach the bad-tempered knight. They spoke briefly and then started moving away from the rest of the party. I think the two young men must be the knights that were so loudly carousing in the guest hall, Aileen decided. Brother Jocelin did say that they seemed to know Master Aylwin.

Determined to hear what the dark knight and the two men were discussing, Aileen casually crossed the courtyard in the same direction as the three men. Fortunately, they came to a stop close by a cart loaded with barrels, so Aileen was able to stand on the other side of the cart without being too obviously intent on eavesdropping.

"Lord Marshal," she heard a quiet voice say. "It is good that you have come."

"I owe my liege this service." This voice was deep and more clear, but it seemed as though the men were being careful to remain unheard by any who might pass by them.

Aileen leaned a little closer to the cart and heard a giggle behind her. Aileen spun around, only to see one of the barrel-maker's children staring at her.

"What are you looking at, Aileen?" asked Eda. Aileen put her finger up to her lips to signal silence. She bent down to talk to the little girl and said, "I wanted to see if I could smell the wine in the barrels."

"Silly!" said Eda. "These are not wine barrels. These are for water. Don't you know the difference?"

Looking suitably contrite, Aileen told Eda that she had learned something new today and sent the child on her way, hoping that their conversation had not attracted the attention of the three men standing on the other side of the cart.

She turned back cautiously and peered around the back of the wagon. She was relieved to see that the three men were intent on their own conversation and seemed unaware of anything else that was going on around them. However, they had moved a little further away from the cart, so it was harder to hear much of what they had to say.

Would that midday in the courtyard was not so busy, thought Aileen. I really cannot get any closer. Frowning in concentration, she tried to tune out all the hustle and bustle around her.

"They do not know," she heard one of the knights say. The rest of his words were drowned out by the sound of a horse neighing and rearing as a stable boy tried to lead it into the stables.

"Constantine." This from a man with a deeper voice, but she could hear only odd words and none of them made any sense. I think that must be the man who has just ridden in from Sussex, Aileen thought. His voice suits well his stature.

"It is missing," came a little too loudly from a higher-pitched voice. What is missing? Aileen thought to herself. Almost she wanted to stamp her foot in frustration, but drawing attention to herself in such a manner was not to be contemplated.

"Keep your counsel!" Aileen heard the deep-voiced knight say sharply.

The three men lowered their voices even further. Aileen was no longer able to hear even one word of their conversation.

At length, the men started walking back toward the guest hall, the newly-arrived knight shouting at his servants not to drop anything and to hurry up.

Aileen hung back a little so as to make sure none of the party suspected her of following them. Once she thought sufficient time had elapsed to allow Brother Jocelin to get his guests settled, she approached the entry to the guest hall. Seeing the Guest Master coming toward her, she hurried to intercept him.

"Good morrow, brother," she said. "It would seem that you have many guests to take care of this day."

Brother Jocelin smiled a little distractedly. "Good morrow, Mistress Aileen," he said. "Indeed, I have. I scarce have a moment to catch my breath right now."

Aileen's face fell a little. He is not going to have time to talk to me today, she thought. But in that, she underestimated the monk's fondness for this girl of the Liberty. The Guest Master ushered her into his office, offering her a seat before sitting on his own stool.

"I have much to do, it is true," said the monk. "But talking with you always brightens my day, so pray tell what is it you came to discuss with me?"

"I promise I will not keep you from your duties long, brother," said Aileen, glad that at least the monk did not consider her a nuisance. "I saw the travelers as they rode into the courtyard, and I saw two young knights greet and talk to one of the party. I wondered if you could tell me if these were the same two knights you mentioned as having been recognized by Aylwin."

"I confess, I was too taken up with preparing for such a large party to notice much else," said Brother Jocelin. "But if one of them was fair and the other brown-haired, then it is most likely they were indeed the same." The Guest Master smiled. "We are not so popular with the warriors of the realm that we have many such knights staying within our walls at any one time."

Aileen returned the smile. "Brother," she said. "You told me you did not know whether the young men were distressed upon hearing of the death of the steward."

Brother Jocelin nodded.

"Brother, do you remember anything else that happened in the days before or after the murder that seemed strange to you?"

"Not really, Mistress Aileen," said the monk. "I know

that Sgt. Ralph was much out of sorts the day after the murder, but little else comes to mind."

"Why was the gatekeeper disturbed that day?" asked Aileen.

"I think I told you that my other guests were unhappy with the behavior of the two young knights, did I not?" said Brother Jocelin.

"Yes, brother, you did."

"Apparently, the night of the murder they returned to the abbey long after the gates were closed. They roused the gatekeeper with loud shouts and banging on the door until he awoke and let them in. Sgt. Ralph said they were very much in their cups and very rude. They told him that lords of such importance should not be kept waiting by such as he."

"That was not courteous," said Aileen. "Did they wake the other guests in the hall as well?"

"I know not," said the monk. "None complained of their behavior that particular night, but it is certainly true that both of these men are considered to be something of a nuisance, and I confess I will not be sorry when they leave our abbey to return to their home."

Brother Jocelin thought about it for a moment. "If you are looking for strange happenings. Mistress Aileen..."

"Yes," she prompted.

"Then it seems passing strange that two young men who have caused so much trouble during their stay should of a sudden quieten down and cause no more." The monk laughed as if he had just told a good joke.

"They have changed?" Aileen asked.

"Yes, they have caused no concerns for this old monk

these past few days," said Brother Jocelin. I have scarce seen them in four days and, now that I think about it, I have received no complaints about their conduct from any other within these walls either."

Jocelin's ears turned red. "Indeed, perhaps they were more affected by the death of the steward than I had thought. God forgive me if I have misjudged them," he said, crossing himself.

Brother Jocelin really is a sweet man, thought Aileen. He becomes so flustered whenever he thinks he is being too harsh about anyone.

As she parted company with the monk, Aileen thought to herself that it was unlikely the Guest Master had misjudged the men. More likely these two knights were trying to behave in a manner more fitting for two Sussex knights who were waiting for the arrival of Aylwin's master.

Had they been aware of the course of the discussion between Brother Jocelin and Aileen, the two young knights might have been a little disconcerted. Since they were not so aware, however, the two men conferred together quietly and then headed toward the stables.

"You there," called the brown-haired knight, his strange eyes blatantly expressing his disdain for his surroundings and the scruffy boy in front of him. "Saddle our horses immediately."

The stable lad who was being addressed looked around and mumbled, "Yessir."

"Be quick about it," said the knight. "You may be able to get away with being slow and lazy when it is only the monks you have to please, but we do not have to put up with that."

Being unused to serving such loud and prideful guests of the abbey, the boy stopped and stared at the men, face frozen in open-mouthed apprehension.

"Stupid boy!" said the fair-headed knight, waving his hand and looking toward his friend as though he were seeking commendation for the forcefulness of his demand. "Do you not see that we are important men, not used to being kept waiting?"

The boy snapped out of his shock and scuttled toward the stable.

The two knights laughed derisively.

"I doubt these peasants have ever been honored by the presence of so many high-born men at one time," said the fair-headed knight.

"I know not, Edward," said his friend indifferently, looking around the courtyard. Seeing that no one was near them, he leaned in toward the fair knight.

"Be that as it may, we need to find a good place to talk where we will not be overheard."

"Yes, we do," said Edward. "Walter, do you think that Sir Thomas…"

The man stopped short when his companion frowned at him and shook his head. The stable boy was coming out of the stable with their mounts.

"Hurry up, you clodpoll," said Walter as the boy paused

to let one of the horses take a drink from a trough outside the stable door. "We don't have all day."

The boy brought the horses over to the two men. Cuffing the lad around the ear, Walter mounted his horse. Jerking at the reins, he started toward the gate of the courtyard. "Come on, Edward," he called over his shoulder.

The fair knight shrugged his shoulders, scowled at the boy still holding his reins, and mounted his horse. Stroking the horse's mane, he took the reins from the boy's hands and followed his companion.

The two knights rode eastward for a while, saying nothing. The day was sunny, although the breeze had a chill in it. The men passed only a few dwellings after they left the immediate area of St. Edmundsbury and eventually found themselves surrounded by woods.

"Let us get off the road," said Walter after a few minutes. "I think I see a clearing through the trees."

Guiding their horses in the direction of the break in the trees, the two men came to a small clearing. Dismounting, they sat down beside a brook they found flowing there.

"The marshal was not pleased," Edward, the fair-haired knight said.

"Did you expect him to be?" Walter responded. "The steward is dead, the sword that he carried is missing, and Sir Gilbert is angry and distraught."

"But we are not responsible for the loss of the sword," protested Edward.

"You know Sir Thomas is a hard man," said Walter. "Little surprise then that his first words to us would be to demand answers. He expected us to provide them."

"Have we not done all we could to discover where the sword may be," whined Edward.

Walter was rapidly losing his patience. "Stop sniveling," he said. "The steward died Saturday night, and today is Thursday. Sir Thomas expected more from us. Indeed, I cannot say I much blame him."

Edward flushed at the harsh words and looked as though he might say something in return. Instead, he hung his head and started picking at a blade of grass beside him. His companion gave him a look of disdain.

"Sir Thomas has offered us great preferment," said Walter. "It would behoove us to make sure he continues to favor us."

Edward just looked at his friend. I would that I had Walter's strength, he thought to himself. Yet if following his lead ensures my advancement, I must needs suffer his sharp tongue.

Sighing, Edward turned his focus back to the conversation. "How shall we do that, Walter?" he asked.

"The first thing we need to do is find that sword," said Walter.

"But how?" Edward sounded confused.

"The marshal will be taking charge back at the abbey, and no one will notice if we are there or not," Walter said. "We are going to return to the town and work back from the place where the steward was found. We must see if we can find any likely hiding places where Aylwin may have concealed the weapon."

"But why would he have done such a thing?" asked Edward.

"If he saw a shadow or heard footsteps behind him, he

might have thought it best to stash the sword somewhere until such time as it was safe to retrieve it."

"I suppose that may be so," Edward said doubtfully.

"For the moment, it is the only theory I have," said Walter. "Let's go." With that, Walter rose, quickly mounted his horse, and started to ride away. Edward had little choice but to quickly follow suit.

Had anyone cared to take notice of the two knights cantering toward St. Edmundsbury that day, they might have commented on the grim expression on the face of the taller, brown-haired man and the nervous expression on the face of the other. None did so observe them, however, and so the knights returned to the town to pursue their purpose as clouds scudded across the sky and the good folk of the Liberty began to wind down for the day.

9. Chapter Nine

*Awake, O sword, against my shepherd; and against the man
that is my fellow, saith the Lord of hosts.*

Zechariah 13:7

For a moment no one moved; no one even took a
breath. The grim knight looked from face to face,
perceiving the effect of his abrupt question. He
took a slow breath, eased the tension in his body, and put
up his hand in acknowledgement.

"Forgive me, Father Abbot," he said. "I have ridden
hard in grief and anger. Throughout my journey I thought
of nothing but my friend, Aylwin, and how he had come to
such an end. Yet there is no excuse for the discourtesy of my
entry into your chambers and the lack of respect I showed
by my first words."

The abbot bowed his head graciously. "My lord," he

began. "Your compassion for your friend does you honor, even if your greeting was perhaps a little unexpected." The abbot smiled to take the sting out of his words and gestured for the knight to be seated.

"I believe that I have the honor of addressing Sir Gilbert de Cley," Abbot Samson said.

"Yes, Father," said the knight. "I am Gilbert de Cley. Aylwin was my steward and my friend of many years."

"Before we speak further," said the abbot. "Let me offer you some wine and bread. You have ridden far and must be in need of drink and food." So saying, the abbot told Brother Junius to fetch food from the kitchens and himself poured wine for the knight.

"Thank you," said Sir Gilbert. "In my haste, I took little time to do anything but ensure the horses were watered and fed. Now that I have arrived at your abbey, I find myself suddenly very tired and in need of refreshment."

"Would you rather that we speak tomorrow, after you have rested a little?" asked Abbot Samson.

"No, Father," the knight said. "The questions that I have, and mayhap those you have for me, cannot wait."

"In that case," said the abbot. "Let me introduce you to Master Durand, who is the reeve of the Liberty of St. Edmundsbury. It is he in whom we have placed our trust to solve this most heinous crime."

"Master Reeve," the knight said, turning to acknowledge Durand. "Pray tell me what progress you have made in finding the killer."

Durand returned the enquiring look of the knight. "My lord," he said. "My men and I have not spared any effort to find out what happened to this visitor to our town. We have asked questions of all who were abroad that night and many more besides."

"And what have you learned?" asked Sir Gilbert.

"We have learned that your steward was seen as a kind and devout man by all with whom he spoke."

"This I already know," said Sir Gilbert. "But have you learned nothing of his death or the reason for such a wicked assault upon him?"

"No, my lord," said the reeve. "The motive does not appear to be robbery, for his belt and purse were still in place when he was found."

"But the sword was not?" Sir Gilbert asked sharply.

"No, my lord," Durand walked over to the table and picked up the sword. "The steward had taken it to the blacksmith for repair before presenting your gift at the shrine of St. Edmund."

The knight exclaimed at the sight of the sword and stood to take it from the reeve.

"Then I have the answer to my question," he said, cradling the sword in his hands. "If the sword was not in my friend's possession, then he cannot have been murdered for it."

The abbot and the reeve exchanged glances. "My lord," said Abbot Samson. "I cannot say how many within the confines of our town were aware of the fact that the sword had been taken to the smith for repair."

"Indeed," said Durand. "It would seem that Master Aylwin did not visit the taverns or have much converse with any within the walls of the abbey or without."

"Aylwin was not one for talking," the knight smiled sadly.

"Sir Gilbert, our lack of understanding about the steward and the sword hamper our efforts to seek justice for this worthy man," the abbot said. "Mayhap you can tell us more and thus help Master Durand achieve that justice?"

There was a pause while the knight gathered his thoughts.

"I have known Aylwin my whole life," he began. "He was, as I am sure you know, of Saxon blood?"

The abbot and Durand nodded.

"Aylwin's ancestors were landowners under Harold Godwinson, but they were dispossessed after King William defeated the Saxons at Hastings. They remained on the land, but in service to my great-grandfather, to whom their land was granted."

"Many who lost their land in this way took up arms against their lords," said Abbot Samson. "Was your great-grandfather not concerned that having the former owner of his land so close might not cause such trouble to him?"

Sir Gilbert smiled. "Lord Robert would have said that it is better to have potential enemies close, where you can observe them, than far away where you cannot tell what they may be plotting."

"A wise man, indeed," said the abbot. "Forgive the interruption, my lord. Pray continue."

"As the years passed," continued the knight, "the risk of rebellion also lessened, and my family and that of Aylwin were at peace with each other. By the time my father inherited the land, Aylwin's father was a trusted servant.

"When I was about three years old, there was a very hard winter," he went on. "Rivers were frozen, and many people died of the cold."

"Yes," said Abbot Samson. "I remember that winter of 1150. There had been so much rain in the summer that the corn harvest was destroyed. The winter dealt the final blow to many of the poor."

"My father told me times were hard, but I remember little about that year other than Aylwin's father saving my father's life."

"God's truth!" said Master Durand. "This is a tale I had not foreseen."

"Master Reeve," said the abbot, giving his officer an admonishing look.

"Your pardon, Father Abbot," Durand said. "I was so surprised I forgot myself."

The abbot graciously inclined his head and turned to the knight, signing him to continue.

Sir Gilbert half smiled. "It was in the midst of that winter that my father, Sir Richard, received a message from the king that he should attend upon him in London. My father rode out, together with the messenger the very next day.

"The rivers were frozen solid that winter, and the men sought a shorter way than by the road around our lands. They thought to cross over the icy water, but my father had no sooner reached the middle of the river near our home when the ice broke beneath him, and he fell into the freezing water."

Sir Gilbert paused for a moment to take a drink of wine. His two listeners tried not to show their impatience to hear the rest of the tale.

"Aylwin's father, Cuthbert, was on the riverbank at the time," said the knight. "He was walking toward his house and thought to take the same route as had my father. When he saw my father fall through the ice, he took no heed for his own safety but crawled over the ice toward the hole.

"When he reached the hole in the ice, my father was sinking, borne down by the weight of his clothes. Only his hand remained above the water, reaching out to the sky in desperation."

"What happened then?" This seemed like a tale told by a traveling storyteller, thought Durand, but better.

"Cuthbert grasped my father's hand with his, but he was close to being pulled down by the drowning man and almost thought to let go. But he could not see any man drown when there was a chance of saving him.

"As he slid further toward the hole, the ice cracking all around him, Cuthbert used his free hand to grasp the rope he had used to lead the oxen to the field. He looped it around my father's wrist. That done, he pulled his own hand from the one that was holding on to his so tightly, backed away from the hole and the thin ice and pulled my father out."

"That was bravely done," Abbot Samson said.

"My father agreed," said Sir Gilbert. "He told me that men of honor are often sought but rarely found. Cuthbert was such a man. My father trusted him more than most for the rest of his life."

"And you trusted Aylwin," said the abbot.

"Yes," Sir Gilbert said simply. "Aylwin and I learned our letters and studied beside each other at the order of my father. We became the closest of friends, and when my father died, I kept Aylwin in my household. When the old steward died, I elevated Aylwin to that position, though many sought the power of being steward. I could and did trust Aylwin more than any other."

"You must grieve greatly that he should have died so cruelly," said Durand.

"I do," responded Sir Gilbert. The hand holding his goblet of wine tightened around the stem. "My greatest fear is that I sent Aylwin to his death by sending him to St. Edmundsbury with this offering."

"My lord," the abbot said. "There can be no guilt when a pious man offers a gift to God and His saints. The guilt lies with the murderer, not you."

"I thank you, Father Abbot," said the knight. "Yet I think it is not that easy for me to cast off this fear."

"Sir Gilbert," said Abbot Samson. "We know little of the history of this sword. Mayhap if you can tell us more about it, we can see a path toward solving this mystery."

"If it will help, then I will gladly tell you all I know," the knight said.

Settling back into his seat, he began: "Some months ago, a merchant known to me for many years arrived and stayed at my castle as a guest. He has traveled far and seen much. His tales were a welcome addition at our table.

"Brenier, for such is his name, had traveled from Normandy on a pilgrimage to Walsingham. He brought with him this sword, which he had purchased in Pontarlier."

The abbot started. "Pontarlier? Then he had traveled the Chemin des Anglois, the pilgrim's route from Rome?"

"Yes, Father," said Sir Gilbert. "Brenier is a devout man. Indeed, I met him first on such a pilgrimage."

"Did this merchant tell you the history of the sword?" asked Durand, eager to return to the subject at hand.

"He did not know its full history," said the knight. "He said only that the sword was rumored to be a special sword and extremely valuable. He spoke of rumors that a Christian hero had carried it into battle for God."

"Did he say which Christian hero?" asked the abbot.

"No," said Sir Gilbert. "I do not think he knew for sure. I gained the impression that he may have been ridiculed for giving a name in the past and thought better of risking laughter again. His account made for a good tale, though, and the sword, though damaged, certainly looked as though it could have been borne into battle long ago."

"It is a pity that the merchant was not able to name the hero," said the reeve.

"I agree," Sir Gilbert said. "However, an incomplete tale did not detract from the pleasure Brenier's visit brought us. He stayed with us for some weeks but left somewhat abruptly."

"Truly?" The reeve was interested to hear about this.

"There came a time when I had to ride to visit one of my estates that was a three-day journey." Sir Gilbert went on. "Upon my return, I learned that Brenier had received a message from another friend of his who also wanted to journey to Walsingham. Since that friend wished to leave immediately, Brenier decided to join him."

"He did not take the sword with him?" asked the abbot.

"My elder son, Roger, did tell me that Brenier, as an expression of appreciation for our hospitality, had gifted the sword to our house. Roger said that the merchant was sad that he could not await my return, but that he hoped the sword would speak for him of the depth of his gratitude."

"Indeed, that was a great gift," said the abbot.

"A gift too great for simple hospitality," replied the knight. "I determined to offer the sword at the shrine of St. Edmund. To me, it did seem that a sword that had fought battles for our Lord should find its final resting place at the shrine of a saint of our Lord."

"That was well done," Abbot Samson said.

"I knew that my faithful steward would take great pleasure in being the one to bring the sword to St. Edmundsbury," Sir Gilbert continued. "He had spoken often of traveling here to pray at the shrine. So I placed the sword into his care. I offered to send riders with him in case of ambush by robbers on the way, but Aylwin said he would ride alone. He believed that God would guard a simple pilgrim along the way."

"His faith was justified, my lord," said the abbot. "He was not attacked along the way, and thus you should not suffer guilt as a result of his death. Had you sent a dozen riders with him, they could not have prevented his murder."

"Mayhap you are right," said the knight. "Yet I would find the villain ere I leave your walls."

"We shall do all within our power to find the murderer," the abbot said. Durand nodded his head in agreement.

"Thank you," Sir Gilbert said. "I would ask one further favor."

"You have but to ask," responded the abbot.

"I would have a mass said for my friend's soul," said the knight. "I go from here to light a candle for him, but if you would hold a mass in your great abbey, I would be deeply grateful."

"It shall be done," said the abbot.

With these words the knight rose, thanked the abbot and the reeve for their assistance, and left the lodging to light his candle and return to the guest hall.

10. Chapter Ten

And David lifted up his eyes, and saw the angel of the LORD
stand between the earth and the heaven, having a drawn
sword in his hand stretched out over Jerusalem. Then David
and the elders of Israel, who were clothed in sackcloth, fell
upon their faces.

1 Chronicles 21:16

I don't know how she does it, thought Robert as he walked up Churchgate late that afternoon. Any other time, I'd be doing my best not to meet Mad Meg, but right now I'm looking for her everywhere. Aileen could charm the birds out of the trees. She can certainly charm me into doing almost anything!

It could be worse, he mused. Mad Meg may be mad, but she's harmless. I wonder if it's true she is the widow of a

villein who was caught poaching and thrown off his land by
his master.

Whether it be true or not, it is hard to know where she
may be found. She could be begging on the other side of
town or sleeping off too much ale in an alley somewhere. At
least I know that, if she is awake, I will hear her ranting and
muttering afore I see her. And if I do not find her, I can at
least enjoy the bread and cheese Aileen told me to bring.

Fast upon that thought, Robert spotted Meg hunkered
down in an alley not far from Moyses Hall. The thin, old
woman with mangled, greasy hair and dark eyes was well
below five feet when standing tall. This afternoon, she was
sheltering from the wind in the back corner of the alley,
eating a crust of moldy black bread. Around her was a cloak
with an old-fashioned fastening. I'll wager that cloak is all
she has left of her old life, said Robert to himself.

As Robert approached her, Meg shied away from him,
drawing even further back into the corner.

"'Tis mine," Meg said, grasping the crust of bread close
to her.

Robert slowed down and put out his hand in a concilia-
tory gesture. "Do not be afraid," he said. "I will not harm
you or try to steal your bread."

Meg eyed Robert with suspicion but said nothing, only
muttering under her breath about thieves who come upon
poor, old women and attack them for their pittance.

"Look," he said, untying his bundle of bread and
cheese. "I have brought you fresh bread and some cheese.
The nights have been cold, and I thought you would need
something more than stale bread to keep you warm."

At his words, Meg's face expressed clearly first suspicion, then doubt, puzzlement, hope, and finally cunning. "You want something," she said. "There's none would go out of their way to bring me good victuals. They all think I'm a mad old woman and go the other way when they see me coming. What do you want?"

Perhaps she isn't so mad after all, thought Robert. If she notices how everyone reacts to her, there has to be something left of the old Meg.

"Your pardon," he said. "I am as guilty as any other. As a child, I was afraid when you ran up to me and started talking about devils right in front of my face. But I am grown now, and I hope that I would not react in the same way."

Meg cackled and lunged forward, snatching the bread and cheese out of Robert's hands. Instinctively, he stepped back as she moved, and that just made her laugh the louder.

"Methinks you have not grown so much," she shouted, standing up and dancing around in circles. "I think you want something much. To gift me victuals, methinks you swallowed your fear." So saying, Meg crammed bread and cheese into her mouth, never taking her eyes off Robert while she ate.

I don't know how to do this, Robert said to himself. Aileen is so much better at this kind of thing. Mad Meg is never going to tell me anything. But I have to find a way of making her trust me enough to talk.

Hoping that the woman would feel less threatened if he no longer towered over her, Robert squatted down and waited for her to finish eating.

Gradually the tension seemed to go out of Meg's body, and her noisy chewing slowed. Finally, she sat back down and regarded the young man with narrowed eyes. "What do you want, then?" she asked.

"I wanted to ask you about something," Robert said.

"Ask," Meg said. "I ain't promising to answer, but you can ask."

That's not exactly a good start, thought Robert, but at least she's willing to listen. "Did you hear about a man who was killed in an alley not far from here?"

"No," she said shortly, shaking her head.

Robert looked keenly at the woman. "It was about five days ago," Robert said. "Are you sure you didn't hear about it?"

Meg looked at him steadily for a moment or two. "Why do you want to know?" she asked. "You don't look like the kind that takes pleasure in nasty tales and foul deeds."

"I'm not!" said Robert, shocked that anyone would think that of him. "I ask only because a friend of mine is afraid. I am trying to help him see he doesn't have to be so concerned."Again Meg paused, scanning his face carefully. "I believe you," she said matter-of-factly. Gnawing on a crust of the bread, she was silent for what seemed like ages.

Robert, reining in his desire to urge her to say something, echoed her silence.

"Good folk should be able to lay their heads down at night without being disturbed by neither angels nor demons," the woman burst out.

This sounds like what she told John Thetford, thought Robert, heartened that Meg had finally said something. Mayhap I can coax more out of her.

"I agree," he said, trying to look as sympathetic as possible.

Meg eyed him narrowly. "Most folks in the Liberty care little about themselves and nought about me."

The woman leaned forward, squinting at Robert, her eyes daring him to contradict her. Seeing this as a test, Robert merely nodded. Aileen would be able to come up with a good response, he thought. I judge it better to say nothing!

As though his very silence was a good answer, the old woman sat back. "I ain't stupid," she said. "Folks around these parts call me 'Mad Meg,' and that suits me well enough. I gets food and drink from women who know that, but for the grace of God, they could share my fate. Most others just leave me alone. A tad of shouting and muttering drives away any I don't want to see."

She trusts me, thought Robert in surprise. That must be the longest speech anyone has had from Meg in a long time, and I doubt she has revealed her secrets to many. Aileen will be so proud of me.

Robert was brought out of his musing by the realization that Meg was still speaking.

"You ask about that night," she said. "Shouts and cries, that's what I remember."

"Who was shouting?" asked Robert.

"I may be old, and I may be mad, according to some," Meg said, "but I already told you I ain't stupid. Think you that I would seek out trouble in the dead of night?"

"No," said Robert. "I think you are too sensible for that."

Meg's face cracked into a gap-toothed smile. "Mayhap you are right," she said. "Then again, mayhap you ain't."

Robert said nothing.

"Ye believe in God and His angels?" Robert was startled by the question.

"Yes, of course I do," he replied.

"There's some that do and some that don't," Meg said. "The priest always makes it seem as though Judgment Day was a day far from now."

"You think it is not?" asked Robert.

"Mayhap for some it comes early," Meg said.

Robert's faced reflected his confusion.

Meg cackled and reached up to the sky. "Michael the archangel brings forth his shining sword to defend God's people," she said, her voice rising. "But the devil puts out the light and plunges all into despair and darkness."

What is she talking about? Robert thought. This is madness. Perhaps I was wrong to trust she could tell me anything.

But Meg was no longer seeing the young man in front of her. Her face still turned toward the sky she continued, "The man, the good man, his face shone with God's grace. I remember his kindness."

Her face crumbled in sorrow, and her hand fell into her lap. "The good man reached his hand out to rescue the archangel's sword, but he could not take it. All is lost."

"Meg," Robert said gently, hoping to bring her back to the present. "Meg, did you see the face of the devil?"

Meg just looked at him, her face grim and sad. Try as he might, Robert could get her to say nothing further. Perhaps it would be better to try another day. I don't know that she has been of any help anyway, but mayhap Aileen can make some sense of what I have learned today.

So thinking, Robert rose, bid the old woman a kind farewell, and made his way back home.

Robert little knew it, but he almost met the two young knights from Sir Gilbert de Cley's household as he walked up Churchgate on his way to find Meg. Had he turned off the street just one block earlier, he would have come face to face with the pair. Even had he done so, though, there would have been nothing in their faces of note, and it is doubtful that Robert would have paused in his steps even for a moment.

Walter and Edward were following Walter's plan to search for the missing sword. Starting from the place where the steward's body had been discovered, they walked through the streets of St. Edmundsbury slowly, looking all around them and peering into alleyways and behind stalls and barrels in the streets.

Robert might have noticed nothing unusual in their behavior in the brief time they would have been within his sight, but there were plenty of townsfolk who stared after the young men as they walked.

"What are those two men doing?" said little Sarah Meeker to her mother in her piercing three-year-old voice.

"Shhhh!" said her mother. "They will hear you." She need not have worried. Walter and Edward were too absorbed in their search to pay mind to any who might be passing them on the street or even, for that matter, standing in their way.

"Mind your path," said Hubert Walker, just avoiding falling over as the fair-haired knight struck his shoulder in passing. Edward barely noticed the contact and certainly made no apology.

"Think you they have lost something of value?" whispered Mistress Porter to her husband, unwittingly putting her finger on the truth.

Her husband shrugged and went back to working on his plans for purchasing a new cart.

Walter and Edward had almost reached the bottom of the hill. The abbey gate was in sight, and they were becoming increasingly frustrated.

"He cannot have hidden it this close to the abbey," said Edward. "Had he glimpsed someone following him this soon, he would not have continued on his way."

"I agree," said Walter. "We have searched all likely places. What could we have missed?"

"Mayhap the steward did not conceal it at all," Edward said.

Walter stood still for a moment, deep in thought. "If he did not conceal the weapon on his way through St. Edmundsbury that night," he said at last, "could he have done so before then?"

"But why would he do so?" asked Edward. "And, if he did, where would he have hidden it? The abbey is not so quiet that a stranger could safely conceal something as big as a sword and be sure no one would find it."

"If not hidden, then where is it?" Walter's voice was a little louder than usual, a sure sign of his frustration. Realizing that he had spoken thus, Walter stole a look around him to see if anyone was paying attention to their conversation.

"We will have to search within the abbey grounds," he said quietly, satisfied that there were no eavesdroppers.

Edward sighed. "There must be hundreds of places within the abbey walls where Aylwin could have stashed the sword," he said.

"Then we had better begin now." Walter's tone was grim. "Sir Thomas will not thank us for taking our rest when the sword is still missing."

So saying, Walter strode off in the direction of the courtyard gate, leaving Edward to follow in his wake, as was his wont.

11. Chapter Eleven

Son of man, prophesy, and say, Thus saith the Lord; Say, A sword, a sword is sharpened, and also furbished.

Ezekiel 21:9

"I am sad that I did not know this man in life," Abbot Samson said after Sir Gilbert had left. "Would that I had known such a man was within my walls."

"Truly it seems that the steward inspired others to much trust and friendship," said Durand. "Yet I do not know that the knowledge we have gained from Sir Gilbert will be of much use to us in solving this crime."

"What of this tale of the sword?" asked the abbot. "Think you that this gift is indeed the cause of Aylwin's death?"

"Father, I do not know," said Durand. "It was a strange

tale that Sir Gilbert told. We have a sword of great renown and value, purchased by a merchant who left the walls of the lord's castle suddenly, gifting it to the household for mere hospitality. That it should be borne to our town by a man who is then murdered does seem to be more than mere coincidence."

"I agree," said the abbot. "And I think now that I remember why this sword did seem to me to be so familiar."

"Indeed, my lord abbot," Durand said with interest. "I would be glad to hear of your memories."

The abbot motioned for the reeve to take his seat again. "You have not taken the pilgrimage to Rome?" he asked Durand.

"No, my lord," responded the reeve. "I have listened to the tales of many who have, and I pray that one day I may be so honored as to take the journey myself."

The abbot nodded. "To walk the Chemin des Anglois with other pilgrims is a journey no man can forget," he said. "Meditating on and talking about God our creator and savior as you journey toward the Holy See changes a man. I will ask the Lord that your prayer be answered some day."

"Thank you, father," the reeve said sincerely.

"Now, let me think what I do remember from my time on the pilgrim's way," the abbot went on. "Sir Gilbert de Cley did talk about meeting the merchant in Pontarlier, I believe."

"He did," said the reeve. "I am not familiar with all the stops on the route to Rome. I know the pilgrim's way begins in Canterbury and makes its way through many countries, but I have not heard of Pontarlier."

"There is no one route that pilgrims must follow,"

explained the abbot. "The journey can be beset by robbers and thieves, and pilgrims will sometimes walk a different route if they hear tell of greater dangers. So too will pilgrims to the Apostolic See whose journey begins over the other side of the South Sea and who call their route the Via Francigena.

"Pontarlier is in the area of the Kingdom of Burgundy. It is not a large town, but pilgrims find it a good place to stop either before or after crossing the Jura mountains. Pilgrims and traders take their rest, exchange goods and coin and tell tales around the fires at night."

"So it was that you also took your rest there?" Durand said as the abbot paused to collect his thoughts.

"Yes," responded Abbot Samson. "I took the route through Pontarlier and met many pilgrims and merchants in that town. One of the traders with whom I broke bread was a man named Brenier."

Durand started. "Brenier? The same Brenier who brought the sword across the South Sea?"

"It would seem to be so," said the abbot. "It would be passing strange if there were two merchants of the same name both involved with an ancient sword."

"It would, father," said the reeve. "I would have said that mayhap such a thing would be as strange as two men such as Sir Gilbert and yourself meeting the same man but for the fact that the merchant seems to follow the pilgrim route as a matter of trade." The two men smiled in mutual agreement.

"Father Abbot," Durand went on. "Did Brenier tell you the same tale of the sword as he did Sir Gilbert de Cley?"

"I cannot say whether it is the same tale," said the

abbot. "But I can tell you what he told those of us who sat one cold night around the fire."

"I would be most interested in your account of that conversation," said the reeve.

The abbot paused for a moment and then began his account. "As I said, we were gathered around the fire that night, just a group of four men. Besides the merchant and myself, I seem to remember that there was a Cistercian monk with whom I had a lively discussion concerning the interpretation of the Rule of St. Benedict, and a Norman knight who said little but was gracious enough when asked for his opinion."

"How was it that the merchant came to talk of the sword?" asked the reeve.

"I believe it was actually due to something I said," responded Abbot Samson. "I was intrigued by a story I was told by another pilgrim concerning the saber of the Emperor Charlemagne. The merchant said that he had heard the same tale about the Emperor Otto III finding the sword when he opened the grave of Charlemagne."

The abbot ceased talking at this point and picked up his goblet. Durand wanted to ask more about this interesting piece of information but was loathe to interrupt the thoughts of Abbot Samson.

"The group talked about the story for a short time," the abbot continued. "Then Brenier said that this was not the only legendary blade that had been found. Of course, we were all interested to hear this tale, and so we asked the merchant to tell us more.

"Brenier told us that, by the grace of God, he had been able to acquire the sword of a Christian hero greater even than that of whom we had been speaking. Of course we all demanded to know whose sword this could be. The merchant then drew out of his belongings an object wrapped in cloth, soiled by long travel but yet clearly of fine fabric.

"The trader reverently unwrapped the bundle to reveal an old sword, much damaged by the years. In the firelight, the inlay in the sword gleamed through the dirt and rust that covered it."

Durand was sitting forward in his seat, his attention fully focused on the abbot.

"I must admit that the sight of the sword did somewhat underwhelm me," said the abbot. "I think we all felt the same way, but the merchant gazed upon the sword as though it was the greatest treasure in the world.

"Finally, he looked up at us and said that this sword was the very one held by the Emperor Constantine when he fought and won the battle against Maxentius, thus paving the way for the emperor's conversion to Christianity. Legend says that this sword has the power to make men great and that the Lord defends those who wield it."

"Truly, this is the sword of Constantine?" asked Durand, looking at the weapon with wonder in his eyes.

"This I do not know," said the abbot. "This was the tale told us by Brenier, but in truth I did not get a very good look at the sword. I saw it only that once, and in the fire-light, it was hard to see much before Brenier wrapped it up again.

"The trader told us that the sword had inlay on both sides of the blade and that this was how he knew the sword had belonged to the great Emperor Constantine. Beyond that, I know nothing."

"That you did not see the sword in detail explains why you did not recognize it when I first showed it to you," the reeve said.

"It does," affirmed the abbot. "But I believe it was the word 'CONSTAININUS' on the side of the blade that made me think there was something familiar about the sword."

"Is this another variation of the emperor's name?" Durand asked.

"I had not heard so," said the abbot. "But we know that many names, when they are taken far from their original home, are written or even pronounced differently. Why should this not be so with the names of the great, as with any other? It may be that the emperor was known as Constaininus in some parts of his empire, and that the sword was forged by a bladesmith in such a far land."

Durand frowned. "Your words are wise, father," he said. "And of course there is the benediction on the other side of the blade to be considered. Yet I am still unsure of the history of this blade."

"I share your concern, Master Reeve," said the abbot. "It would seem also that, by the time the merchant arrived in the house of the Lord de Cley, he had thought better of sharing his belief as to the identity of the original owner of the weapon. I think I shall talk further with that worthy lord. Mayhap he has thought of more information he can give me of the tale he heard from the merchant and of the life of his steward. It is possible that he knows more than he realizes of the circumstances that led to his friend's death."

"And I will talk further with Master Short," said Durand. "He is skilled in the art of swordsmithing, and I believe he may be able to tell me more about his doubts as to the origin of the sword."

"A good plan," the abbot said. "I shall look forward to hearing what the smith has to say."

With a benediction from the abbot, Durand left the abbey. He was more determined than ever to succeed in his investigation. This Saxon steward had been a good man, and justice must be had for his murder.

12. Chapter Twelve

Behold, I have created the smith that bloweth the coals in the fire, and that bringeth forth a weapon for its work.

Isaiah 54:16

F riday morning, as he made his way toward the blacksmith's forge, Durand was worried. Tomorrow would be a week since murder was done, and he was not confident that the killer would still be found within the precincts of St. Edmundsbury. Still, all he could do was to continue to seek answers to the questions surrounding this death. God grant that I find out the truth and bring the murderer to justice, he thought as he turned in to the forge. There he was greeted by Guy Short and Adam, who was pumping air into the forge to keep the fire alight.

"Good morrow to you, Master Durand," said the black-smith. "I hope that you are well?"

"Thank you, Master Short," said the reeve. "I am well, but I hope to hear that you are quite recovered from the attack upon you."

The blacksmith rubbed his head ruefully but acknowl-edged that he was quite well enough to work, and thus he could say that he was recovered.

"What can I do for you, Master Reeve?" he asked Durand. "I know full well that you came not only to ask after my health."

Durand smiled. "We have known each other for too many years for me to be able to hide much from you, Master Short," he said.

"Sit you down," said Guy. "Let us have a drink of ale and you can tell me what it is that you need from me."

"I thank you," Durand said. "I would like that." He seated himself on a stool away from the fire and waited while Adam left the forge to fetch the tankards for both men.

"Master Short," the reeve began, "You have said that the sword Aylwin brought to you for repair did not seem to match the account he gave you."

"Almost I regret making mention of this matter," said the smith. "My distress at hearing of the death of Aylwin made me place too much importance on small concerns. I should perhaps had better been silent."

"Master Short," said Durand. "I doubt not that you are a man who does always that which he believes to be right." Guy smiled a little and nodded his head. "Whether there be any connection between the sword and the murder of this good man I cannot yet tell. Thus I must pursue any possible route to find his killer."

"If I can be of any help, then of course I will do my best," responded the smith. "I do not know what else I can tell you but ask what you will."

"I need to know more about the sword and its origins," said the reeve. "Like many men, I have carried a sword and of course seen many others, but I am not expert in their forging and the changes in the form of swords over the years. I would be most grateful if you could talk to me about the sword itself, and mayhap you could tell me more about the root of your concern."

Guy took a long pull at his ale and then, going over to the other side of the forge, he brought back a sword and held it in his hands as he turned to the reeve. Adam, who had been quietly pumping air into the forge, hoping that his father would not take notice of him and tell him to leave them, strained to hear the conversation over the sound of the bellows.

"This is a sword similar to those carried by the brave knights who answer the Holy Father's call to take up arms for the Cross," Guy said.

Durand nodded.

"This weapon is over three and one half spans long," the smith continued. "At the guard, the blade is over five barleycorns wide. These measurements are similar to those of the sword brought to me by the steward, although not exactly the same." He stopped and looked at the reeve.

"I confess I do not see the significance of these facts," said Durand. "Some differences between one sword and another are clear even to those who, like me, are unskilled in the art of bladesmithing, but I understand little of the reason for those differences."

"I fear I am not explaining myself very well," said the smith. "It is in the forging that I demonstrate my skill, not in words. Let me put it this way. The size of a sword and other small details may well vary a little from one to the next, but the general look of swords in any era changes little."

"That would seem to make sense," said the reeve. "Pray continue, Master Short."

"I tell you all this merely to introduce the differences in sword-making over the course of history. Even though the sword brought to me by Aylwin was not so different in size from this sword, I would say that the forging of the weapon was not in the style of the bladesmiths of our time."

"Would that not make his tale of it being an ancient sword the more likely?" asked Durand.

"I believe that only a smith with experience in the forging of swords would look at the blade and wonder about the claim as to its age," said Guy.

He settled on his stool and, seeing the puzzlement in Durand's face, continued. "Although I spend most of my time now making nails and farm implements, I was fortunate in my youth to be apprenticed to a swordsmith. He was known throughout the land as a fine craftsman, and from him I learned all that I know."

Durand nodded for Master Short to continue.

"Around the fire of an evening, he would recount tales of heroes wielding fine swords. He would talk also of the changes in forging and design through the many eras of warfare."

"This is how you came to know so much about swords then," Durand said.

"It is," said the smith. "When the steward brought me the sword for repair, he seemed to believe the blade was from a time before invaders drove the Roman soldiers out of our land. Even though the sword was damaged, it seemed to me that it was not so old as that."

"Please explain," said Durand.

The smith thought for a moment before speaking further. "I do not doubt that those who have guarded the sword for many years truly believed it to be an ancient sword," he said. "The swords carried in the days when Rome ruled this land were forged of mixed metals layered together to harden the outside. The swords were made light and easy to wield by forging in grooves on either side of the blade. They were of similar length to the sword that Aylwin brought to offer at the shrine of our blessed St. Edmund." Guy crossed himself as he spoke the name of the saint.

"I still do not understand your misgivings in this matter," Durand said, becoming a little frustrated.

Guy sighed. "Forgive me," he said. "I am a little long-winded in my explanation. The more I talk about it, though, the more I am sure the sword is not ancient, but merely old. Speaking of it out loud to you makes more clear to me the full extent of my doubts."

Eagerly he turned to the reeve. "It is in the method of forging that the seed of my misgivings lie," he said. "For many eras now, swordsmiths have forged weapons by heating the metal to a high temperature, quenching it in water to harden it, and then reheating it to a lower temperature to make sure that the blade holds a sharp edge while at the same time retaining its flexibility. This process makes the blade more reliable than did the process followed in ancient times. Craftsman such as the swordsmith who taught me all I know were experts in judging the temperature of the forge at each stage of the process. Is this clear?" he asked Durand.

The reeve voiced understanding.

"When I saw the sword the steward wanted me to repair, it did seem to me that the blade showed signs of having been forged in this more modern manner," Guy went on. "The grooves on each side of the blade were wider and more shallow than I believe was the case in ancient times. The cross guard seemed to be wider than in the Roman era. While it is possible that rare swords of that time may have possessed at least some of these features, I deem it unlikely that both the forging and the design of any of these ancient swords would be so different from the common run of swords."

"Master Short," said the reeve, "I am in awe of your knowledge. Bladesmithing is indeed a skill beyond the understanding of the man who wields the weapon. I would like to ask, however, if it would not have been possible that these features that so trouble you could have been added to the steward's weapon at a later time, mayhap when the sword was repaired?"

The smith smiled. "Think you not I did ask myself the same question?" he said. "It may be that is the case, but I do doubt it."

Guy held up the sword he had brought from the other side of the forge. "See you this slight difference in color where the pommel is attached to the sword?"

The reeve looked hard at the sword and then acknowledged that he did.

"The pommel that was forged at the time of the making of this sword was broken at an earlier time. How I do not know. That second pommel has shown signs of weakness, and the owner of the blade has brought it to me for replacement. I shall be proud to replace this weak member with a good, strong pommel." The smith's pride in his work was obvious.

"It was in a manner similar to this that you came to the conclusion that the sword to be offered at the shrine of St. Edmund had no repairs?" the reeve asked.

"It was," said Guy. "I may be mistaken, but I could see no signs of repair, or of changes in the design of that weapon. Indeed, the steward brought it to me because the weapon was in need of a new pommel, the old one having been broken off, and the original metal standing out stark and raw."

"Master Short," said Durand, rising as he spoke. "You have given me much to ponder. I thank you and hope that I may not trouble you any further."

"Master Reeve," said the smith. "My son and I are at your disposal whenever you may need." As he spoke, Guy turned to his son whose interest in the conversation had caused him to pump less vigorously. Adam's face colored, and he returned to his task with energy.

"Fare thee well," Durand said, leaving the pair to return to their duties.

I am not sure that I am any further forward, thought Durand as he trudged toward his home. If the sword was not as old as Aylwin had thought, then how could it be the cause of his murder? But what if the steward was not the only one who had believed it to belong to a great Christian hero, possibly the Emperor Constantine? In that case, it may still be the motive for the murder.

The reeve knew that the abbot was sure to ask him later that day what he had found out from the smith. Abbot Samson had granted Sir Gilbert de Cley's petition to be permitted to bury his faithful steward in the Anglo-Saxon cemetery to the west of the abbey. Aylwin was to be laid to rest alongside his ancestors that very afternoon, and many would attend. If the murderer were still within the walls of the town, he may be there as well, thought Durand. Too much to hope that I will spy guilt on any face in the crowd.

My poor head is aching, Durand thought to himself. Too many strands of thread lie scattered all around, and I can make no sense of them at all. I had better lie down with a poultice on my head when I get home. There is much thinking to do, and a sore head is no way in which to do it.

13. CHAPTER THIRTEEN

Think not that I am come to send peace on earth: I came not to send peace, but a sword.

Matthew 10:34

The procession, grim and silent, made its slow way through the streets of St. Edmundsbury, the plain wooden coffin borne on the shoulders of men who had worked with Aylwin for many years. Behind the coffin walked his grieving master, followed by his household and monks of the abbey. It was a testament to the impression that the Saxon steward had made upon the town in so few days that a long line of the people of the Liberty came behind those who had known Aylwin best.

The sky was heavy with dark clouds that seemed ready to weep alongside the mourners at any moment. Yet, when the procession reached the old cemetery and the abbot began to read the words ordained for the burial of the dead, a beam of light shone down through the clouds and warmed the cold wood of the coffin.

Almost it seems as though Aylwin himself is thanking the people of St. Edmundsbury for their compassion and generosity, thought Aileen.

Almost it seems as though Aylwin himself is trying to help us find his murderer, thought Durand. He looked around the gathered crowd, most standing in silent stillness, some shuffling slightly as though to warm themselves on this chilly morn. The reeve hoped to see guilt, or possibly even fear, on the face of someone close by. In this he was disappointed, but nevertheless the reeve felt somehow heartened by the ray of light so perfectly timed on this grey and sorrowful day.

The abbot looked around the crowd as he intoned the all-too familiar words of comfort and hope of salvation. Sorrow I see, he thought, but also sidelong glances at acquaintances as well as strangers. It is not good for our town that this crime be not solved. Suspicion of those around you will only beget more arguments between neighbors, and mayhap even more violence.

Abbot Samson's gaze fastened upon one man in the crowd. For a moment he faltered in his words, causing some of his flock to look up in surprise. Samson quickly recovered, but his expression remained thoughtful and his brow furrowed.

Soon enough, the worthy steward was consigned to the grave. The good people of St. Edmundsbury walked slowly back to their duties to the sound of clods of damp earth hitting the wood of the coffin as the gash in the smooth soil of the cemetery was filled in.

Aileen and her coworkers, all of whom had joined the robemaker in walking in the procession, returned to the abbey in a subdued mood. Mistress Taylor, chivvying her ladies to hurry up and get back to work, surreptitiously wiped a tear from her eye.

These are strange times, thought Aileen as she worked. Our town mourns for a man few had even met and eye with suspicion those whom they have known all their lives. Until the murderer is discovered, the folk of the Liberty will not be at peace with themselves. Pray God Master Durand catches him, and if there is anything that Robert and I can do to aid him in that task, pray God we will find a way to do so.

I t was afternoon before Aileen had the chance to follow her plan to visit Brother Jocelin. Walking quickly across the courtyard toward the guest hall, she encountered two of Sir Gilbert's servants running in the direction of the infirmary, faces set in anger.

"Your pardon," said one of them, stopping short as he almost ran into Aileen.

"I took no harm," Aileen said, smiling at the pair. "I think you must have an errand of great urgency to rush so in the abbey."

Her encouraging smile smoothed the frown on the

young man's face. I thought not to see a pretty girl in this old abbey, he thought.

"Hold up, Tom," he called to the other servant who had continued on his way. The man turned and, seeing his friend talking to Aileen, retraced his steps.

"John," he said, "We don't have time for this. Sir Thomas will be calling for us any time now, and you know how he is if everything is not done as he ordered."

"There is no need to be rude, Tom," said John. "I stopped merely because I near ran into this young lady. It is only courteous to apologize." He smiled at Aileen, achieving the reward of an answering smile directed at both young men.

"Sirs," said Aileen, "There is nothing to forgive. But I see that you are in a hurry. Is there any way in which I may be of help? I am not only of the Liberty, but I work here in the abbey."

"You do?" asked John. "Then can you tell us where we can find the infirmarer? The Marshal has cut himself and has need of some salve."

"Aye," said Tom. "And the Marshal is not known for his patience."

What an opportunity to learn more of this household, thought Aileen. "I think it is easier if I walk with you and show you the way," she said. "Our infirmarer, Brother Adam, is on pilgrimage now, but Brother Francis has assisted him these many years and is very skilled. He may be in the infirmary, but at this hour, it is possible he is within the cloisters. It serves little purpose if I tell you only how to find the one and not the other."

Receiving the thanks of the two young men, Aileen set off in the direction of the infirmary.

"I think you are of the household of Sir Gilbert de Cley?" Aileen began.

"We are," Tom said. "Our master is Sir Thomas Warren, the Marshal."

"There did seem to be many riders in your party," Aileen said. "I think Sir Gilbert must have held his steward in high esteem."

"Aye, he did," said John. "When he received the news of Aylwin's death, he was sore troubled. Nothing would serve but that he and his sons ride to St. Edmundsbury immediately. The Marshal would not allow that the lord and his heirs ride alone without the protection of his knights. So it was that more than a dozen of us set out."

"This Sir Thomas sounds like a stern man," said Aileen.

"He is!" said Tom with feeling. "He rules the fighting men with an iron fist, and his moods are as black as his hair and his eyes. You can imagine John and I were not best pleased when we were told we must ride to St. Edmundsbury with him. At least back home we are not the only targets of his ire."

"Tom," said John. "We should not speak to strangers of such things."

Tom was abashed. "My pardon, mistress," he said to Aileen. "I pray you will not think the worse of us for my hasty words."

"Have no fear," said Aileen. "We all must needs obey the orders of those for whom we work. I am blessed that my mistress, although stern, is of a kindly disposition. Why would I make things harder for you by sharing your words with others?"

"Thank you," said John simply.

As he spoke, Aileen spied Brother Francis crossing the courtyard. A pity, she thought. I had thought to learn more of the household of Sir Gilbert de Cley. Yet I know that I may seek out these two young servants should I have need of them again.

"Brother Francis," she called. The monk turned toward her voice. Smiling, he came over to the trio.

"Mistress Aileen," he said. "Good morrow to you."

"Good morrow to you, brother," Aileen responded. Turning to the two men beside her, she explained that they were of the household of Sir Gilbert de Cley.

"Brother, we have need of the services of the abbey's infirmarer," said John. "We are told that Brother Adam is not within the walls at this time, but that you may be able to assist us."

"If it be within my power, I will gladly do what I can," Brother Francis said.

"Sir Thomas Warren, who is the marshal to Sir Gilbert de Cley, has cut his finger," John went on. "It is bleeding and he sent us to find the infirmarer and obtain some salve."

"I will come at once," said Brother Francis. "Such cuts, if made by contact with old knives or tools, can fester and become serious."

"The knife was not old," Tom said. "Sir Thomas was having loud conversation with another knight while peeling an apple with his dagger. The dagger slipped and cut his thumb, but it was a clean weapon."

"That is good," said the monk. "Let me return to the infirmary and collect a salve and some bandages, and I will come to the guest hall right away."

"Thank you, brother," said John. Turning to Aileen, he smiled and bowed. "Thank you also, mistress. Without you, I am sure we would have taken longer to find help, and Sir Thomas would have become even more distressed."

"I am glad that I was able to help," said Aileen.

The monk went one way to find what he needed to treat the marshal's wound, and the two servants went another to return to the guest hall. Following them in that direction slowly, for she did not wish them to think she was following them, Aileen thought over the conversation. So the marshal was having "loud conversation" at the time he cut his finger. I wonder what the conversation was about, she thought.

Reaching the door of the guest hall, she almost ran into Brother Jocelin.

"Your pardon, Mistress Aileen," said the monk. "I fear I was paying too little attention to where I was walking and too much to the number of loaves I must needs have to feed all my guests."

Aileen smiled at the harried Guest Master. "I took no injury, brother," she said. "It is unusual for the guest hall to be so full at this season of the year, is it not?"

Brother Jocelin sighed. "Indeed it is," he said. "I had thought that I might be able to take some time to check on the state of our linens and cots before the next feast day. I even thought to write in my journal. So many unusual events have occurred in our Liberty of late that I did wish to record them truly. But it was not to be."

"Mayhap the arrival of such a large party as that of Sir Gilbert de Cley did interfere with these plans?"

The monk nodded, and then looked embarrassed. "The guest hall is here to receive all who come to the blessed shrine of St. Edmund," he said. "Even more so should those who grieve the sudden death of another be welcomed within these walls."

"None could complain of the welcome given them by you, brother," Aileen said gently.

"Thank you, my child," said the Guest Master.

"As I came across the courtyard I met two servants to Sir Thomas Warren," Aileen said.

"Young John and Tom, I imagine," said Brother Jocelin.

"Yes," said Aileen. "They were in a great hurry to seek out help for their master."

"Would that the worthy knight had come to me to ask for assistance, I could have sought out Brother Francis with greater haste." The monk seemed distressed at his perceived failure to provide service.

"Do not worry yourself, brother," said Aileen. "I took them to the infirmarer. Brother Francis will be here with his salve and bandages without delay."

"Thank you," Brother Jocelin said. "My mind is greatly relieved to hear this." He looked across the courtyard, clearly hoping to see the young monk coming toward him.

"Brother," Aileen said.

The monk turned back to Aileen, smiling to excuse his inattention. "How may I help you, my child," he said.

"Brother Jocelin," said Aileen. "I have seen a few members of this party now. Grief is clear in the faces of some, but some of those who rode with Sir Gilbert do not appear to be so affected as others."

"That is the way with all things in this world, my child," said the monk. "Grief does not show itself in the same way in all men. Some few weep openly, and some show sadness clearly in their faces. Other men maintain a stony countenance, but one should not judge them uncaring. That may simply be their way."

Aileen nodded her head. It is true, she thought. I remember when the miller lost his baby son. His wife was inconsolable, but the miller himself showed little grief. Only when I saw him early one morning kneeling by the grave, tenderly pulling weeds from the grass, did I understand that his grief was the equal of his wife's.

Unaware of Aileen's musings, Brother Jocelin continued to follow his train of thought. "It must also be the case that any man, especially a man with power, will not be loved by all," he said.

"Yet this man does appear to have been held in high regard," said Aileen.

"This is so," agreed the monk.

As they spoke, a tall young man came out of the doorway, deep in thought, walking toward the stables. He was thin, with brown hair and eyes to match. Methinks he has a kindly face, thought Aileen.

"He is one of the party, is he not, brother?" asked Aileen.

"Yes," said the monk. "He is one of the sons to Sir Gilbert. His name is Stephen, and I believe he is the younger son."

"Is the older son also of the party?" asked Aileen.

"Yes," said Jocelin. "Yet I think that you would not believe the two young men to be brothers of the same father were they to stand side by side." The monk smiled at his own attempt at gentle humor.

"Are they so different then?" Aileen asked.

"In both temperament and appearance," confirmed Brother Jocelin.

"It seems that happens in many families," said Aileen. "The same could be said of my sister and myself. I do love her dearly, and I am certain that she loves me. Yet we can rarely talk to each other without arguing. Our mother has on occasion had to remind us that our father would be most displeased if she was to tell him of our quarreling."

Jocelin smiled. "Indeed, Mistress Aileen," he said. "I fought often with my brother when I was young, and yet we had great love for each other."

Aileen caught the tone of his voice. "That is not the case with the sons of Sir Gilbert de Cley?" she asked.

"Mayhap I should not have given that impression," said Brother Jocelin, always eager to see the best in all. "I know little of this family beyond the fact that they are close allies of the great Lord de Warenne. What I see of their behavior and their manners is but a small part of the whole."

The de Warenne family, thought Aileen. Truly these guests have powerful connections.

Not wishing to be distracted from her purpose, Aileen asked the Guest Master what it was that made him think there was little love lost between the two brothers.

"It may be nothing," said the monk. "It does seem to

me that Sir Roger, the older son, does tease his brother a little too harshly. Yet Stephen responds scarce at all."

"Mayhap he finds a response not appropriate in public?" Aileen asked.

"Mayhap you are right," said Jocelin. "His lack of response seems to make his brother even more angry though. I have seen him actually push his brother when Stephen refuses to acknowledge the sting of his words."

Before Aileen could ask another question, the Guest Master spied the infirmarer crossing the courtyard. "Mistress Aileen, please excuse me. I see Brother Francis coming, and I must conduct him to the injured knight."

Saying her farewells, Aileen started back across the courtyard. She had gone only a few yards when she spotted one of the lay servants from the guest hall coming across the courtyard, a basket of bread on her arm. The girl's pinched face and limp blonde hair made her look even smaller than she was.

"Sarah," Aileen called.

The girl stopped and, seeing Aileen smiling at her, walked slowly over to greet the older girl.

"Good morrow," said Aileen.

Sarah, head down and eyes on the ground, could be heard to mumble a greeting in return.

"It is a long time since we have talked," said Aileen. Indeed, Sarah and she had never really been friends. Sarah was only a year younger, but where Aileen could always be found laughing and enjoying the companionship of many friends, Sarah was painfully shy and rarely spoke unless spoken to first. Aileen liked her well enough, but they had little in common and therefore rarely spent time with each other.

Sarah merely nodded in response. Unabashed, Aileen went on, "I had heard that you were now working in the abbey, but this is the first day I have had the good fortune to see you."

Sarah was not used to such attention being paid to her. She blushed to the roots of her fair hair.

"I have been a lay servant in the guest hall these past three months," Sarah ventured. "Brother Jocelin is very kind."

"I agree," said Aileen. "I have just been talking to him about the party of guests that came from Sussex."

"Sir Gilbert de Cley," said Sarah. "He is a very great lord."

"Great lords have great demands," Aileen said. "No wonder it is that you are so busy."

"Sir Gilbert is not very demanding," responded Sarah. "He is quiet and says little. He accepts what service we can provide without complaint."

"A kindly master, then, for a steward who seems to have been of a similar disposition," said Aileen.

Sarah nodded. "Would that others of his party were so inclined," she said with feeling.

"They are not so?"

"Sir Gilbert has with him two of his sons," said Sarah. "The younger one does seem to take after his father. The older son is very different. He is cruel and arrogant, and..." Sarah stopped and put her hand to her mouth, clearly shocked at the way in which she was talking.

"Sarah, do not worry that I will betray your words,"

said Aileen. "The good Lord knows that I have sometimes been so tried as to say something out of my ordinary speech."

Grateful to have found someone to whom she could pour out her feelings, Sarah continued. "As I said, the younger son—his name is Stephen de Cley—is very courteous. He never strikes out in anger at any servant. Tom says..." Once again Sarah blushed, and Aileen had to hide a smile with a cough.

"The lord marshal's servant told me that Master Stephen, as the younger son, was to take the cowl and be a monk. But though he is most serious, he has told his father he would prefer to attend the court of the king. His father, who for certain seems to be on good terms with this son, is said to be seeking a suitable position for Master Stephen."

"That is most interesting," Aileen said sincerely.

Sarah smiled. She really should smile more often, thought Aileen. She looks so different when she does.

"You said that Master Stephen's brother was not of the same temperament," Aileen encouraged the girl.

"Indeed he is not," Sarah said, the smile wiped from her face. "Sir Roger may be the heir, but he favors his father little, and to hear them talk to each other, Sir Gilbert thinks little of his conduct."

"That must be a sorrow to Sir Gilbert," said Aileen. "What is it that Sir Roger has done, do you think, that has so angered his father?"

"I do not know," said Sarah. "I have only seen them a few times when I have been bringing food to the guest hall, but yesterday Sir Roger turned suddenly when I was behind him and knocked a flagon out of my hand. He shouted at me and would have struck me but for his father. Sir Gilbert told him to hold his passions and behave as befits a man of his rank."

"What happened next?" asked Aileen, intrigued.

"Sir Roger became even more angry, if such was possible, and he pushed me aside. He strode up to his father at the head of the table, and it seemed almost as though he would strike Sir Gilbert himself. Sir Roger is as tall as his father, although not as broad. His angry grey eyes bored deep into those of Sir Gilbert, like thunderstorms about to break, and when he spoke, it was through clenched teeth."

"Almost I can see it, you describe the scene so well," Aileen said, shocked to hear of a son speaking so to his father. "Please go on."

Sarah had rarely had such a rapt audience. She looked around and then drew Aileen down to sit on some barrels.

"Sir Roger told his father that he should not speak so to his son and heir in front of people of such low account. Sir Gilbert stood face to face with his son, more as though they were enemies than family. He told Sir Roger that he would not speak so if his son and heir were a man to be held in higher regard."

Sarah paused for a moment and Aileen leant forward, eager to hear more.

"You could almost hear Sir Roger's teeth grinding, he was so angry," said Sarah. "He accused his father of placing more trust in his Saxon steward than he did in his son, and told him he could not grieve the death of a man who stood between him and the honor and power that was his due. There was a silence after he spoke those words. It was as if the whole room was waiting for the storm to break."

"Go on," said Aileen as Sarah came to a halt. The servant girl gave a slight shake of her head and looked down at her hands.

Wondering what had happened to cause her silence, Aileen looked around to see a tall, thin young knight coming toward them. His brown hair, just a little longer than was the norm, gleamed in the sunlight. She thought he might be one of those who had arrived the day after Aylwin. As he neared them, Aileen was startled to see that the man had one blue eye and one brown. How very unusual, she thought. I have never seen anyone with such eyes, though I have heard tell of such a thing.

For a moment, she thought he was going to speak to them, but those strange eyes looked right through the two girls, and the knight merely reached down into one of the barrels close to them. Taking out an apple and the dagger which hung on the right side of his belt, he began to peel the apple. Then, without acknowledging either girl, the man sauntered off putting slices of apple into his mouth as he walked.

"That was close," said Sarah, a little shaken by the encounter.

"Who is that knight?" asked Aileen. "Is he one of the household of Sir Gilbert de Cley?"

"Yes," said Sarah. "I have seen the marshal speaking to him so, even though he did not arrive with Sir Gilbert's party, I am sure he must be one of the knights of that house. The marshal called him Sir Walter."

"I have seen him before in the abbey courtyard, though I did not know his name," said Aileen. "But Sarah, please go on with your story. It is fascinating."

Sarah settled herself more comfortably on the barrel and continued with her tale. "Sir Gilbert looked at his son for a long moment, and then, as if he had only just realized that there were many people in attendance, he told Sir Roger that the bitterness displayed by such a speech must be the result of undigested food since jealousy was unbefitting one of his rank. Sir Gilbert went on that he was sure Sir Roger would think better of his words in a short while and that they would continue the conversation then."

"What did his son say to that?" Aileen asked.

"Nothing," said Sarah. "Sir Gilbert walked out of the hall, and Sir Roger just stood there looking after him."

That was a bit of an anticlimax, thought Aileen. Nevertheless, the tale told by Sarah was illuminating.

"I must get back to the guest hall," said Sarah, getting up hastily. "I have dallied too long and am behind my time."

"I must get back to the linen room as well," said Aileen. "Mistress Taylor will not be pleased if I am late."

The two girls said their farewells, promising to talk more in the future.

As Aileen hurried toward her destination, she heard a voice calling her name. Turning, she saw Hugh running up to her.

"Aileen," said Hugh, "What news have you for me?"

"Hugh," she said. "I am sorry, but I will be late if I tarry any longer."

The boy looked so disappointed, Aileen could not just walk away without giving him some reason to hope. "Robert and I are meeting on the riverbank near to the meadow before the sun sets," she said. "Would you like to join us? We can discuss what progress we have made and decide on what we should do next."

"Yes, I would," said Hugh, happily. "Thank you."

The two exchanged smiles and, with the promise of more to come, went their separate ways.

14. Chapter Fourteen

Ye have feared the sword; and I will bring a sword upon you.

Ezekiel 11:8

"He did not even have the sword with him." Edward was clearly distressed as he and his friend walked in the vineyards behind the abbey. It was Friday morning, and the mist was only now clearing from the banks of the river as the sun melted the frost on the ground.

"Keep your voice down," said Walter angrily. "There is nothing to be gained by alerting the whole world to our concerns."

Edward gulped and took a deep breath. "What should we do now?"

Walter looked at his friend. Edward is weak, he thought.

I know not what Sir Thomas sees in him unless it be that Edward's father has many useful connections of which we can make use as we rise in power.

"We do whatever the marshal tells us to do," Walter said bluntly. "The sword is found. We wait until Sir Thomas tells us he has need of us again."

"I know not what other service we may perform for the marshal now that we have failed to produce the sword," said Edward gloomily. "He does not regard us kindly right now, and that speaks ill of our chances of preferment."

"Sir Thomas will have other tasks for us to perform," replied Walter. "He is a man of powerful moods. He will always plan for the best future within his grasp, not only for himself, but for the lord's family and all those around him. When he is ready, he will tell us what he needs us to do to help achieve that future."

"Mayhap we would be better asking Sir Gilbert how we can help," said Edward.

"Sir Thomas is our leader," Walter said sharply. "He is to whom we report. We would be ill advised to anger him, even were we to gain the favor of his master."

"The marshal's anger can be brutal once aroused," agreed Edward.

"In the meantime," said Walter, "we should be available as needed and ensure that we do not attract any unpleasant attention. That is the best way in which we can be of service."

The two knights turned to head back to the guest hall, dissatisfied and deep in their own thoughts.

As the pair crossed the courtyard, Brother Francis approached them.

"Good morrow, sirs," said the monk.

The knights looked at the infirmarer disdainfully. "What is it that you want, brother," Walter said.

Even Brother Francis, young and naïve as he was, could sense that the two men did not wish to be interrupted by a lowly monk.

"Please excuse the interruption," he stammered. "I merely wished to ask after the health of Sir Thomas Warren. I know you are of his party, and I was concerned about the cut on his hand."

Edward and Walter both relaxed a little. The monk may be a foolish peasant, thought Walter, but there is no point in making a scene.

"I believe the cut is healing well, brother," he said. "Forgive us if I was short with you. Sir Edward and I simply did not expect to be interrupted in the middle of our discussion."

Edward looked at his companion in surprise. It is unlike Walter to apologize for anything, he thought. He must have a reason for doing so, but I'm dashed if I can see it.

"Of course," said Francis. "I should not have approached you thus."

Walter inclined his head graciously toward the monk.

"Thank you for the information," said Francis. "Please do let me know if I can be of further assistance to any in your party."

So saying, the monk walked away hurriedly. Walter and Edward, with nothing further to say to each other, returned to the guest hall and set themselves to wait for further instructions.

W hile the two knights were considering how they should move forward, the abbot and Durand were closeted in the abbot's chambers.

"Sir Gilbert seemed strangely troubled when I had conversation with him this morning," Abbot Samson said. "I thought at the time his mood was somber due to the funeral for his friend, especially as he asked as a courtesy to the memory of his steward that I be the one to read the words of the funeral service, but I do believe there is something more to it than that."

"I doubt not this is a hard day for him," said Durand.

"It is," the abbot said in agreement. "However, after he left I realized he had asked no questions about the progress of the investigation. In fact, he seemed to be preoccupied with the conduct of certain members of his household rather than in discussing Aylwin's sad fate."

"That is strange," the reeve said. "When he arrived, all he could talk about was finding his steward's murderer. That he would so quickly allow internal matters to overtake his mind does seem to be unlike the man as he appeared to us."

The two sat in silence for a moment, the abbot sipping from his goblet and the reeve taking a deep draught from his tankard.

"Father, what was it Sir Gilbert discussed today if not the death of Aylwin?" Durand said.

"The first thing he said was that a man can do only what he believes to be right," said the abbot. "I merely said that against such a sentiment there could be no argument."

Durand said nothing. He looked at the abbot quizzically.

"Sir Gilbert then talked about how the lord of a great estate cannot know everything that takes place on a daily basis, but that he did wonder at the fact that two of his knights had decided to come to St. Edmundsbury within a day of his good steward."

"They had not obtained permission from the lord?" Durand said.

"They had not," said the abbot. "Sir Gilbert told me that the marshal had given them permission to come to our great abbey on pilgrimage. There are many knights within the walls of the lord's estates, so he would not necessarily have been told of such a journey. He did think it was ill-timed, however. Had he known that the two young knights were so eager to visit St. Edmund's shrine, he would have insisted that they ride with Aylwin."

"It would have made more sense had they ridden together," said the reeve. "They must have traveled the same route just one day apart."

"Indeed," said Abbot Samson thoughtfully.

"Was that the full extent of the lord's concern?" asked Durand.

"No," said the abbot. "He questioned also why you had had to send a rider to inform him of the death of Aylwin when there were two knights within these walls who knew the steward well and could have ridden to Sussex themselves."

"That is a good question," Durand said. "I confess I have had the same thought myself. I had hoped to talk to Sir Edward Strode and Sir Walter de Nantes today and ask of them why they did not come forward earlier to identify the dead man."

"Sir Gilbert has already talked to the two young knights," the abbot said. "He told me they were distressed that they had found out the identity of the murdered man too late to set out for Sussex before you sent your rider. Sir Walter told his lord that they were at prayer most of the Sabbath and therefore heard of the death of Aylwin only the day after."

"They did not wonder at the steward's absence from mass, or even from the guest hall on Sunday?" asked the reeve.

"It would seem that you and Sir Gilbert are of the same mind," the abbot said with a slight smile. "He did ask them the same question. Their response was that the steward did not spend much time with them, and therefore they had no reason to wonder why he was not in their presence."

"A very pretty explanation," said the reeve. "It may even be the truth."

"You have reason to be suspicious of their account, Master Reeve," said the abbot.

"No, Father Abbot," Durand said. "It may be merely a function of my job that I am always suspicious of neat explanations when I am in the middle of an investigation."

The abbot chuckled. "Mayhap that is why you are so good at your job, Master Reeve," he said.

Durand inclined his head in acknowledgement of the compliment. "Was there anything else that Sir Gilbert said that gave you cause for concern, father," he asked.

"There was nothing else that he said," responded the abbot. "It was more what he did not say."

Durand raised an eyebrow and waited for Abbot Samson to continue.

"You will recall that Sir Gilbert was almost overcome by the thought that he had unwittingly sent the steward to his death by entrusting him with the sword to place at the shrine of our blessed saint," said the abbot.

"I do recall, father," said Durand. "Your wise words reminding him that the fault lies with the murderer did seem to offer him some comfort."

"I did hope that to be the case," Abbot Samson said. "And yet I wonder."

"I do not understand, my lord abbot," said the reeve.

"In the course of our conversation this morning, I asked if any within Sir Gilbert's household could suggest any reason for this foul crime. The lord's reaction took me by surprise. He appeared almost angry and said only that there had been little discussion beyond the fact that the sword was not lost. He told me that some had asked where it had been hidden, and his reply had been to tell those present that it was not hidden, but merely in your possession. I gained the impression that the response of some within his household to that information had not been as he expected it to be."

"He said nothing more?" asked Durand.

"No," said the abbot. "Almost immediately after that he stood up, thanked me for my hospitality and the efforts of all who have honored his old friend, and left. Sir Gilbert told me that he and his household will return to Sussex on Monday. He did not ask me whether I thought it might be possible to solve this crime before then."

"This is strange indeed," said Durand. "Mayhap he has some concern that some within his household know more of the circumstances surrounding the death of Master Aylwin."

"Sir Gilbert is an honorable man," responded the abbot. "I think that, if he truly believed anyone known to him had done this deed, he would surrender them over to you. Yet there is something that bothers him, and he is eager to leave the Liberty and return home. Mayhap he has convinced himself that he can resolve whatever the matter is there, on his own territory."

"I think you may be right, father," said the reeve. "In the meantime, I will keep investigating and see if I can yet find this murderer and put at ease the mind of this noble lord before he rides home."

So saying, Durand rose, took his leave of the abbot, and set out for home.

Walking up Churchgate Street, Durand was deep in thought. These young knights have done something to earn the disfavor of their lord, he mused. Yet I can see no reason why they would have done harm to the steward. Had they wanted to take the sword, they could have done that before he ever left Sussex. They could have overtaken him on the road and done him to death there. Why wait until he is within the Liberty and risk being seen by others. No, whatever it is they have done, it is unlikely to have anything to do with Aylwin's murder.

Durand's thoughts were interrupted by the sound of raucous laughter coming from a group of men leaving the tavern he was passing. He frowned at them but let them be. The men are in their cups, he thought. They are causing no trouble.

The reeve had gone only a few yards more when a snapping sound to his left alerted him. Instinctively, he darted a glance in the direction of the sound just in time to see barrels rolling off the wagon he was passing. Three big barrels crashed to the ground, the first one smashing to pieces as it hit the ground. The other two, catapulting over the first, headed straight for the startled reeve.

15. Chapter Fifteen

Is there not here under thine hand spear or sword? For I have neither brought my sword nor my weapons with me, because the king's business required haste.

1 Samuel 21:8

The riverbank that evening seemed even more peaceful and calm than usual. Aileen was the first to arrive, and she took the time to enjoy the light breeze and the scents of the grass and flowers around her.

"Aileen," called Robert, interrupting her thoughts. "I am sorry I am a little late. I was delayed by a maidservant at the abbey."

"A maidservant at the abbey," Aileen said in pretend shock. "Pray tell how that came to be?"

"It was not as it seems," Robert said quickly, his hand

raised as though to stop Aileen's thoughts going in the wrong direction.

"Of course it was not," Aileen said, barely able to conceal her smile. "If it was not what it seems, then what was it?"

Robert's blushes were spared by the arrival of Hugh, and the three wasted no time in beginning their discussion.

"So many people came to see the steward buried," said Aileen. "He touched many lives here in St. Edmundsbury, and I feel we owe it to him even more to make sure those who killed him do not go free."

"I agree," said Robert. "Hugh, we began this journey with the goal of making you and your family more at ease in your minds. We had no intention of seeking out a murderer, and Master Durand made it clear to us that he did not want us doing so."

"I understand," said Hugh quietly. "I asked too much of you."

Aileen leaned over and put her hand on top of the Hugh's as he sat on the riverbank looking miserable.

"But then your father was attacked in his own forge," Robert went on, not quite sure how he felt about Aileen's gesture toward the boy. "Aileen and I could not stand by while your family was so afflicted, and so we talked to some people that perhaps Master Durand would not think to interview."

"I am sure you have learned much that could be of help," said Hugh, raising his chin and looking much happier.

Aileen and Robert exchanged glances, aware of the ample trust placed in them by their friend.

"We have learned many interesting things about the sword, and about the family whom Aylwin served," said Robert. "Like Aileen, I feel as though it is our duty to do whatever we can to help Master Durand bring the killer or killers to justice."

"Hugh." Aileen thought it was time to get down to practicalities. "Whenever we can, Robert and I meet here at the end of the day to exchange whatever we have learned. By doing so, we hope to glean something that may be of help in identifying the murderer."

"So did you learn anything of interest today?" asked Hugh.

"I had hoped to learn something of interest by watching the people who attended the funeral," said Robert. "I was disappointed, however. I could discern no guilty or fearful look."

"Not even in that moment when the sun broke through the clouds and seemed to shine upon Aylwin's coffin," added Aileen. "Had I been the murderer, that moment would have betrayed me, I do believe."

Robert smiled. "Aileen, you look guilty if you are caught picking more wild mushrooms than you need for one day's cooking. I cannot even imagine you in the role of murderer!"

"I suppose if you are capable of doing such a foul deed, you would have to be able to hide your true character from those around you," said Aileen.

"That is a good point," said Robert. "Think you the killer is hiding in plain sight and that it may even be someone we know?"

"I pray not," said Aileen. "I mean, whoever it is, there

will be some who love him and who will be filled with sorrow when he is brought to justice, but I confess I do hope that it will not be someone with whom we have shared bread or good companionship."

Hugh broke the silence that followed Aileen's words. "When I asked for your help, I did not realize that this was going to be so difficult. I thought only of finding some information about the sword and its bearer that would make my father less sad. I am sorry that I have been the cause of so much trouble."

"You did right, Hugh," Aileen said. "This is a riddle for sure, but if we can help solve it, I believe both Robert and I will be glad."

"That is truth," said Robert.

"So let us begin," said Aileen. "Robert, I want to hear about this maidservant who delayed you this evening."

I really set the hawk among the sparrows with that one, thought Robert. I had better choose my words with more care or I will definitely be in trouble.

"The encounter was not of my choosing, Aileen," he said. "Sir Gilbert had ordered a gold brooch from my father, and he sent me to deliver it. Sir Gilbert and most of his party were riding out, so one of the monks fetched a maid-servant who was of the lord's household. That is how it came about that I was delayed."

Robert could feel the color in his face rising as he spoke. Why can't I stop that happening? he thought. Aileen cannot fail to notice.

"I understand how it came about that you spoke with this maidservant, Robert," said Aileen. "What I do not understand is why the simple task of delivering a package for your father should have so delayed your arrival this evening."

I knew it, thought Robert disgustedly. Aileen is too clever. I cannot hide anything from her.

"I think it was only that few people take note of the girl," he said. "She was eager to talk to someone other than the servants around her. Molly said that it was interesting to talk to someone from the Liberty."

"Molly?" asked Aileen, eyebrow raised and laughter in her eyes.

"Aileen, please," said Robert, glad that at least she seemed to be amused. "I promise I dallied no longer than necessary. I confess, I think the girl was overly friendly with a stranger, but in the end it was to our advantage. She told me something that I think you will find of interest."

"I'm sorry, Robert," Aileen said. "I could not resist teasing you just a little."

Aileen reached out and placed her hand on top of Robert's for a moment. He flushed to the roots of his hair again and then recounted what he had to tell.

"It was as I said," he began. "Sir Gilbert had sent word to my father asking that he visit him in the guest hall to discuss a commission. He gave my father a drawing of a brooch and asked if it would be possible for it to be made within a matter of days."

"Surely it takes longer than that for a craftsman such as your father to complete such a commission," said Hugh.

"In the usual course of business, that is indeed so," replied Robert. "This was a special commission, though, and my father told the lord that it could be done if he put aside all other work. Sir Gilbert offered him a good price, saying he had heard of my father's skill and would be grateful if the task could be carried out."

"What was so special about this brooch?" asked Aileen.

"Sir Gilbert told my father that the drawing was of a brooch that had been passed down by the steward's forebears and that it was of great value to Aylwin. He wore it on his cloak always."

Aileen thought for a moment. "Was not the cloak stolen on the night of the murder? I remember thinking it strange that a cloak would be taken but not the money in the steward's purse."

"Yes," said Hugh eagerly. "I thought the same thing myself."

"Mayhap this is the answer to that part of the riddle," Aileen said. "The thief may have seen the brooch and not the purse. He stole the one and left the other without even realizing that there was coin worth taking."

"It may be so," agreed Robert. "A gold fastening can be seen by all, whereas a purse hanging from a belt underneath the cloak cannot. If the murderer was afraid of being caught, he might not have taken the time to search his victim."

Hugh looked admiringly at the pair. It seems almost as though they think as one, he said to himself.

"Let us leave that aside for the moment," said Aileen. "I want to hear more of your tale."

"There is not much more to tell," Robert said. "My father did wonder at the urgency of the commission and offered to send it to Sir Gilbert in Sussex once it was finished. He told the lord that he usually liked to take more time over the fine details.

"Sir Gilbert said he would wish the commission to be completed before he left St. Edmundsbury because he knew that Aylwin's son would be traveling to Sussex from across the South Sea, and he would like to be able to present him with the brooch upon his arrival."

"A son," said Aileen. "We heard nothing about the steward's family. How terrible for them."

"Why did the son not travel to St. Edmundsbury with Sir Gilbert?" asked Hugh.

"My father said Aelfric, for so is his name, was taking care of Sir Gilbert's estates in Normandy when the tragedy took place. He sent word to Aelfric but did not wish to tarry long enough to await his arrival."

"How sad," said Aileen. "Are there any other children who will grieve the loss of their father?"

"I know not," Robert said. "My father did not ask."

"Of course he would not," said Aileen. "Whether there be more of Aylwin's line to grieve does not change the task we have before us."

"No," agreed Robert. "But I have more to tell you. I have not yet spoken of what it was that Molly told me."

"No indeed, you have not," said Aileen, smiling.

"The maid took the package from me and promised to keep it safe until Sir Gilbert's return," Robert said. "She told me that she would hand it to none but Sir Gilbert, for there were some of the household who might not think to keep it from damage as well."

"Truly?" said Hugh.

"Truly," said Robert. "She told me that there were some among the party who were jealous of the power of the steward. She could not speak of how they would care for a copy of Aylwin's brooch were she to hand it to one of them."

"Did she say of whom she was speaking?" asked Aileen.

Robert looked a little shamefaced. "No, she did not," he said. "I confess, I was a little too eager in asking that very question. Molly became shy of talking more about the household, and in the end I had to leave without learning more."

"Never mind, Robert," said Aileen. "This was all good information. We must see how it fits into the rest of our picture."

"I have one more thing to tell you about," said Robert. "I think it may be important."

"What is it?" asked Hugh.

"I cannot wait to hear what it is," said Aileen at the same time.

Satisfied that he had made quite an impression with his last statement, Robert launched into an account of his encounter with Hadric. "So," he concluded. "What do you think of that?"

"Hadric is certainly not popular with the townsfolk here," said Aileen. "He is oftentimes a little too pushy, and he has a reputation for not being completely truthful."

"My mother says he has a hard life and she feels sorry for him," said Hugh. "At the same time, I have heard her tell my father that she cannot entirely trust him."

"That is our difficulty," said Aileen. "But well done, Robert. You drew him out very well."

Robert positively glowed at the compliment, although some might have called the beetroot color that rose to his hairline something else.

Aileen, pretending not to see his embarrassment, returned to the thought she had been expression before Robert mentioned Hadric. "We need to look at the rag and bone man's story as another part of the overall picture that we can paint once we have all the information we can obtain," she said.

"Speaking of which, Aileen," Robert said, rallying. "What did you learn today? You meant to talk to Brother Jocelin. Were you able to do so?"

"Yes," said Aileen. "But I spoke to others of the household of Sir Gilbert and learned much from them as well."

"What did you learn?" Hugh could barely contain his excitement. Robert and Aileen were so good at finding out what was going on. He had certainly asked the right people for their help.

Aileen told the others all about her conversations with Brother Jocelin.

"So Sir Gilbert de Cley is an ally of the Lord de Warenne," said Robert. "Even I have heard of that family."

"Who are they?" asked Hugh.

Aileen frowned at Robert. I should not even have mentioned the connection, she thought. This can have little or nothing to do with the murder of the steward.

"You have never heard of the de Warenne family?" Robert was shocked. "They are only one of the most powerful families in the realm. They own most of Sussex and have many manors in this part of the country as well."

"Oh, that de Warenne family," Hugh said unconvincingly.

Aileen took pity on the boy.

"Robert is always interested in battles and weapons,

Hugh," she said. "Your interests lie elsewhere, so there is no reason why you should have as much knowledge of this noble family as does Robert." She scowled at Robert as she spoke.

"Your pardon, Hugh," said Robert. "Aileen is right. I have always been fascinated by the tales passed down in my family about the time of the Conqueror and his fighting men."

"My father also told me stories he had heard from his father and he from his father before him," said Aileen.

Feeling a little sorry that she had spoken so sharply to Robert, she smiled at him. "Why do you not tell Hugh about Sir William de Warenne and how he came to be lord of so many lands."

Robert was happy to take up the tale. "Hugh, I am certain you do know how William the Conqueror fought the Anglo-Saxon king Harold to win England."

"Of course," said Hugh. "I have not lived in a hole all my life!"

Oh dear, thought Robert, I have put my foot in the mire once again.

"Of course not," he said. "I was only setting the stage for my story."

Hurrying on before anyone could interrupt him, Robert continued, "Sir William de Warenne was one of the lords who came across the South Sea with the Duke of Normandy and fought at his side at the Battle of Hastings."

Warming to his tale, Robert became even more animated. "Side by side with his lord and his fellows he fought, sword clashing on sword, horses baying and men falling. All day they fought, blood and sweat combined running down their faces. As night drew near..."

"Robert," said Aileen. "I think we are perhaps straying a little from the main story."

"Your pardon," said Robert, flushing in embarrassment. "Where was I?" he said. "Oh, yes. Well, after the Conqueror became king, he rewarded Sir William by making him the Earl of Surrey and granting him a lot of land. He gave him the Rape of Lewes which, as you know, is close by the area where Sir Gilbert de Cley lives. He gave him many other estates, including some in the areas east of us. Sir William de Warenne was a mighty warrior."

"But I think I heard tell he was a devout man also," said Aileen. "My father did tell me that he went on pilgrimage to Rome and that, when he returned to England, he founded a priory on his lands."

"I may have heard something of the same," said Robert, clearly not as interested in the founding of priories as in the clash of weapons.

"So it is the heir of this great man who now holds the title of Earl of Surrey?" said Hugh.

"Not a direct heir, I think," said Aileen. "I believe I heard my father say that the male line died out in his father's time. The daughter of the third earl, I think it was, married a relation of King Henry II."

"I doubt not the relation was glad of such a desirable match," said Robert. "For I have heard tell that he was born not of the lawful line of succession,"

Aileen frowned her disapproval, spurring him to add, "But then are many fine men born so. The Conqueror himself was born of such a union but still was declared his father's heir."

I am making a mess of this, thought Robert. I had better stop before Aileen gets really angry.

"Hamelin, for that was the man's name, did take the name of de Warenne upon his marriage," said Aileen, deciding to ignore the gaffes of her friend. "Thus the Earls of Surrey still retain the name, and they are still powerful lords in our land."

"And Sir Gilbert de Cley is friend to this earl," said Hugh. "I cannot imagine how such a man could be involved in the death of his faithful servant."

"I doubt not that he is entirely innocent of any knowledge of this crime," said Aileen. "That does not mean that all within his household are as free of guilt."

Aileen returned to her account of the day's events, telling Robert and Hugh about her conversation with Sarah. "So it seems that there is more than one person within the household who displays ill temper," she finished.

"Yes," said Robert. "But what does this have to do with the murder of the steward? After all, if a bad temper were the sign of a murderer, there are several people I know who would be under investigation by the reeve."

Aileen and Hugh laughed.

"Of course you are right," said Aileen. "The moods of the marshal and Sir Gilbert's son do seem to have little to do with Master Aylwin's death. It would seem that Sir Roger bears a greater grudge against his father than the steward. Both the marshal and Sir Roger were in Sussex when the murder occurred, and in any case, I cannot see why Sir Thomas Warren would wish Master Aylwin dead."

"So do you think this information is of any use at all?" asked Hugh.

"I think that where there is one person with dark intent, there are bound to be more," Aileen said. "Although we cannot see a motive for murdering Aylwin in what we have learned thus far, there may well be another close by for whom a motive does exist. We cannot stop here."

A lively discussion then took place on their next steps. Robert was eager to see if he could learn anything more from Molly.

"I am sure she knows more than she told me," he said. "I only need be careful how I ask her questions. I'm sure I can learn more from her."

Aileen did not much care for this idea. "You have probably learned as much as she knows already, Robert," she said. "Molly sounds as though she is a little too fond of good-looking young men."

Aileen stopped short, and Robert blushed once again. Hugh laughed at the expressions on the faces of his two friends.

"What about me?" he asked. "Surely I can do something to help."

Glad to change the subject, Aileen said she was not certain there was anything Hugh could do to help. He did not have the same opportunities to ask questions that she and Robert had.

"But the knights are returning to the forge tomorrow," he said. "I can talk to them."

"The knights who asked your father about the bit for the horse?" Robert asked.

"Yes," said Hugh.

"Why are they coming back?" said Aileen.

"For the new bit, of course," Hugh said. "They asked that father make one before the Sabbath. Tomorrow is Saturday. They have not returned yet, so they must be coming then."

"I am not sure it is wise for you to ask questions of these knights," Robert said. "They do not sound as though they are kindly disposed toward any outside their kind, and we do not want them to become suspicious."

"I will be careful, I promise," said Hugh. "After all, we are only trying to find out more about this strange group of men surrounding Sir Gilbert de Cley. I am sure I can find out something without making it seem as though I am just nosy."

"Mayhap it will be better if you do sound nosy," said Aileen, laughing. "People take no account of those they see that way. Only if you take your questions too seriously are they likely to pay much attention."

"Good," said Hugh. "Then it is settled."

Neither Robert nor Aileen was entirely happy with this situation, but they realized there was little they could do to stop Hugh. Better he be guided by their directions than that he go out on his own and risk getting into trouble.

"As for you, Robert," Aileen said, frowning. "I think mayhap it is better if you talk to Molly again than that I try to talk with her. She sounds like the kind of girl who is more likely to respond to a man than to another woman."

Not wishing to provoke another scolding Robert merely said Aileen's words made sense. With that, the trio parted company and made their way back to their homes, each with their head deep in plans for the morrow.

16. Chapter Sixteen

*And to the angel of the church in Pergamos write; These
things saith he which hath the sharp sword with two edges.*

Revelation 2:12

The ring of a hammer striking an anvil greeted the
three men who entered the forge on Saturday
morning.

"Good morrow, my lords," Guy said, straightening up
and putting the horseshoe upon which he was working
back in the forge to heat.

"Good morrow, blacksmith," said Edward Strode, who
was the knight who had asked Guy to make the bit. "My
companion and I have brought with us he who has
command of all the knights of the household of Sir Gilbert
de Cley." He gestured toward the third man of the party,
who stood a head taller than either of the two young

knights and wore a dark and forbidding expression with eyes as black as his hair.

A man who expects to be obeyed, thought Guy, looking at him closely.

"Good morrow, my lord," he said mildly. "I have of course heard tell that you were of the party but had not expected to receive such a great lord in my humble forge."

A wintry smile crossed the face of Sir Thomas Warren. "Blacksmith, I was speaking with these two knights this morning when Sir Edward realized he needed to come and complete the purchase of his new bit. I merely accompanied them in order to finish our conversation."

Strange that such a lord should think to offer an explanation to a humble smith, thought Guy. Mayhap there is more to this visit than meets the eye.

Mentally shrugging his shoulders, Guy fetched the bit he had worked for the younger knight.

"This is beautiful work," said Sir Edward. "I did not know that St. Edmundsbury could boast of such a skilled blacksmith. I am glad indeed that I chose to have the bit made here."

Taking the bit from his companion and examining it, the second knight also praised the work as very fine indeed.

It is a bit, thought Guy to himself. I do good work, but these words seem too flowery for the situation.

The marshal, who had stood just inside the door of the forge looking around him in a disinterested way, came over to stand with the other knights.

"I must see this bit," he said. "Rare it is, master smith, to hear such compliments from my knights."

I'm sure, thought Guy. Rare it is for such compliments to be given, from knights or any others.

Sir Thomas did not handle the bit, but he peered at it over the shoulder of Sir Edward.

"Indeed, it is fine work," Sir Thomas said. "Where did you learn your craft, master smith?"

Now why would this lord want to know something like that? Guy wondered.

"From a craftsman greater than I could ever be," he answered. "It was a long time ago and a long way from here." Guy smiled at the knights as though he did not realize he had not really answered the question. Let us see where we go from here, he thought.

Sir Thomas scowled, but quickly recovered his attentive expression. "Then he must have been a great craftsman indeed," he said. Pausing, he looked around the forge.

"You have a delicate touch for a blacksmith who handles more farm tools than fine swords," he said.

"I thank you, my lord," said the blacksmith. I do not like playing a fool, thought Guy. But mayhap they will come to the point now.

Frustrated, Sir Thomas said shortly: "Do you know much of swords, master smith?"

Ah! That is what he wants, thought Guy.

"Not a great deal, my lord," he said. "Like all smiths in towns such as ours, I have seen my fair share of weapons needing a new pommel or a new guard."

"Such as in the case where Sir Gilbert's steward brought you the sword he was to offer at the shrine of St Edmund," Sir Thomas said.

"Yes, my lord," Guy responded.

"What know you of the history of the sword?" said the marshal.

"I know only what was told me by the good steward when he brought the sword to me for repair, and what has been the general rumor since his foul murder," said Guy.

The two young knights shuffled their feet and looked at their master nervously.

"But you must have thought the sword was something beyond the usual run of swords, because you gave it to the reeve after the steward's death," stated Sir Thomas, ignoring his companions.

"Did you take it to the reeve because you thought it to be important to his investigation?" the marshal continued.

"No, my lord," said Guy in a surprised tone. "The sword was not mine to keep. It belonged to the murdered man, or at least to his lord. I thought only to ensure it was kept safe until such time as it could be claimed by that lord. It seemed best to give it to the reeve for safekeeping."

Sir Thomas looked hard at the smith. Finally, his expression relaxed, and he laughed.

The laugh is as false as the smile, thought Guy. I do not understand what it is they hope to learn by talking to me.

"Well," the marshal said. "I am glad to know that you were not fooled by all the rumors about the sword being a powerful relic of a great hero."

That is an interesting choice of words, thought Guy. The sword is supposed to be a "powerful relic?" Most of the rumors are simply about it being the sword of a great Christian hero.

Sir Thomas Warren appeared to be unaware of the effect of his words. "I am afraid that the steward was of a superstitious nature," he said. "It may even be that he spun a fair tale to some fellow pilgrim of the rewards to be gained by owning the sword. I doubt not that he was killed by a man who believed the story and wanted to gain those rewards."

"I know not, my lord," said Guy. "It may be as you say. I am sure the reeve would be most interested in hearing what you have to express. He is working very diligently to solve this crime, and I am sure he would like to have any information that would be of help."

Sir Thomas merely nodded and walked out of the forge. Sir Edward Strode took out his purse to pay for the bit before following the marshal.

As the knight counted out coins into Guy's palm, Hugh came in the forge door from the street.

"Father," he said. "There are three beautiful horses outside." The boy stopped when he saw the knights.

"Do they belong to you?" he asked. "I think I have never seen such shining coats and such glinting tack."

In spite of themselves, the two knights were unable to resist owning that the horses were theirs.

"And father has just made you a bit for your horse," said Hugh. "How proud you must be to know that your work will be borne by such a mount, father."

Guy looked at his son, wondering what had happened to the shy boy he had spoken to only that morning.

Before he could say anything, the two knights took their leave and started toward the door.

"May I stroke the horses?" Hugh asked, prattling on about their noble heads and manes.

"Hugh," said his father sternly.

"It is of no matter," said Edward Strode in an offhanded manner. "Let the boy do as he asks."

Proud as a peacock, thought Guy, and about as clever.

As they walked outside, Hugh saw that the dark man who had been mounting his horse as Hugh approached the forge had gone. I am glad, he thought. That man scared me.

"I am sure you have heard many of the townsfolk exclaim about the beauty of your horses as you went about the Liberty," he said.

"They had little chance to do so," said Sir Edward. "There was small need to ride where we were going."

"You did not ride out then," said Hugh. "That is a pity."

"Within the town a horse is too easily noted," said Sir Edward.

"You spent time walking around the town then," Hugh said.

The young knight began to speak, but his companion did not let him.

"Enough," said the other knight. "It is time we left."

"Of course, Walter," said the sociable knight. Seeing Walter frown at him and nod his head slightly toward Hugh, he turned to look at the boy also.

"You ask a lot of questions," said Sir Walter. "I thought you wanted merely to stroke our fine mounts."

"Your pardon, sirs," Hugh said. "I know I talk a lot. It is rare for me to have the chance to see such horses and talk to their riders. Please forgive my being so forward." Hugh dipped his head in a small bow.

The knights, saying nothing further, mounted their horses and rode in the direction of the abbey.

That was close, thought Hugh. For a moment there, I thought I had gone too far.

Hugh went inside to get on with his chores for the day. I am not sure I learned very much that will be of help, he thought. I did learn that they did not want to be seen around town much, however. I think Aileen and Robert will be proud of me.

17. Chapter Seventeen

If, when evil cometh upon us, as the sword, judgment, or pestilence, or famine, we stand before this house, and in thy presence . . . and cry unto thee in our affliction, then thou wilt hear and help.

2 Chronicles 20:9

"He could have been killed," were the first words Aileen heard Saturday morning as she walked into the linen room of the abbey.

Mistress Taylor came bustling up to her, face flushed and hair peeking out of her wimple. "Will there be no end to the misfortunes of our poor town?" she said, taking Aileen's arm and fairly pushing her toward her work-table. "But we must all calm down and get on with our work. There is nothing to be gained by our adding to the chaos."

"What has happened?" asked Aileen. "Who was nearly killed?"

"Master Durand," said the robemaker. "I cannot believe you have not heard about it."

If she only knew how fast I had to run to the abbey this morning, thought Aileen. It seemed to take me twice as long to get the morning chores at home done, and I was sore afraid I was going to be late.

"I had little chance to hear about anything on my way," Aileen said. "But please tell me what has happened to the reeve. Is he injured?"

Glad enough to be the first person to pass on the news, Mistress Taylor sat on the stool next to Aileen. "Barrels rolled off a cart just as Master Durand was walking by on his way home last night," she said. "Why, there must have been a dozen barrels, all as heavy as they could be, heading straight for the unfortunate reeve."

Had it not been for the seriousness of the situation, Aileen might have smiled. A dozen barrels from one cart, she thought. No tale ever loses anything in the telling.

"But was Master Durand hurt?" she asked.

"Praise the Lord, he was not," Mistress Taylor said. "He was able to leap out of their way. Master Durand said. Had he not paused to see what a bunch of rowdy drinkers coming out of the tavern were doing, he would not have been able to avoid the barrels."

"That was a lucky thing," said Aileen.

Mistress Taylor sniffed. "First time I can think of

anything good coming out of that tavern door late on a Saturday night!"

Aileen smiled to herself. I really am fond of Mistress Taylor, she thought. She has a kind heart, but sometimes her words do not match her goodness.

"So the reeve was not hurt?" she asked again.

"He twisted his ankle as he landed, but a twisted ankle is nothing to being crushed to death," the robemaker stated bluntly.

There was little Aileen could say to that other than to agree that Master Durand had been lucky to escape greater injury.

"It was the fault of that lazy carter," the robemaker continued. "He cannot have secured his load properly. The barrels were full of wine made from our very own vine-yards, and I'm sure the abbot will have a lot to say to him about wine running in the streets and the loss of income to the abbey."

Having had her say, the robemaker stood and clapped her hands to silence the babble of voices in the linen room.

"We have wasted enough time," she said. "Ladies, there is work to be done. Please be seated and get on with your tasks."

Aileen worked diligently on the new linen altar cloth she was embroidering. The fine gold thread was expensive, and she had little time to think of anything but placing her needle properly.

Toward the end of the workday, the cloth was done. Mistress Taylor having approved the work, Aileen carried it to the sacristy and placed it in the press.

It is so peaceful in here, Aileen thought, as she turned

to leave. There is so much noise all around, it is sometimes hard to think. In here it is possible to be quiet and focus on what is important.

Aileen knelt in front of the altar and offered up a quick prayer for guidance. Rising from her knees and offering an obeisance to the altar, she turned and headed toward the door. Before she could reach it, however, the door creaked open, and a young man entered.

That is Stephen de Cley, Aileen thought. I did not think to see him here.

As the young man passed her, Aileen almost tripped over the raised edge of a flagstone. Her arm brushed against that of the young man, and he stopped to steady her.

Aileen dropped a curtsy. "Your pardon, sir," she said. "I would that my clumsiness did not disturb your peace."

Stephen de Cley smiled. "It is of no moment, mistress," he said. "I have taken no harm."

Aileen curtsied once again and turned to go.

"This place is so peaceful," said Stephen. "In here it is possible to leave behind all the noise and anger beyond these walls and think only of what is important."

"That is just what I was thinking a few moments ago," said Aileen in surprise.

The young man looked at her. Aileen was embarrassed but stood her ground, smiling tentatively at the young lord.

Stephen sighed. "I come here to pray for our poor lost steward and for peace in my family," he said. "I gain strength from praying thus."

He looks so sad, Aileen thought.

"Sir, I am blessed in my family. We argue and laugh and

work hard, but there is always love between us. I will pray that you and your family will be so."

Stephen said nothing. Why can I never think before I speak, Aileen thought to herself!

"My lord," said Aileen. "I beg your forgiveness once again. My father says that my nature is to be too forward, and I fear that he is right."

"There is nothing to forgive, mistress," Stephen said. "I can take no offense at your generosity. It is kind of you to offer to include my family in your prayers. Thank you."

Aileen, believing herself to be dismissed, dropped another curtsy and turned to go.

"It is strange, is it not," said Stephen. "God is a generous God. The Bible tells us that He rewards good deeds and punishes those who do evil."

"Yes, my lord," agreed Aileen, not sure whether she should stay or whether this young man was merely saying out loud what he was thinking.

"Yet sometimes it seems as though evil goes unpunished," Stephen continued.

"It does seem that way, I agree," said Aileen. "Yet I must believe that there will come a time of reckoning for all evildoers, even if it be not in this life."

"Yes," said Stephen, looking closely at this surprising young woman. "I can see that you truly do believe that. I have always believed so as well, but I must confess that recent events have caused me to doubt that such is the case."

This is most interesting, Aileen thought to herself. I had not thought that this younger son would know anything that would be of help. Mayhap I was wrong.

"Sir," she said. "I do not mean to be forward, but your words trouble me. I would understand what it is that you mean."

Stephen looked at the girl before him for a moment. Seeing only open-faced honesty, he made a decision. "I will tell you," he said. Drawing Aileen away from the center of the church and toward the Lady Chapel, he smiled at Aileen.

"You talked of your family and how you squabble and laugh in love," he said. "God may not have granted you wealth and power, but He has nevertheless blessed you far beyond those earthly qualities."

I never quite thought of it in that way, thought Aileen, but he is right. We are blessed. "Yes, my lord," she said. "What you say is true."

Stephen sighed. "My family has been greatly blessed for many generations," he said. "We have both wealth and power. Yet I would exchange all of that were we to have such good accord as does your family."

"I am sorry to hear this," Aileen said gently. "Is there a particular grief that causes you such distress?"

"I am not sure if you know anything of our family," said Stephen. "My father and mother are good and loving. I have a younger sister at home who is the image of our mother, both in appearance and temperament. I also have an older brother, who traveled this sad road with us to St. Edmundsbury."

"I did hear that Sir Gilbert rode with his two sons from Sussex," Aileen said.

Stephen nodded. "My brother Roger is my father's heir," he continued. "He is three years older than I. I love him as a brother should, but I think my mother is correct when she says that we are as different as chalk and cheese."

Stephen looked so unhappy Aileen was moved to try to comfort him.

"I believe that is not so unusual, sir," she said. "My sister and I are very different and yet we would defend each other to any stranger, come what may."

"That is the way it should be," agreed Stephen.

Aileen waited. He is trying to decide whether to say more, she thought.

Stephen turned to her. "I think that I did not ask your name," he said. "May I ask the favor of your name now?"

"My name is Aileen, sir," she said. "I am one of the embroiderers of the clerical linens here in the abbey."

"I am sure you are very good at your job," Stephen said, smiling.

"I hope that I may be, my lord," she said.

"The sons of lords sometimes have little useful function," he went on. "I think on occasion that is why my brother is so often angry. He is not patient by nature, and he resents his lack of authority. Yet coming into his inheritance must needs involve the death of our father."

"That must be very hard," Aileen said sympathetically. "But I imagine that your father values the time he has with your brother, teaching him what he will need to know when he becomes the Lord de Cley."

Stephen barked a laugh. "My father and my brother are rarely in accord," he said.

"That must be a great sorrow to your mother," said Aileen.

"It grieves her, I know," Stephen said. "She is ever the

peacemaker. My father is a man of equable temper, but Roger does sorely try him. In recent times their disagreements seem to have become more explosive."

"Is that why you talk of the blessings of close families?" Aileen said.

Stephen seemed to consider her question seriously. "In part, yes," he said after a moment's pause. "But in speaking with you, I realize it is more than that."

Again he hesitated. Aileen did not wish to disturb the young man. He was so clearly struggling to express emotions that he himself did not totally comprehend.

"You must understand that my brother is a strong man," Stephen said at last. "He is strong in body and opinions." Stephen smiled wryly. "He and I are totally unlike," he continued. "I do not like to put on armor and wield a sword. Roger says that I am no better than a woman with my books and my pen." Stephen looked up suddenly, his ears turning pink, his hands rising to cover his face momentarily.

"Your pardon, mistress Aileen," he said. "I intrude upon your kindness too much. It is unforgiveable that I should share such personal thoughts in your company."

"Sir, do not distress yourself," said Aileen. "We are talking of the differences in families. I think you would not wish to hear my sister's opinion of me." She laughed gently in an effort to ease the young man's embarrassment.

Stephen smiled tentatively. "I thank you," he said.

"May I ask why these family differences are so on your mind now, my lord?" asked Aileen. "The loss of Master Aylwin is sorrow enough for the time, yet it would appear that the journey you have made to St. Edmundsbury has increased the weight of your concern about your brother."

Stephen's head jerked up, and one hand was raised again, this time to cover his open mouth. "You have placed your finger on the truth," he said. "I have struggled to understand my apprehension. In one brief meeting, you have explained it to me."

"I have?" Aileen was surprised.

"Yes," said Stephen. "The battles between my father and my brother, and my brother's behavior toward me, have remained unchanged for so long that I scarce noticed them any longer. But in recent months the arguments have become louder and more bitter, and my brother's attitude toward me has become contemptuous, not merely uncaring."

"That is strange indeed," said Aileen. "Why do you think it should be?"

"I do not know," Stephen said. "If I knew mayhap I would be less anxious."

I know not whether this has anything to do with the sword, let alone with the murder of the steward, Aileen said to herself. It is a puzzle within a puzzle, though, and I would like to help this young man find a little peace in the midst of all this turmoil.

"Please forgive me if I am speaking beyond my privilege, sir," she said. "I do wonder if mayhap there was some change within your household in the last few months. Sometimes people do not react well when things do not remain the same."

Stephen took a moment to think before answering. "I can think of nothing in particular," he said. "There have been no difficulties with the crops. We are on friendly terms with the neighboring manors. The steward reported no problems with tenants, and the marshal's tutelage of my brother and control of the fighting men has remained unchanged."

Aileen was not one to be deterred by one setback. "So no unusual event has been reported?"

"Not unless you include the visit of the merchant Brenier," said Stephen.

"The trader who brought with him the sword that Sir Gilbert wished to offer at the shrine of our blessed saint?" As she spoke, Aileen suddenly realized Stephen might find it strange that a mere girl of the Liberty should know so much about how the sword came into the hands of the Lord de Cley. Fortunately, Stephen did not appear to notice her lapse. Relaxing, Aileen returned her attention to what Stephen was saying.

"Yes," he said. "The merchant did stay for more than a month, which is unusual for our visitors. I think he would not have stayed so long had not my father enjoyed the tales of his travels and trades."

"It must have been so interesting to hear those tales," Aileen said sincerely. "When I hear the stories of those who have gone on pilgrimage beyond the Liberty, I can almost see the faraway places they describe."

Stephen smiled. "A good story can have that effect," he said.

"Do you think that some of those within your household did begin to resent not being able to travel as does the merchant?" Aileen asked. "Could that be the source of your uncertainty."

"I do not believe so," Stephen said. "Mayhap some of the servants did envy the merchant's ability to go wherever he desired, but none other would. My father and Roger both travel to our far estates, whether they be on this side of the South Sea or the other. Sir Thomas Warren often accompanies one or other of them and is, of course, free to travel wherever he may wish. I do not often feel the need to go beyond our estates unless it be to London, but there is none who would stop me if I should decide to go elsewhere."

"Then mayhap the tension you feel has more to do with your father growing less tolerant of your brother's lack of patience and cordiality," Aileen offered.

"That could be," said Stephen slowly. "I find myself more in sympathy with my father than with my brother. It is my temperament to take on the emotions of those around me. Perhaps I have absorbed my father's dismay and thus see my brother's conduct in a more serious light."

"I am sure you are right," said Aileen.

Stephen straightened his shoulders and smiled at Aileen. Almost it seems as though he is shaking off his cares, she thought. I am glad. His account may not have contributed much to our knowledge of the steward and the sword, but I hope that I have helped him just a little.

"Mistress Aileen," Stephen said as if reading her thoughts. "I am grateful to you. You have helped me greatly."

"It gives me pleasure to know that I have been of some help," said Aileen demurely.

"Mayhap one day I may be able to show my gratitude," said Stephen. "For now, however, I must wish you God's blessings on you and your loving family." Stephen ducked his head in a small bow, turned and made his way to the altar.

Not wishing to disturb the young man's prayers, Aileen went on her way back to the linen room to complete her tasks for the day.

As she walked home that afternoon, Aileen saw a knight entering the shop of Edric Clover the glovemaker. *That is the knight from the courtyard the other day,* Aileen thought, *the one that scared Sarah. I think he is the one called Walter de Nantes.*

Aileen waited, interested in seeing what the knight was doing and where he may be going.

After a few minutes, the young knight came out. He had gone into the shop gloveless, but now he was wearing a pair of fine leather gloves. *Why would anyone be spending coin on expensive wares at such a time,* thought Aileen. *A man he knew well has been murdered. His lord is preparing to return to Sussex, and he is in the town purchasing fine gloves.*

Deciding to see where the knight might be going next, Aileen followed Sir Walter as he strolled back toward the abbey. *I probably should go home,* she thought. *It is clear that this knight is merely going back to the guest hall. There is nothing more to be learned.*

I cannot just leave, she thought. I must make sure he has no other plans before I can go home.

Passing through the gate into the courtyard, Aileen spied Sir Walter greeting the marshal and Sir Roger de Cley. Sir Gilbert's son was clearly disturbed about something. His face was set in anger, and his fists were curled into balls as he waved them around. Sir Walter took a step backward as the man turned toward him. Sir Thomas Warren leaned close to the furious man and, speaking softly, placed his hand on Sir Roger's shoulder, clearly trying to calm him. Sir Roger shook off the hand and, turning on his heel, stalked off toward the stables.

Sir Walter de Nantes turned to the marshal and started to say something to him. Sir Thomas shook his head and, taking Sir Walter by the arm, headed toward the cloister. Aileen would have followed them, but the marshal kept looking around him as though suspicious of any who might overhear their conversation. The risk of discovery was too high.

Frustrated, Aileen made her way home, deep in thought.

18. Chapter Eighteen

*He that hath a purse, let him take it, and likewise his scrip:
and he that hath no sword, let him sell his garment, and
buy one.*

Luke 22:36

"I thank you, Father Abbot," said Sir Thomas Warren. "I know that the Sabbath eve is for you a time filled with duties."

"My son, God is never too busy to talk with his children," Abbot Samson said. "His servants must obey the commandment to follow in His way."

The marshal cleared his throat. "Nevertheless, I thank you for agreeing to talk with me on a matter that is of great concern to me."

The abbot gave the knight an encouraging smile. "Pray continue," he said.

"My concern is for my lord, Sir Gilbert," said Sir Thomas.

This I did not expect, thought the abbot. Sir Thomas does not strike me as a man of great insight into the cares and woes of others. Mayhap I have maligned him.

Unaware of the musings of the abbot, Sir Thomas continued to talk. "I think you may know that Sir Gilbert and the steward had been close since childhood," he said. The abbot nodded in acknowledgement.

"Sir Gilbert is a powerful lord," said Sir Thomas. "He is well trusted by the Earl of Surrey, Lord de Warenne. Indeed, my lord's firstborn son was named after one of the earl's ancestors."

"I doubt there is anyone in the realm who does not know that the Lord de Warenne is one of the most powerful men in the kingdom," said Abbot Samson. "Sir Gilbert is truly well-connected to be close to such a man."

"I myself come from a family close to the Earl of Surrey," said Sir Thomas proudly. "It was the Lord de Warenne himself who sent me as a young man to be trained for knighthood within the house of Sir Gilbert."

"A sign of trust indeed," the abbot said.

"Then you understand how important it is that Sir Gilbert be not overtaken by emotion surrounding the death of his servant," Sir Thomas said forcefully.

"Surely this tragic event will have no effect upon Sir Gilbert's relationship with the Earl of Surrey," said the abbot.

"In itself, the death of the steward would be as nothing to such a powerful man as the Lord de Warenne," said the marshal. "However, a messenger from the earl arrived only a day before your rider. He told Sir Gilbert that the earl required that he ride with his knights to join him in defense of his lands over the South Sea."

"Who would dare attack the lands of so powerful a lord?" said the abbot.

Sir Thomas' face darkened. "In the houses of many great lords, there are those who would challenge their right to hold lands, or even titles," he said. "Howsoever that may be, the Lord de Warenne expects his close friend and ally to gather his knights and attend upon him without delay."

"I am sure that Sir Gilbert did inform the earl of his need to journey to St. Edmundsbury," the abbot said.

"Of course he sent word," the marshal said impatiently. "But the fact remains that my lord's grief over the death of this Saxon is leading to decisions that delay his responding further as ordered and may cause a rift with the earl."

Sir Thomas never calls the steward by name, thought the abbot. Rather he seems angry that the death of this "servant" has affected his lord's actions in a way that is disagreeable to him.

"Has the earl expressed his displeasure to his friend's actions?" the abbot asked.

"No," said the marshal. "He sent word that he would await Sir Gilbert's arrival in due time."

"Then I do not understand your concern," said Abbot Samson.

"Powerful lords can never show weakness," said Sir Thomas. "This excessive grief over the loss of his steward makes Sir Gilbert appear weak. That puts at risk his position and that of his line."

So we come to it at last, thought the abbot. Sir Thomas

is not concerned about the man. He is concerned about the man's position.

"Sir Thomas," he said. "I will pray for Sir Gilbert and for you. I think, however, that you should cease your fear over your lord's grief. If the Lord de Warenne has not expressed any concern, then it would seem that the position of the de Cley line is secure."

The marshal's face expressed his lack of agreement with the abbot's words. He remained seated, however, eyes on the ground and hands clasped tightly in his lap.

"Is there some other way in which I may be of service to you, my son," said the abbot.

"About this sword," said the marshal. He seemed not to know how to go on.

Interesting, thought Abbot Samson. I did wonder at the marshal discussing with me such a personal issue as his lord's conduct surrounding the death of Aylwin.

"The lord de Cley has indicated that he will fulfil his vow to present it to the blessed saint," the abbot said.

"I know," said Sir Thomas, frowning. "That is not what I want to discuss."

The abbot gave the marshal no help. He merely sat quietly, waiting for Sir Thomas to continue.

"It would seem that there are many wild stories about the history of the sword being told all over the Liberty," said the marshal.

"So I have been led to believe," Abbot Samson said.

The marshal paused. "Do you believe that this sword is one of legend?"

"I have heard some of the tales," the abbot said. "I cannot know what is truth and what is rumor, but I do know that it is for God to determine what instrument He may use for any given purpose. If the sword was wielded by an ancient Christian hero, it would have been only at the direction of our Holy God."

Sir Thomas seemed dissatisfied with this answer. "Brenier talked at length of his pilgrimage to Rome while in our house," he said. "He seemed much affected by the journey and by those with whom he met on the way."

"I am not surprised to hear that," said the abbot, ignoring the sudden change of direction in the conversation. "The way to Rome is in many ways as great a holy journey as the last steps to the shrine at the end of it."

"Have you yourself taken the Chemin des Anglois?" asked the marshal, looking closely at the abbot.

"I have," responded Abbot Samson. "It has been many years since I traveled the road, but the memories of that experience have never left me."

The marshal's eyebrows rose slightly. "Memories of experiences along the way?"

"Yes," the abbot said. "The way was rough and dangerous in places, of course. Yet I have many good memories of the camaraderie and the long nights of conversation."

"Are there any you met along the way with whom you still correspond?" The marshal leaned forward as he asked the question.

"Monks such as I have little correspondence outside these walls," said the abbot blandly. "My travels have rarely allowed me to attend upon those who do not have the same vocation."

Sir Thomas sat back.

"I too desired to travel to Rome along the same route,"

he said. "Perhaps Sir Gilbert mentioned that I once began such a pilgrimage but was forced to turn back due to illness."

"He did not mention it in our discussions," said Abbot Samson.

"It was a great sorrow to me that I was not able to finish the journey," said the marshal.

"If it is God's will, then I am certain you will complete your pilgrimage in due time," Abbot Samson said.

With this, Sir Thomas rose and made his farewells, thanking the abbot for his hospitality. As the marshal closed the door behind him, the abbot stared into the fire, his eyes seeing beyond the flames. He sat there a long time, musing over the visit of the marshal and the events of the past few days.

19. Chapter Nineteen

But in the end she is bitter as wormwood, sharp as a two-edged sword.

Proverbs 5:4

Robert's Saturday was eventful and illuminating. Having finished his morning chores he decided to take advantage of the noonday break and visit the abbey. He wanted to see if he could find Molly and glean more information from her.

I'm in luck, he thought happily as he spied the maidservant coming from the kitchens loaded down with bread and cheese for the guests' lunchtime repast, a flagon of ale hanging precariously from one hand as she balanced the basket.

"Molly," he called, running up to her. "Let me take some of that load from you."

"Thank you," she said gratefully, passing him the basket. "I thought I could carry both bread and ale without having to return to the kitchens, but I am sure I would have dropped one or the other had you not come along." She smiled flirtatiously at the young man.

Take care, Robert, he said to himself. You have need of more information from Molly, but no need of more embarrassment in front of Aileen.

"I am glad to be able to help," he said as the pair began to walk slowly toward the guest hall.

"I did not expect to see you in the abbey today," said Molly. "Do you have another delivery to make?"

"No," Robert said. "I came to see you." Aileen always says it is better to keep as close to the truth when seeking information, he thought, and it is certainly true that I came to the abbey to see Molly.

Molly patted her hair and smoothed her apron. "Truly? I am glad."

Now what do I do? Robert thought. This is going to be awkward.

"I enjoyed our conversation yesterday," he said. "I thought that perhaps we could sit in the courtyard and talk some more today."

"Oh," said Molly, looking a little disappointed. "I have to take these victuals in to the hall," she said. "Once I have served the guests, though, I should be able to come outside for a short time. Can you wait a little?"

"Of course," said Robert, smiling at the girl and hoping he didn't look as uncomfortable as he felt.

Molly asked one of the lay servants who was by the

guest hall door to take the basket from Robert and then went on inside happily with her flagon of ale.

Robert sat down on the ground with his back to the wall and closed his eyes, enjoying the sun for a few minutes. What I do for you, Aileen, he thought. How am I ever going to glean information from Molly without getting involved with her or hurting her feelings. Life can be so difficult.

Half an hour later, Molly came rushing out of the guest hall door. "I was sure you would not still be waiting for me," she said.

"I told you I would wait," said Robert, getting to his feet. "I would not that you think me untrue to my word."

"No, of course not," Molly said. "You are most kind, unlike some within the hall."

"Something has happened to make you unhappy," Robert said, trying to sound sympathetic.

"It is nothing," said Molly, pouting a little.

Robert said nothing.

"I will be so happy when all these guests go back to Sussex," the girl burst out. "I tire of their moods and their arguments."

It seems as though I will not have to prompt the maid into talking more, thought Robert. This may go better than I had feared.

"You have suffered no more threats?" he asked.

"No," said Molly. "But that Sir Roger seems always to be arguing with someone. He shouts at his servants to go away, tells his brother he should just take the cowl and be done with it, and pretends not to hear when his father speaks to him."

"This knight does sound like a man not to be crossed," said Robert.

"Even the marshal takes care in speaking to him, and I would not have thought that man would be afeared by anything," Molly said.

"I wonder why Sir Roger is so angry," said Robert, hoping to learn more.

"I know not," said the maid. "All I know is he dislikes it when anyone gives orders, even if it be his father or the marshal. He behaves as though it is he who is in charge. I try my best to stay out of his sight."

"Pity those over whom he rules when he inherits his father's land," Robert said.

"I do not like to think about it," Molly said. "Perhaps my lot is not so bad after all."

"Does Sir Roger have no friends among the company?" Robert asked.

"I know not if they be friends," the girl said. "He does spend time with the two young knights who were here before Sir Gilbert arrived, and he and the marshal seem to talk a lot."

"I wonder what conversation they have," said Robert.

"I doubt any could tell you," Molly said. "I've seen Sir Thomas and the two young knights gather in some corner of the courtyard, heads down and voices low. Another time I saw the marshal and Sir Roger talking quietly in a corner of the guest hall. But what they talk of I cannot say."

"The marshal has charge of the knights, so it may be he is issuing orders to them," said Robert.

"If so, they are slow to respond," said Molly. "That day I saw them talking in the courtyard, they did nothing after the marshal returned to the guest hall than talk to each other and scold a groom for his failure to curry their horses to their liking."

"I have not seen these knights around the town much," said Robert. "I suppose that is because they came to St. Edmundsbury on pilgrimage to the shrine of St. Edmund."

Molly snorted, a sound that was not exactly becoming to her, thought Robert.

"Those two knights," she said. "They may say they came as pilgrims to our Liberty, but as far as I can see, they have spent more time at the taverns than in the church."

"Mayhap they have had need of wine to help their grief over the death of the steward," Robert said.

"Not they," Molly said. "They were drinking late into the night before the steward was ever done to death if their condition in the morning is anything to go by."

"You are very observant," said Robert as Molly fell silent. "Even while you work so hard, you notice things such as how people behave toward each other and what mood they are in."

Molly simpered a little at the compliment.

"At times, it is necessary to watch what is happening around you," she said. "Had I not stepped back that day when Sir Roger nearly struck me, I might have been hurt."

"That is true," Robert said. "Mayhap that is why Sir Thomas spoke quietly to him in the corner of the hall."

"That was not the same day," said Molly. "In any case, I doubt that even the marshal can improve the mood of that unpleasant man."

At that moment, Brother Jocelin came out of the entry to the guest hall.

"Molly," he said. "I have need of you."

Sighing, Molly stood up and said her farewells to Robert, telling him she hoped they could speak more on another day.

Robert was saved from responding by the voice of Brother Jocelin calling to Molly once again. I never thought to like the Guest Master more than I do right now, he thought, as he set out for home.

It was not to be. Robert had scarce left the abbey grounds when he was hailed by Mistress Oliver, the wife of one of the most prosperous tavern-keepers in the Liberty.

"Master Robert," said the good woman. "It is God's blessing that I have met you today."

"Mistress Oliver," Robert said. "How fare you this day?"

"I will fare a great deal better if you will take these parcels from my arms," said Mistress Oliver. "I fear I have purchased too many wares today and am like to drop them if no one helps me."

Robert hastily took the packages from the lady's arms. Matilda Oliver was a buxom woman who was constantly trying to push her flyaway hair under her wimple. Right now her cheeks were bright red rather than their usual rosy color, and she was breathing rather hard.

"Thank you, Master Robert," she said. "Will you walk with me to my home?"

"I will be glad to do so," said Robert.

So saying, they began to walk slowly in the direction of Ralph Oliver's tavern.

As they passed along Mustow Street, the two knights

about whom Robert and Molly had only just been speaking rode past.

Mistress Oliver waved one hand in their direction and frowned. "Glad I am that those two young men will soon be gone," she said.

"Truly?" said Robert. "You know of these knights?"

"I know more than I care to know," said Mistress Oliver. "Being a tavern-keeper's wife is not always easy, you know."

Robert could not hide his interest. "I am sure it is not," he said. "But what is it that these two knights have done that you would say so?"

Mistress Oliver stopped a moment to once again try to push stray hairs under her wimple. "I do not know how other women manage to keep their hair properly arranged," she grumbled. "Father Peter is constantly glaring at me in church. Cannot he understand that hair is hair and not everyone has straight, flat hair that does what they tell it to do!"

Robert had to try hard to keep his face straight. "I am sure you are right," he said sympathetically. "But you were telling me about the two knights..."

"In our business, we are used to seeing men in their cups," said the tavern-keeper's wife. "Most men cause no trouble, even when they have taken too much drink."

Robert acknowledged that such was the case.

"But these arrogant knights cannot carry well their drink," the woman said. "Knights they may be, but in their case, nights are no good." Mistress Oliver laughed at her own joke.

At least she has returned to her usual good humor,

thought Robert. "It would seem that you have a good story to tell concerning these men," Robert said.

"Aye, I have," Mistress Oliver said. "It is of no surprise that visiting pilgrims visit our tavern, for all men know that we have the best quality ale and wine to be found within the Liberty." The good woman nodded her head in agreement with her own statement.

"I am certain that none are long in town before they learn of your tavern," Robert said.

"So it was that these men came to our tavern early and stayed late for several nights," Mistress Oliver continued. "Their coin was welcome, but as the evenings went on they would become loud and troublesome."

"I imagine that this is not an uncommon thing for you," said Robert.

"My man Ralph can take care of any troublemakers," said Mistress Oliver. "He is, as you know, a large man and lacks the patience and good humor for which I am so well known. Why, if it were not for me, I am certain our business would not be as good as it is."

In this case, Robert thought, such words were not boastful. Ralph Oliver was a good ten years older than his wife and distrustful of just about everyone. How he ever came to be in a business which needed to be welcoming Robert could not say, but it was certain sure that marrying Matilda had been a good thing.

Mistress Oliver, unaware of Robert's momentary lack of attention, continued: "Their conduct began to annoy even some of our milder customers. When the men of the Liberty start complaining that they cannot enjoy even a simple drink with friends at the end of their long labors, my husband will not let it be."

I have heard that Master Oliver has no hesitation in throwing troublemakers out of his tavern, thought Robert. If that is what happened here, it does not sound as though there is much to this tale after all.

Mistress Oliver did not often need much in the way of a response from her audience, and thus she was blithely unaware of the sudden loss of interest in her story on the part of her companion.

"One night, these two young men began to become even more loud," she said. "They were sitting with some others from the abbey guest hall and began to boast of how they would soon be supping wine in better establishments than this lowly tavern."

"That cannot have made your husband happy," said Robert.

"It did not," Mistress Oliver said. "I could hear him growling under his breath, and almost he did stamp over to them and shout at them to leave."

Robert was becoming a little more interested again by now. Mayhap there was more to this story than had at first appeared.

"I calmed him down," said the good woman. "But then one of the young knights pushed Peter Fuller out of his way and started waving his tankard around, shouting that the old man was going to get his just reward and that their master would soon raise them up, so they didn't have to spend time with such peasants."

"That was unkindly done," Robert said. "You said rightly that they could not keep in their cups."

Mistress Oliver laughed. "Ralph would not be stayed. He marched over to them, stood with his arms akimbo, and told them to leave."

"Were your husband to say that to me, I would not hesitate to do so," said Robert.

"Yes, but you are not in your cups," laughed Mistress Oliver.

"The knights stood their ground then," said Robert.

"For a moment. The younger one swayed to his feet and, waving his tankard in front of Ralph's nose, said he didn't have to listen to any squinty-eyed old man and was going to stay right where he was."

Robert stopped in his tracks and just looked at his companion.

Mistress Oliver was well satisfied with the effect of her narrative on the young man beside her. "Ralph may have to squint to see beyond the end of his nose, but he has no liking for anyone who comments on that," she said. "Roaring like a boar in the forest, he reached out both arms and grabbed the young men. Before they knew what was happening, he had thrown them out of the door and onto the street."

"What happened next?" said Robert.

"Nothing," said the tavern-keeper's wife. "They have not tried to return, and my husband will not talk more of it."

"Mistress Oliver, this was a most interesting account," he said. "These men have been within the walls of our Liberty for some time, and I had not heard of such an event. Do you remember on what night this happened?"

"Oh yes," she replied. "That is not hard to remember. It

was the night that poor man was done to death. Such a terrible thing to happen, but it did fix in my mind other events during that time."

"That would be why there was no tale around town of the bad conduct of these knights," said Robert. "The murder overtook all other events."

"That poor man," sighed Mistress Oliver.

Having arrived at the door of the tavern, Robert returned the packages to the arms of the tavern-keep's wife, and, accepting her thanks for his help, he bade her farewell and once again set out for home.

20. Chapter Twenty

*God judgeth the righteous, and God is angry with the wicked
every day. If he turn not, he will whet his sword; he hath bent
his bow, and made it ready.*

Psalm 7:11-12

I t was a somber group who met at the riverbank that
evening. Only one more day, thought Aileen, and
then all those most likely to know anything that will
aid us will be gone.

Only one more day to learn more, thought Robert.
Why can I not put these pieces together for Aileen...and for
the sake of the poor steward.

Only one more day, thought Hugh. Are my friends
going to be able to solve this riddle in time?

"There is only one more day left," said Aileen. "I know
not what Master Durand has learned, but I think we should

talk of what we know and whether anything may be of help to the reeve."

"I agree," said Robert. "Aileen, do you want to begin?"

"If you wish," said Aileen.

Making herself more comfortable and rolling a blade of grass in her fingers, Aileen thought for a moment before speaking. "I did meet the younger son of Sir Gilbert de Cley today," she said. "He has seemed to be the one person in this who has always somehow been like a figure in the mist; unclear and not completely real."

"I am not sure I thought of him in that way," Robert said. "But true it is that know little of him but what other people say. What did you learn of him when you met him?"

"Whoever else of Sir Gilbert's household may know something about this murder, or even the events of the past, I do not believe that Stephen de Cley is anything other than what he seems," said Aileen. "He is quiet and sad, and I think he grieves not only for Aylwin but for the rift in his family."

"I did hear tell that his father wished him to take the cowl, but Stephen did persuade him otherwise" said Hugh.

"I heard the same thing," agreed Robert.

"After speaking with him I can how that would be so," Aileen said. "Yet I think the persuasion was that of a beloved son and not that of a deceitful man. I think we may say that our attention should be turned elsewhere."

"I always trust your instincts, Aileen," said Robert.

"Me too," Hugh put in.

Aileen smiled. "Thank you both," she said.

Once again collecting her thoughts, she picked up her account of that day's activities. "It was after I had spoken to

Stephen de Cley that I saw the one they call Sir Walter de Nantes entering the glover's shop," she said.

"It seems unusual for one such as he to be looking at the wares our merchants have to offer when his party is preparing to ride home to Sussex," said Robert. "I could better understand it if he was seeking victuals, or even salves for sore joints."

"I thought the same thing," Aileen said, smiling at her friend.

"So what happened next?" asked Hugh after a pause.

"When Sir Walter entered Edric Clover's shop he wore no gloves," Aileen said. "When he came out only a few minutes later, he was wearing a pair of fine leather gloves."

"Then mayhap he had lost his gloves and sought out another pair before returning home," Robert said, a little disappointed.

"That may be so," agreed Aileen. "Yet it is still another strange fact to add to those we already have."

Robert and Hugh nodded their heads.

"Go on," said Robert. "I am sure that is not all that you have to report."

"No, not quite," Aileen said. "I decided to follow Sir Walter after he left the shop and see where he went next. At first, it did seem that the instinct you so trust, Robert, had failed me."

"But it had not, of that I am sure," said Robert.

"Perhaps not," she said. "Sir Walter made his way back to the abbey straight from the glover's shop, and I thought to just go home and not take any more time to follow him inside the gates."

"I would have left, too," said Hugh.

"Yet I did not leave," said Aileen. "As Sir Walter entered the courtyard, he was met by Sir Thomas Warren and Sir Roger de Cley. The lord's son was greatly angered by something, and some of that anger seemed to be directed at the younger knight. He was waving his arms around, and were it not that they were in a public place, I believe he would have shouted at him. Instead, it looked as though he was hissing something at him."

"Could you hear what was being said?" Robert asked.

"No," said Aileen. "There were many people in the courtyard, and I was not that close to them."

"That is a pity," said Robert.

"I doubt I could have heard their words even had I been more near to them," said Aileen. "They clearly did not wish to be overheard. Or, at least, the marshal did not want it. He tried to quieten Sir Roger, but the man would have none of it. He stalked off, leaving the marshal and the young knight standing in the middle of the courtyard."

"From what I hear, this son of Aylwin's lord is ill-tempered. Mayhap there is nothing more to this episode than another bout of phlegm."

"That may be," said Aileen. "Yet it did not appear so, and the concern on the marshal's face did seem to be greater than that you would expect of a man dealing with yet another tantrum."

"So another fact for us to add to our list then," said Robert.

"Yes, another fact," Aileen replied.

"Have you more to tell us, Aileen?" asked Robert.

"No," said Aileen. "Do you go next, Robert?"

Robert was not sure he wanted to go next, given the

circumstances. "Let us hear from Hugh first," he said. "I would like to hear about the visit of the knights to his father's forge."

Aileen was not fooled by Robert's words. She lifted her hand to smell the fresh grass and hid her smile behind it.

"I am not sure that I have much to tell," said Hugh in a somewhat dispirited manner.

"Even small facts help build the whole picture," Aileen said.

Thus encouraged, Hugh launched into his story. "Father sent me on an errand this morning, and so I was not there when the knights arrived," he said.

"Oh no," said Aileen. "Did you not see them at all then?"

"I got back home while the two knights were still within," Hugh said. "But the marshal had come with them. He was mounting his horse as I ran up to the forge."

"We did not expect that," said Robert.

"Did he say anything?" asked Aileen.

"No," Hugh said. "He seemed to be unhappy about something. He looked right through me."

"From all that I hear, he is rarely anything but unhappy," said Aileen.

"I confess I was glad that he did not say anything to me," Hugh said. "The marshal is a man I would be happier never to see again."

"I cannot blame you for that," said Aileen.

Relaxing a little now that he had got started, Hugh picked up his tale. "I ran into the forge and found the knights talking to father. One of them was taking out his purse, so I knew I had little time before they too rode away."

"What did you do?" asked Robert.

"I could think of little I could do, so I said whatever came into my head first," Hugh said. "I babbled something about how beautiful their horses were and how I thought never to see such grand mounts. I could see father was surprised and about to stop me, so I asked the knights if I could stroke their horses."

"That was clever of you, Hugh," Aileen said. No wonder his father was surprised, she thought. Hugh rarely puts more than two sentences together.

"What did the knights say?" asked Robert.

"I think they were amused by such silly talk, but they were also too proud to realize this was something out of the ordinary," Hugh said. "They told me I could do as I asked.

"I walked outside with the knights," Hugh continued. "The marshal had already ridden away, and neither of the other two seemed to care that he had not waited for them to conclude their business."

"That the marshal was no longer there must have made it easier for you to talk further with the knights," Robert said.

"It did," said Hugh. "While I was stroking the horses I thought to talk about how people must have been impressed by their horses in the town. I could think of nothing else to say."

"That was well done, Hugh," Aileen said kindly.

"I do not know if it is important," Hugh went on. "But from the way the knights talked, I think they walked around the town, rather than ride."

"From what we have seen of these two men, I am surprised that they would not feel their status demanded they be seen on their mounts," said Robert.'

"I agree," said Aileen. "What was it they said that made you believe this, Hugh?"

"The younger one said something about it being too easy to be seen if you are mounted," said Hugh. "The other one stopped him from saying any more."

"So they wanted to be unseen," said Aileen. "Mayhap they did not want to be seen by anyone who might recognize them."

"If that be the case, it may be that these two knights know much about the murder of Master Aylwin," Robert said. "Hugh, you may have solved this crime yourself."

Hugh beamed with pride. Then his face clouded over.

"What is it?" asked Aileen.

"I think they may have been suspicious of me," Hugh said reluctantly.

Aileen and Robert looked at each other.

"Why do you say that?" Robert asked.

"Sir Walter said that I asked too many questions," said Hugh. "I told him that I had a habit of talking too much and begged their forgiveness."

"Did they seem satisfied with your answer?" Aileen said.

"I think so," said Hugh. "At least, they mounted their horses and rode away without pressing me further." Hugh's pride had now clearly dissolved into fear.

"Hugh, do not be frightened," said Aileen. "These knights may well know something about the murder of the steward, but that does not mean they did the deed themselves. There is no reason for you to fear harm to yourself just because they thought you were nosy."

"Aileen is right," said Robert. "Do not take notice of my wild theories. I became too excited and allowed my mouth to lead my head."

Hugh looked unconvinced.

"Robert has the right of it," Aileen said, putting her arm around Hugh in a sisterly gesture. "We cannot leap to conclusions when there is still so much to learn."

"If you say so, then I believe you," said Hugh, brightening a little.

Aileen decided it was time to move on. "Robert," she said. "I am sure you have something interesting to tell us about your further conversation with Molly."

Robert shot a quick glance at Aileen's face, happy to see that there was no sign of disturbance in her expression.

"I did speak with the maid," Robert said. "She had little more to tell me, but she did say that Sir Thomas and Sir Roger could be seen talking together secretively on occasion. She also told me that the two knights we have been talking about did seem to have conversation with the marshal, but that if he was giving them orders, they took little notice."

Aileen was a little disappointed. "I had hoped for a little more detail."

"I did as well," said Robert. "But she also told me that the knights spent too much time in the taverns and that the signs of their drinking were obvious in the morning."

"I am not sure how that helps us," Aileen said.

"By itself it may not," said Robert. "But Molly was not the only person with whom I talked this morning."

Aileen and Hugh looked interested.

"I ran into Mistress Oliver after I left the abbey," said Robert. "She had been visiting the merchants and needed help carrying her parcels."

Aileen laughed. "Mistress Oliver does like to visit the merchants," she said. "It may be one reason why Master Oliver always seems so out of sorts."

Everyone in the Liberty knew about the shopping habits of the tavern-keeper's wife. Robert and Hugh smiled in agreement with Aileen's words.

"That is not all, though," Robert said. His expression told the others that he was waiting for someone to ask him what more there was to tell.

"Please go on, Robert," said Aileen accommodatingly.

Robert went on to tell the others about the night the knights were thrown out of the tavern. "And when I asked her what night this was, Mistress Oliver told me it was the night that the poor steward was murdered," he ended with a flourish.

"Now that is indeed interesting," said Aileen.

"It is," said Hugh. "But how does that help us solve the crime?"

"It is one more fact among the many we have gathered," said Aileen. "Mayhap we should take a look at what we know and see if we can fit these pieces into any of the theories that have been put forward around town."

"That sounds like a good plan," said Robert. "Where do we start?"

"One theory that I have heard being discussed by the ladies in the linen room is that another pilgrim listened to the stories about the sword and wanted it for himself. From what the ladies have been saying, I think that theory is one being put forward by some within Sir Gilbert's household."

"We need to look at that carefully then," said Robert. "If the murderer is one within the household itself, there must be some flaw with the theory."

"I agree," said Aileen. "Mayhap that flaw could lead us further toward the truth, since anyone putting forth a false theory would do their best to lead us in the opposite direction."

"I would never have thought of that," said Hugh. "What do you think is wrong with the theory of the pilgrim then?"

Aileen and Robert exchanged glances.

That was the question, thought Aileen. I am not sure we have the answer to it...yet.

I hope Aileen will be able to answer that question, thought Robert.

"Let us think about it," said Aileen. "The theory depends on another pilgrim knowing the details about the sword. That pilgrim, who surely made the journey to the shrine of St. Edmund to offer devout prayers, must be someone who is willing to commit murder in order to obtain the sword."

"When you put it that way, it does not really make sense," said Robert. "Why would someone journey all the way to St. Edmundsbury in the hope of receiving favor from our holy saint only to commit a deed so foul he could never expect to receive such a blessing?"

"Exactly!" said Aileen. "I think we can set aside this theory of the murder."

How do they do this? thought Hugh. I would never have been able to argue away the theory in such a way.

"So, let us move on to the next theory," said Robert.

"Do we think that the rag and bone man may have done it?" Aileen asked.

"Hadric is a man filled with cunning and greed, I think," said Robert. "He did hesitate several times when he was telling me his story. Mayhap he feared he would say something to give himself away."

"Or he might just have wanted to avoid having to admit he's cunning and greedy," said Aileen.

Robert smiled. "That is probably more likely," said Robert.

"The rag and bone man is not a large man," Aileen said. "If he wanted to do harm to the steward, I think he would have to take him by surprise."

"I agree," said Robert.

They sat in silence for a moment. Hugh looked expectantly between them.

Aileen stirred. "Master Aylwin was looking all around him according to Hadric," she said.

"Yes," responded Robert. "Hadric thought he must have seen the second man, and that is why he started to run."

"Would that not mean that Hadric could not have taken the steward by surprise, even if he had caught up with him and avoided the second man?" asked Hugh, getting into the spirit of the discussion.

"Not necessarily," Aileen said. "Hadric appears to be very good at hiding from people. If he is to be believed, he was not seen by either Aylwin or the second man."

She turned to Robert. "Did you believe him when he said he had not been seen?"

"Yes, I did," said her friend. "He looked triumphant, as though he had done something very clever."

"Then let us assume he remained unseen," said Aileen. "I am not sure that helps us much."

"You mean because we cannot tell from that fact alone whether he gave up following the two men or continued on and murdered Aylwin?" asked Robert.

"Yes," Aileen said. "Is there anything else he said that might help us on that point?"

Robert thought for a moment. "Not really," he said reluctantly. "I am just trying to remember when he hesitated before speaking. Mayhap that will give us some direction."

The others nodded their heads but said nothing that could interrupt Robert's train of thought.

"I think the first time he slipped up was when he told me he started to follow Master Aylwin," said Robert finally. "He started to say that he followed him for one reason, but then in the middle of the sentence he suddenly changed whatever it was he was going to say to asserting that he wanted to help the steward."

"That sounds unlikely," Hugh said.

"That was what I thought," Robert stated.

"That is interesting," said Aileen. "If he had no bad purpose in following Master Aylwin, why would he need to change what he was going to say?"

The three friends looked at each other. They could see all were thinking of the same possible answer to that question.

"Please go on, Robert," Aileen said. "What happened next?"

"That is exactly the question I asked of Hadric after he tried to get me to go with him to the tavern," said Robert. "It was when I asked what happened after he saw the second man that the bone-grubber wavered over answering me."

"Was that when he told you the two men started to run?" asked Aileen.

"Yes," said Robert. "Why do you think he would pause before telling me that?"

"I do not know," Aileen said. "It seems likely that he was telling the truth when he said they ran, does it not?"

"Yes," said Robert. "I did not feel he was lying at that point."

"Then mayhap something else happened after he saw the second man but before they started to run," Aileen said.

"But what?" asked Hugh.

"I cannot tell," said Aileen. "It may be nothing, or it may be something. Mayhap it relates only to some advantage Hadric thinks he can gain by withholding the information."

"Do you think Hadric may actually have seen the face of the second man when he started hurrying after the steward?" asked Robert.

"Possibly," said Aileen. "If so, he may be hoping to get some coin out of that man in order to keep quiet. It does not seem likely to me that Hadric will willingly tell Master Durand his story."

"It does not seem likely to me, either," said Robert. "I think that we should do so."

"I agree," Aileen said. "We will do so tomorrow."

Robert kept going over that meeting with Hadric in his head. "I do remember that he paused one more time in our conversation," he said. "It was when I asked him what he did after seeing the two men running. He hesitated and then quickly brought the story to an end by saying he lost them among the alleyways."

"Yes, when you said that, it struck me that Hadric had been enjoying himself too much to put such an abrupt end to his tale," Aileen said.

"So do you think he had to finish his story thus because he could not confess to having followed the steward and killing him?" Hugh asked.

"It is something we have to consider," said Aileen. "Hadric is an unpleasant man, but it takes more than being unpleasant to be a murderer. It may be only as we said before: Hadric wishes to gain something by not revealing all he saw that night."

"In other words," said Robert. "We need to learn more."

"Possibly," responded Aileen. "But first we need to tell the reeve about this chance meeting of yours. Mayhap he can find out more easily what the rag and bone man knows."

"You have a good point," said Robert. "Master Durand has more authority to demand answers than do we."

"Yes," Aileen said.

"Then should we move on and talk about something else?" asked Robert.

"I think we need to talk about the theory none of us wants to be true," Aileen said.

"You mean that the murderer is one of us," Robert said gloomily. "One of the folk of the Liberty."

"Yes," said Aileen.

"I cannot bear to think that someone we know would do such a thing," Robert said.

"And I cannot think that my father was almost killed by someone we might see every day," Hugh added.

"I feel the same way," said Aileen. "But it is a theory that we must address otherwise it will always be in the back of our minds."

"You are right, of course," said Robert. "And in facing it, we might be able to rule it out."

"Exactly," Aileen said.

"I don't even know how we can start looking at all the people around us," said Hugh.

"I think we should look at it in another way," Aileen said after a moment's thought. "Let us start with the murder and work backwards to see who among the towns-folk would even have enough knowledge to think of doing such a deed."

"That is a good idea," said Robert. His chin in his hand, he took a minute to put together his thoughts. "Anyone from St. Edmundsbury would know where a man might be waylaid in the dark of night with small risk of discovery," he said. "That is a mark in favor of the theory,"

"That is true," said Aileen, "But would any man from the town know that the steward would be abroad so late in the night, or where he would be bound?"

"No," said Robert. "Few people of the town had much conversation with the steward beyond the normal words of trade. That is a mark against the theory."

"But tales of the sword are all around the town," Hugh said. "What if the steward had talked of it to one of the townsfolk. After all, he talked of it to my father."

"Yes, Hugh," said Aileen. "But he talked of it to your father because he wanted the sword to be treated with reverence. His recounting of the history was not mere chatter."

"I agree," said Robert. "From what we have learned of the steward, he was not a boastful man who talked more than was necessary."

"That is my impression as well," Aileen said. "So let us assume that Master Aylwin did not talk to people he met on the street about the offering he had brought to our abbey. Is there any other motive for someone within the town to offer violence to him?"

"I can see none," said Robert. "The only way in which the steward could have come into contact with a thief and murderer would be if he chanced upon such a felon as he walked through the town that night."

"Yes," Aileen said. "But then we must ask ourselves this question: Why was he walking through the streets that night? Master Aylwin did not spend his time in the taverns. He was a pilgrim who came to our town for a certain purpose. We do know that he seemed anxious when he was in town during the day of his death. If he was not assured of his safety during the day, why would he walk abroad during the night?"

"He would not," said Robert.

"No, he would not," said Aileen. "That means he must have left the safety of the abbey for a reason."

"What reason?" asked Hugh.

"We cannot know that for sure," responded Aileen. "To

me, the only likely reason is that someone persuaded him to leave the safety of the abbey that night."

"It would have taken a powerful argument to induce the steward to leave the guest hall," said Robert.

"I agree, and we should give some thought to what form that persuasion may have taken," said Aileen. "But do you see what this means?"

Robert and Hugh shook their heads.

"I believe it means that the murderer was not of the town," said Aileen. "Few but those within the walls of the abbey had any chance to coax the steward out of the guest hall. I think we must look within the walls of the abbey for the murderer."

"You have the right of it, Aileen," declared Robert. "How you think of these things I do not know, but you have the right of it."

Aileen blushed slightly at Robert's enthusiasm. "Thank you," she said. "But let us move on. There is at least one more theory of the murder that we must discuss."

"What theory?" Hugh asked.

"That would be the idea that there were two murderers," Aileen said. "Those two murderers would be Sir Walter de Nantes and Sir Edward Strode."

Robert and Hugh said nothing but looked at Aileen in an encouraging way.

"We have learned a great deal about these two young knights," she said. "We know that they arrived only a day after the steward, and that Sir Gilbert did not know of their pilgrimage before he saw them here. We have also heard from several people that they spent more time drinking than praying, and now we have the account from Mistress Oliver of their drunken boasts."

Turning to Hugh, Aileen focused her next words on him. "Because of your courage, we also now know that Sir Walter and Sir Edward did not wish to be too noticeable in town," she said. "That could be significant."

"So you believe that the knights murdered the steward?" asked Hugh, blushing at the compliment he had little thought to receive.

"I am not ready to say that," said Aileen. "We are just putting together facts right now. We will see where they lead us."

She sat in silence for a moment, thinking. Then, with a sigh, she sat up and turned to the other two.

"The facts are suspicious in regard to the two knights," she said. "I think, however, that there are too many explanations for their behavior that do not include murdering a man over a sword."

"What other explanation can there be?" asked Robert.

"These knights are undoubtedly not nice men," Aileen said. "They are braggarts, and they drink too much. Neither quality is desirable."

Robert tried hard not to smile. Aileen sounded just like his mother when she was complaining about the young men of today.

"Howsoever that may be," Aileen went on, "being proud and arrogant does not necessarily make you a murderer."

"That is so," said Robert.

"I suppose not," said Hugh.

"Before we could even talk to the reeve about them, we must have more information," Aileen said.

Robert groaned. "More information," he said. "What else can we possibly discover before the Sabbath, let alone Monday morning, when the whole party takes their leave of our Liberty?"

"You have a point," said Aileen.

"Everyone we know will be at mass tomorrow," said Hugh, looking eagerly at the others.

For a moment, Robert and Aileen looked at their friend in confusion. Then Aileen's face cleared.

"Hugh," she said. "You are even more clever than your tutors could know."

Hugh looked gratified, though Robert still looked puzzled.

"We do not need to wait until Monday morning to ask further questions," Aileen said. "Anyone of whom we have more questions will be in church tomorrow."

"You mean we can talk to them outside the church after mass," Robert said, his brow clearing.

"Yes," Aileen and Hugh said together.

"That is all very well," said Robert. "But who is it we need to seek out?"

Good question, thought Aileen. Who indeed?

"Edric Clover for one," she said finally. "I had no chance to talk to him about Sir Walter de Nantes and the new gloves. Mayhap finding out if Master Clover knows what happened to the old gloves will be of help to us."

Robert and Hugh were forced to agree that asking some questions of the glover could be helpful.

"I will seek him out after the mass tomorrow," said

Aileen. "My father and he are friends, so we nearly always see him there."

Robert's attention had strayed during Aileen's last words. All of a sudden, he struck his forehead with his palm.

"What a fool am I," he exclaimed.

"What is it, Robert?" Aileen said.

"The brooch," he said. "The old brooch."

"What about the brooch?" said Hugh.

"Your talking about the gloves did it," Robert said.

"Did what?" Hugh was confused.

"Made me remember where I had seen the brooch before," said Robert. "When father brought back the drawing of the brooch Sir Gilbert wanted him to make, I had thought it looked familiar, but I couldn't think why that would be. I decided the brooch must be similar to something my father had made in the past."

"But it was not," Aileen said, clearly following Robert's train of thought.

"No," said Robert. "I saw the brooch much more recently than that. I know where we can find Master Aylwin's brooch right now!"

21. Chapter Twenty-One

Thus saith the LORD; Behold, I am against thee, and will draw forth my sword out of his sheath, and will cut off from thee the righteous and the wicked.

Ezekiel 21:3

"Guy," said his wife, "Hugh has a fever. I have given him chamomile tea, but I think he should not attend mass with us this morning."

"You know best of such matters, my dear," said her husband. "We shall go without him."

Guy looked at Abigail, his face creased with worry.

"What is it, Guy?" said his wife, her hand stroking his face. "What worries you so?"

"I am not sure," said Guy. "This past week has been filled with violence and suspicion. I wonder if our town will ever be the same again."

"Do not fret so," she said. "St. Edmundsbury has survived worse than this. Master Durand is a clever man, and I am sure that he will discover who the felon is."

"I would that I had your faith, my dear," said Guy.

"Well, even if the murderer remains undiscovered, the Liberty will survive," his wife said practically. "Fear and suspicion will not be with us forever."

"I am sure you are right," said Guy. "Yet I cannot shake off this feeling."

As he spoke, Adam came down the stairs. "Father, do you want me to stay with Hugh? I know mother is worried about his fever."

Abigail looked at her husband and nodded her head.

"Very well, Adam," the blacksmith said. "We shall return as soon as the mass is over."

"I have prepared a poultice of chamomile and coriander seeds, Adam. Place it on Hugh's forehead and make sure it stays there. I know what Hugh is like. He hates the smell of these poultices. As soon as you turn your back, he'll have it off his forehead and on the floor.

"Yes, mother," said Adam.

"And whatever you do, do not let him get up, even if he says he is feeling better. If he is too ill to come to mass, he is too ill to be running around the house."

"Yes, mother," Adam said, smiling. "I promise I will do as you say."

As Adam closed the front door behind his family, he thought about the concern he had heard his father express as he was coming down the stairs. I am not used to seeing my father thus, he thought. I have never seen him other than as a man of strength and few words.

Shrugging off the weight of his thoughts, he fetched the poultice his mother had told him to take up to Hugh and went upstairs. Hugh was sleeping when he entered the room, so he carefully placed the poultice on his younger brother's head. At least I won't have to fight him about the poultice for now, thought Adam.

Adam went back downstairs, carefully stepping over the tread which creaked loudly every time anyone stepped on it. I love my younger brother, Adam thought, but he can be as annoying as a gnat. I would much rather spend my morning in peace than in arguing with him.

So it was that Adam enjoyed two hours to himself before his brother woke up.

"Mama," Hugh called out.

Sighing, Adam went back upstairs.

"They're at mass, Hugh," he said as he entered the room.

Hugh was sitting up. The poultice was, as anticipated, on the floor, but the flush skin that had worried his mother was gone.

"How do you feel?" Adam felt Hugh's forehead. It seems normal to me, he thought, but I am not an expert.

"I'm thirsty," said Hugh.

"I'll get you something to drink," said his brother, turning to go back downstairs.

As he reached the bottom of the stairs, he heard Hugh coming down behind him.

"Oh no you don't," he said, turning and blocking the way. "Mother said that you were to stay in bed. You know what will happen if she finds out I did not do as she said."

"Please, Adam," said Hugh. "The sun is not high in the

sky yet, and you know they will not be back for ages. The Sunday sermon warning us about the many ways in which we can condemn ourselves to eternal damnation is as nothing to the ache in my joints from staying still for hours listening to it!"

"Hugh," said Adam. "Do not talk in that way. The priests try to help us avoid that terrible fate."

Hugh opened his mouth to reply but thought better of it. If he wanted Adam to allow him downstairs, it was not a good idea to get in an argument with him. Getting out of the stuffy house was more important than getting into a debate with his brother.

"You are right, Adam," he said. "It must be the remains of the fever that made me talk that way."

Adam looked at his brother closely. "Are you sure you are not still feverish?"

"I am well," Hugh said. "But it is such a sunny day I really do believe I will feel better if I can sit outside for a little while."

Adam looked at him doubtfully.

"Please Adam."

Hugh looked so pathetic that even Adam found it hard to say no.

"Oh, very well," Adam said. "You go and sit outside on the bench, and I'll bring you something to drink. But it's only for a few minutes. Then you must go back upstairs."

"I promise, Adam," said Hugh.

Hugh made his way outside while Adam went to fetch the promised drink.

Suddenly Adam heard a noise outside, followed by a cry.

Dropping the cup he held, Adam rushed outside, only to see his brother with a sack over his head, being dragged away by two men in cloaks. Hugh was kicking and screaming, but his strength was not equal to that of the two men.

As Aileen exited the abbey church, she looked around for Edric Clover. Sure enough, he was talking with his wife close by the wall of the abbey.

Whispering to her mother that she was just going to go over and say hello to Master Clover, Aileen strolled over and greeted the couple.

"Mistress Aileen, I have not talked with you in many days," said the glover. "How do you and your family fare?"

"We are well, Master Clover," said Aileen. "Is your family well also?"

"Yes indeed," he said. "The baby keeps us up each night with the colic, but otherwise we are all in good health."

"I am sure my mother could suggest something to help with the colic," said Aileen. "I know my brothers both coughed and cried all the time when they were babes. Mother gave them something that stopped it in a few days."

"That would be most kind," said Mistress Clover. "Will you excuse me if I go and have a word with your mother now, Aileen?"

"I know she would be most pleased to see you," Aileen said.

As the glover's wife moved away, Aileen turned to Master Clover. "I hope you do not mind my interrupting you," she said.

"I am glad of it," he responded. "My wife has been sore worried about the baby. Useless to say that all babies get colic. This is our first bairn, and my good wife feels she is to blame for every wail and sniffle. I am certain she will be more easy in her mind once she has talked to your mother."

"I do hope so," Aileen said. She hesitated a moment before going on. "Master Glover, I would not wish you to think me forward, but I would like to ask you some questions about someone who visited your shop yesterday."

Edric Clover looked closely at Aileen. "'Tis passing strange that you would seek to ask questions about my business on the Sabbath morn," he said.

Aileen blushed.

"Yet I see no reason why I should not talk of this as I would talk of any other matter," the glovemaker continued, smiling. "It is the least I can do when you have eased my wife's mind so well."

"Thank you, Master Clover," said Aileen. "I will not delay you long."

It is probably best just to ask the glovemaker direct questions, thought Aileen. I have not much time, and there is little point in beating around the bush. "I wanted to ask if you could tell me anything of a young knight who is, I believe, a member of Sir Gilbert de Cley's household," she said.

Edric's eyebrows rose, almost disappearing into his thick thatch of black hair.

"And why would the doings of such a man interest you?" he asked.

Fair question, thought Aileen, and one I should have anticipated. Perhaps direct questions were not the best idea after all.

"My pardon, Master Clover," said Aileen. "I should have given you a little more information about the reason for my questions."

Aileen gathered her thoughts. "I am sure you know what happened earlier this week at the forge," she said.

"You mean Master Short being attacked?" said Edric. "I think there can be few in St. Edmundsbury who have not heard about that disgraceful attack, coming so soon upon the shocking murder of the Saxon steward."

Aileen nodded. "Master Short's son, Hugh, had asked my friend Robert and I if we could help put his family's minds at ease about there being no connection between the sword that the steward had brought to the blacksmith for repair and his death," she said.

Again Master Clover's mobile eyebrows rose. "Why would he ask of you such a thing?" he said. "Surely such questions should be asked of the reeve, not two young people such as yourselves."

This is not going to be as easy as I had hoped, thought Aileen. "We have known Hugh since we were young," she said. "He had gained the impression that we had more to do with the finding of the holy relic that was stolen from the Abbey than we did."

"So he thought to ask you and Master Palgrave to do more investigating?"

"It did not start that way," Aileen confessed. "We just

sought to find out more about the sword itself. In our minds, we were convinced that knowing more about the weapon's history would be all that was necessary."

"But it was not?" asked the glover.

"Once Master Short was attacked, we realized there was more to it than mere knowledge of the sword's history," Aileen said.

"But surely that was the time to step away and allow the reeve to do his job," Master Clover said gently.

"We have talked with Master Durand," Aileen said. "We do know that we have no power or ability beyond that of the reeve."

The glover chuckled. "Do not take offense, Mistress Aileen," he said. "I simply wanted to be sure that you are not putting yourselves in danger when handing over whatever you have learned to the reeve is all that is needful."

"I thank you, Master Clover," said Aileen. "I assure you that any information we find out in the course of our daily activities will be given to Master Durand."

"And in the course of your daily activities you have come across one of the knights of the household of Sir Gilbert de Cley entering my place of business?" said the glover.

"Yes," said Aileen. "I was returning home yesterday and saw the knight."

"I see," said Master Clover. "Well, I see no harm in telling you what transpired."

Aileen waited as the glover thought back to the day before. "I do not know the knight's name," said Edric. "He did not deem it important to tell a mere merchant more than was necessary to conduct his business." The glover's tone was wry. Clearly he did not think much of the manners of the knight, thought Aileen.

"This was not the knight's first visit, however," said Master Clover.

"It was not?" Aileen was surprised.

"No," responded the glover. "The knight came to my shop three days ago and asked me to repair a glove. Yesterday, he returned and seemed to find my work satisfactory. He paid me for my work and left. I fear I can tell you little else."

"What was the repair you carried out?" asked Aileen.

"One of his gloves had a tear in the index finger," said Edric. "The gloves are of fine leather, and I can understand that any man would wish to have a tear repaired rather than break in a new pair."

"A tear in the index finger," Aileen said thoughtfully. "Which glove was it that was torn?"

"The right glove," said Edric. "The knight told me he had been peeling an apple with his dagger. The knife slipped and bit through the leather into his finger. It was an easy task to clean the leather of the blood and repair the slit. The glove was almost as good as new by the time I had finished."

Aileen was deep in thought as the glover finished his narrative. "Mistress Aileen," Edric said. "Is something wrong?"

"Oh no, Master Clover," said Aileen. "Your pardon. Nothing is wrong. Thank you so much. Please excuse me," with which confused response, Aileen bobbed a curtsy and ran off, leaving the glover staring after her.

22. Chapter Twenty-Two

A man that beareth false witness against his neighbour is a maul, and a sword, and a sharp arrow.

Proverbs 25:18

Pausing only to pick up a hammer hanging by the door of the forge, Adam shouted at the two men and ran toward them. Seeing that it was not going to be as easy to kidnap Hugh as they thought, the two men dropped the boy and ran away.

Adam was tempted to go after them, but his brother's health was of greater concern.

"Hugh," he said, kneeling by his brother and removing the sack from his head. "Are you hurt?"

Hugh spit out dust and straw from the sack. "I am all right," he said.

Adam helped his brother up and half-carried him back

into the house. Sitting him down on a stool, he fetched another cup and made Hugh drink some of the small ale.

"Thank you," said Hugh. "I am better now."

"What happened?" asked Adam.

"I am not sure," said Hugh. "It was so nice outside, I closed my eyes and leaned back against the wall. All of a sudden, I felt something rough come over my head, and then I felt hands grabbing me.

"It seemed as though they were trying to drag me down the street," he continued. "I fought as hard as I was able and yelled as loud as I could, but they were too strong for me."

"Did you see their faces at all?" asked Adam.

"No, the sack was over my head before I knew they were there," Hugh said.

"I did not see their faces either," said Adam. "It is a pity, for we cannot say for sure who it was without more than a cloak to describe."

Hugh started shaking, the memory of his fear overcoming him.

"Hugh," said Adam. "You did well."

"I did?" asked his brother.

Adam put his hand on his brother's shoulder and patted it awkwardly. "You gave them no opportunity to steal you away before help could arrive. I think most people would be so scared they would be frozen in place if such a thing should happen to them. You did well."

Hugh smiled, his chin quivering only a little. "You rescued me, Adam," he said. "Thank you."

"I could not let two ruffians carry off my nuisance of a brother," Adam said. "Were you not here to irritate me, I do not know what I would do."

They both laughed, yet they could not quite shake off the fear.

"Do you think they will return?" asked Hugh quietly.

"I do not," said his brother. "They know that we are warned now. I am sure they will seek out other victims rather than return to our house."

"Then you think it was mere chance that they seized me?" said Hugh.

"What else?" Adam said. "The men saw you sitting outside, eyes closed, and thought perhaps to take you away and rob you of whatever they could take from you."

"But I have nothing," said Hugh. "Surely they could see that."

"Hugh," Adam said. "To some men, a pair of hose or a jerkin is worth more than a life."

Hugh looked alarmed.

"It is truth," said Adam. "But those thieves take advantage of a weak or sleeping victim. They do not return to the scene and try again once others are alerted."

"No, I suppose not," said Hugh. "Yet I am not convinced that this attack was mere chance."

"Why would it be anything other than chance?" asked Adam.

"You know that I asked Aileen and Robert to see if they could find out anything about the sword father repaired, do you not?" Hugh asked.

Adam was puzzled. This seemed to have little to do with what had just happened.

"I do," he said. "But I see little connection between the sword and some ruffians attacking you."

"Mayhap you are right," said Hugh. "But yesterday I

talked to the knights who had questioned father about the sword. I think they may have thought me a little too curious."

"Why?" Adam said. "What was it you talked about?"

"I spoke only of their horses and whether they had ridden them around town at all," said Hugh.

"Is that all?" asked Adam.

Hugh hung his head a little.

"You know how nervous I get when I have to talk much," he said. Adam nodded.

"I think perhaps in my hope to learn something to tell Aileen and Robert I may have been careless in the asking," Hugh said.

"You believe it was two knights who attacked you?" asked his brother.

"No...yes...I do not know," Hugh replied.

"I saw only cloaks," said Adam. "They were perhaps not the rough fabric of the usual kind of ruffian, and yet I find it hard to believe that two such important men would seek to harm a young boy who was merely asking a lot of questions."

"You are probably right," said Hugh, brightening. "My imagination took me too far."

"I believe it did," said Adam. Nevertheless, he thought, with all that has been happening in our town recently, it may be a good idea to tell the reeve of Hugh's fears.

Before they could talk any further, they heard the sound of their parents returning from mass.

Walking into the room Abigail saw her younger son sitting on a stool, dusty and clearly distressed. Adam held a cup in his hand and looked as disturbed as his brother.

"I told you to stay in bed, Hugh," she said, rushing over and putting her hand on his forehead. Praise God, she thought, he has no fever.

"What have you been doing to get so dusty?" Abigail went on. "Did you go outside?"

Turning to her older son and giving no one any chance to respond to her questions, she gave Adam what the boys called "the look."

"How could you allow him to get out of his bed, Adam," she said. "I gave you strict instructions not to do so."

Guy decided to stay silent. I have heard it said that stillness is wisdom when a woman becomes angry, and I believe that to be well said.

"Mother," said Hugh. "It was not Adam's fault. I woke up feeling so much better for the chamomile you gave me. It was such a nice day outside that I asked Adam if I could just sit outside for a few minutes."

"My instructions were not followed, whatever you may say," Abigail said severely.

"No, mother," Adam said. "I am sorry." I have little hope that contrition will reduce the discipline, he thought. Yet it is worth a try.

"You are old enough to know better, Adam," said his mother. "And you are not so young that you cannot know it is wrong to disobey your mother's orders," she continued, looking at Hugh.

"Yes, mother," Adam said.

"Yes, mother," said Hugh.

Satisfied that she had sufficiently conveyed the seriousness of their fault, Abigail looked more closely at her younger son.

"If you were only sitting outside in the sun, Hugh," she said, "how did you get so covered with dust and dirt?"

"It happened when two men tried to drag me away," Hugh said, trying to avoid his mother's hands as she swept her hands over him to remove the dust.

His words had the effect of stopping his mother, but they also brought his father into the fray.

"Two men did what?" Guy said forcefully.

"Two men dropped a sack over my head and started dragging me away," Hugh said.

"Are you hurt?" Abigail brushed her hands over him, peering at any disarrangement that might hide an injury.

"No, mother," Hugh said. "Father, two men did try to steal me away. Had it not been for Adam, they would have succeeded."

"Is this truth, Adam?" said Guy.

"Yes, father," Adam said. "Hugh cried out when they grabbed him, and I ran out in time to see them trying to take him away. They dropped him when they saw me."

"Can you tell who it was that did this?" the blacksmith said.

"No, father," said Adam. "The men were cloaked, and I saw only their backs. Hugh could not see them because of the sack."

"Mayhap the sack was used so that Hugh could not tell who they were," said Guy. "You are certain you have taken no hurt, son?"

"I am certain, father," said Hugh.

"Very well." Guy had made up his mind as to what he had to do next.

"Adam," he said. "Run and fetch Master Durand. I saw him last talking outside the church, but by this time he may have returned to his house. Wherever he may be, I need you to bring him back here."

"Yes, father," said Adam, glad at least that whatever punishment his mother had planned for his disobedience was for now forgotten.

"Make sure to hurry," called Guy after his son as he ran through the forge.

"I will, father," said Adam.

***

While Aileen was talking to the glover, Robert went in search of the reeve. Spying him over the other side of the courtyard talking to some friends, Robert headed in that direction.

"Master Palgrave," he heard a woman's voice calling to him.

Surprised, Robert turned to see Mistress Oliver hurrying toward him with her husband in tow. Ralph Oliver looked as unhappy as always. Even in the midst of his rush to talk to the reeve, Robert was amused at the sight of the tavern keeper trying to pry his wife's fingers off his sleeve as he had perforce to trot behind her.

"Good morrow," said Robert to the two of them. "I trust that you are well today."

"Oh yes," said Mistress Oliver happily. "We are quite in the rudest of health, are we not, my dear." Ralph shot him a look of irritation but said nothing.

Nothing daunted, Mistress Oliver beamed upon the two men, pushed her hair back under her wimple and turned to Robert.

"Master Robert," she said. "I did have such a pleasurable conversation with you the other day."

"It was my pleasure, Mistress Oliver," said Robert, thinking that it had in fact turned out to be a very interesting conversation.

"I did tell Ralph here all about it," she said, patting her husband's arm. "He was most interested in everything I told him, weren't you, my dear?"

Robert understood the sound that came from Ralph's lips to be "Arggg."

"Well," rattled on Mistress Oliver, "you will never guess who I saw in church today."

"I am sure I cannot, Mistress Oliver," said Robert, casting a quick look over his shoulder to make sure that the reeve was still within view.

"Those two awful men," said the tavern-keeper's wife. "They were sitting in the pew with that great lord whose steward was so foully done to death."

Robert did not think it strange that Sir Gilbert and his party would have attended mass in the abbey church, but he politely responded: "Most interesting."

"I did think so as well," said Mistress Oliver. "You know how little seating there is in the church, and that only for the favored few. Honestly, I think it is most unfair that hard-working folk should have to stand, but there it is. We can do nothing about it and so, as the good book says, grin and bear it."

Robert was not so sure this expression came from the Bible, but he would not have disappointed the good woman for anything.

"So the two knights were sitting with Sir Gilbert and his family?" he asked, more out of a desire to say something that would show interest than for any other reason.

"Behind them," she said. "And it did seem that they were little better behaved in the Lord's house than in ours." Mistress Oliver was clearly offended on the Lord's behalf.

"What was it that they did that was so lacking in respect?" asked Robert.

"The fair-headed one kept on leaning forward and talking to the tall dark man that seems to be close to Sir Gilbert," she said.

"The marshal," Robert said.

"I know not his position, but I have heard some call him Sir Thomas," she said helpfully.

Robert nodded. "It was indeed lacking in respect to talk in church," he said, thinking that as a child he had often been cuffed about the ears by his father for doing the exact same thing during mass.

"Yes," the tavern-keeper's wife said. "That other man, the brown-haired knight, kept on trying to pull the other one back, but he did seem to make little difference."

"Did the marshal say anything?" asked Robert, finding himself to be a little curious about the actions of the young knight.

"Well, even though we always try to stand near the front, we were not close enough to hear any words,"

Mistress Oliver said regretfully. "He did seem to be a little impatient, I will say. At first he did not even seem to hear the young man. Finally he turned with a look of thunder and swatted at him. Then he said something to the brown-haired knight."

"What happened next?" asked Robert.

Mistress Oliver, once again pushing her hair under her wimple, looked sad. "After that, the young one sat still as a stone, but I do not think he paid any attention to that excellent sermon that was preached today." Clearly the good woman was sorry that there was not anything more to tell.

"I wonder that Sir Gilbert did not put a stop to the young knight's behavior," Robert said.

"We saw him as he walked in to the church," said Mistress Oliver. "He looked so sad. Mayhap he did not even notice what was going on only a few feet away from him."

Turning to Ralph, who was looking around the courtyard with a bored expression, she gave him a playful push to bring his attention back to her.

"Do you not agree, Ralph?" she said.

"I care not what those young wasters do or do not do," said Ralph irascibly.

"Oh you," laughed Mistress Oliver. "We just need to get you home and feed you. Please do excuse my husband, Master Robert," she said. "He is loathe to wait too long for his lunch after mass"

"I completely understand," said Robert. "I thank you for all that you have been able to tell me and wish you a restful Sabbath and good health."

"And to you and your good family as well," said Mistress Oliver. She pushed her hair back under her wimple and, taking her husband's arm, walked happily off in the direction of the gate.

Robert, glad to see that Durand was still talking to his friends, hurried in that direction. Seeing the expression on the young man's face as he came to a stop in front of him, the reeve made his farewells and walked a short distance away with Robert.

"What is it that causes you to seek me out on a Sunday morning?" Durand asked Robert.

"Your pardon, sir," said Robert. "I would not have disturbed you thus had I not believed that I have some information you need to know."

"What is it that you have to tell me, Master Robert?" asked Durand, intrigued in spite of himself.

"Sir, I know where the steward's brooch has gone," Robert said.

"What!" exclaimed the reeve. "How can you know such a thing, and why have you not told me before?"

"Master Durand," said Robert, "I did only realize last night. I have sought you out as soon as I could."

"My pardon, Master Robert," said the reeve. "I did not intend to accuse you of withholding important information from me. I was simply shocked at your words."

Robert smiled. "Mayhap I was a little bold in my wording," he said.

"Tell me what you have to say," said Durand, returning to the matter at hand.

"When Aileen, Hugh, and I were talking last night, the subject of the brooch came up," Robert said. "We were talking about motives and old gloves and new gloves and..." Robert drew a deep breath.

"None of that matters now. Only, that's why I suddenly remembered."

"Remembered what?" Duran was getting a little impatient.

"Remembered where I had seen Master Aylwin's brooch recently," said Robert simply.

Seeing the reeve's face getting a little red, Robert hastily continued. "Sir Gilbert de Cley came to my father earlier in the week asking him to make a brooch similar to the one that went missing at the time of the murder," said Robert. "He made a drawing for my father to copy."

Durand deemed it wise to allow the young man to continue with his tale, even though his desire to ask questions was strong.

"Since I am apprenticed to my father, I saw that drawing. Last night, I realized that I had seen the original the night I talked with Mad Meg."

"Mad Meg!" said Durand.

"Yes, Master Reeve," said Robert. "I talked with her several days ago. I found her in an alley sheltering from the cold, hugging a big cloak around her. The cloak was fastened with an old, worn brooch. I gave it no thought, for it seemed fair to think this was all that remained of her former life, but now I realize that the brooch was the one from the drawing."

How do these young people discover so much? thought Durand to himself. It seems as though God himself blesses their naïve enquiries.

"Master Robert, are you certain?" he asked, gravely.

"Yes, Master Durand, I am certain," responded Robert in like manner.

"Very well," said the reeve. "I had not thought that our murderer might be an old woman thinking only of warmth and bread. Yet in desperate times, mayhap we are all capable of terrible violence."

Robert was aghast. "Master Durand," he said. "I cannot believe that Mad Meg could be the killer. Surely she is too small and frail to kill a strong man."

"One might think so," said the reeve. "Yet a man may be taken unaware if faced by a small, old beggar woman. Mayhap he refused her alms and she acted out of fear and anger, regretting instantly what she had done. That could explain why Meg took only the cloak and not the coin."

As he spoke, Aileen came up to the two men, eager to share the information she had just gleaned from the glove-maker. Hearing Durand's last words, she gasped.

"Master Durand, surely you do not believe that Mad Meg is the killer!" she said.

A little stung by the disbelief of the pair, Durand said, "What other explanation can there be, if Master Robert is right in asserting that Mad Meg has the steward's cloak and brooch?"

"What if she came across the body after the murder," said Aileen. "It was bitter cold that night. I can see Mad Meg taking the cloak but honoring the death of the man by taking nothing else. Can you not?" Aileen looked straight at the reeve, her eyes almost daring him to contradict her.

Sighing, Durand picked up Aileen's argument. "It may be as you say," he said. "If so, then it is possible that the beggar woman saw something that may be of use to me in my investigation." If there was a slight emphasis on the word "my" the other two gave no sign of noticing it.

"It is hard to make sense of what that old woman says at the best of times," said the reeve. "Yet I must make the attempt."

"Will you do so today?" asked Robert

"On the Sabbath, one should rest from one's labors," said Durand. "Yet this is a matter of urgency, so mayhap I can do a good deed and take the woman some succor for the Lord's Day."

The reeve looked as though he was about to leave Aileen and Robert that very minute.

"Master Durand," said Robert. "I have something more to tell you. Please wait!"

The reeve turned back to the young man. "What more have you found out while you were simply helping your friend," he said somewhat ironically.

Robert looked a little abashed but was determined to continue.

"The other day, when I had been talking to some friends of mine on my way home, Hadric came up to me in the street."

"Hadric," said the reeve. "The rag and bone man?"

"Yes, sir," Robert said. "Did he come to see you as well?"

"No," responded Durand. "I have not seen him in many months."

Aileen and Robert exchanged glances. It was as we thought, Aileen said to herself. The man was not interested in sharing his knowledge with the reeve.

Quickly Robert told Durand all about his conversation with the old man. The reeve listened intently and frowned as Robert came to the end of his account.

"Hadric did not take your advice and report these events to me," he said. "I must needs ask him for an explanation of that neglect."

"Do you think mayhap he has a guilty reason for not wishing to talk to you?" Robert asked.

Durand barked a laugh. "Methinks the bone-grubber has many reasons for not wishing to talk to me," he said. "Yet I would not have put him down as a murderer before now. This puzzle grows more complicated by the day," the reeve continued. "I thank you for your information. I must now consider how this fits in with all other pieces of knowledge I have gleaned over this past week."

"Master Durand," said Aileen. "I have something I would like to tell you to add to your knowledge. Harkening back to what Robert had to say about the brooch, mayhap it will explain why I am so reluctant to think of Mad Meg as a murderer."

"What is it, Mistress Aileen?" asked the reeve.

"I have spoken with Master Clover this morning," said Aileen. "He has told me that Sir Walter de Nantes brought to him a glove for repair."

"Yes," said Master Durand. "And why is this remarkable? Surely this is a normal part of the glover's business."

"I am sure that is so," Aileen said. "But in this case the glove was bloody, and the index finger of the right glove was torn."

Durand and Robert both stared at her. "The glove was bloody?" asked Durand.

"Yes," said Aileen. "Master Clover did tell me that the knight told him that he sliced through the glove with his dagger when he was peeling an apple, but I do not believe that."

"It would seem a reasonable explanation to me," said the reeve.

"Mayhap it would to me as well," Aileen said. "But Sir Walter de Nantes is right-handed. If you peel an apple with your right hand and the knife slips, do you not cut your thumb?"

"How do you know the knight is right-handed?" Durand demanded.

"Because I saw him peel an apple only the other day," said Aileen. "I was in the courtyard at the Abbey, and he took an apple out of the barrel and peeled it with his dagger. He used his right hand."

Deep in thought, Durand's hands moved as though mimicking first the peeling of fruit and then the thrust of a dagger. "A man who peels an apple may be more likely to cut a thumb than a finger," he agreed. "A man thrusting a dagger into another man may find his grip slip and cut his finger."

Durand turned on his heels. "I must seek out this knight and talk to him," he said. "Mistress Aileen, Master Robert, I thank you."

Durand turned on his heels, but as he made to leave, Adam came running through the gate of the courtyard. Pausing only to seek out the reeve, he sprinted up to him. Panting, he said, "Master Durand. You must come at once. My brother has been attacked!"

23. CHAPTER TWENTY-THREE

So he drove out the man; and he placed at the east of the Garden of Eden Cherubims, and a flaming sword which turned every way, to keep the way of the tree of life.

Genesis 3:24

"Aileen," her mother called as Aileen ran after the three men on her way out of the courtyard. "Where are you going in such a hurry?"

Aileen stopped. "Mother, Adam has just brought news that Hugh has been attacked."

Anne Arundel was shocked. "Then I must fetch some herbs and see if I can help," she said. "Go you now and let Mistress Short know that I will be there shortly."

"Thank you, mother," said Aileen, and set off again for Hugh's home.

Arriving at the Short home, Aileen found pandemonium. Hugh was sitting on a stool, the reeve was barking questions at him with Guy Short as Adam tried to talk over him. Abigail Short was trying to tell all of them that Hugh just needed to go upstairs and go to bed, vainly waving her arms in an attempt to quieten the loud voices of the men. Robert was standing to the side looking a little embarrassed.

As Aileen approached, a loud voice suddenly broke into the babble. "Be quiet!" it commanded.

For a moment, there was total stillness. No sound, no movement. It was the silence of shock. All those who were present had known Abigail Short their whole lives. As a child, she would hide behind her mother's skirts if anyone so much as raised their voice anywhere nearby. As a young woman she had worshiped the big blacksmith but would be tongue-tied if he even wished her "good morrow." When that same blacksmith asked for her hand in marriage, she turned so white that both Guy and her father had stepped forward in anticipation of her fainting. Abigail did not faint, but she couldn't speak. She could only nod her head.

All eyes upon her, Abigail stood defiant.

"My son does not need any more disturbance this night," she said. "He has been attacked, dragged, and dropped. He can tell you nothing more than he has already told us. He is going to bed right now."

Suiting her actions to her words, Abigail took her son by the arm and, gently pulling him to his feet, led him to the stairs.

Turning to the reeve as they reached the bottom step, she said: "Master Durand, if you have more you wish to ask my son on the morrow, please return. You are always welcome to our house." With these words, mother and son mounted the stairs, the party behind them still standing speechless.

A knock at the door broke the spell. Guy walked over to greet the visitor, Adam tried hard not to laugh, and the reeve let out the breath he appeared to have been holding. Aileen and Robert looked at each other and, seeing the glint of laughter in each other's eyes, quickly looked away again.

Anne Arundel, basket in hand, walked in on the scene. "Whatever is happening here?" she asked. "Is Hugh all right? You all seem to be in some sort of daze."

Adam, Aileen, and Robert could no longer hold their laughter in. They broke into giggles, earning a frown from Guy Short and a clear attempt on the part of Durand not to join the younger folk in laughing.

"All is as well as it could be, Mistress Arundel," said Guy. "My good wife is upstairs with Hugh as we speak."

"Mother," said Aileen. "I am sorry. I did not have a chance to tell Mistress Short that you would be coming."

"That is of no matter, Aileen," said her mother. "With your permission, Master Short, I will go up to see if I can be of help."

"Thank you, Mistress Arundel," said Guy. "You are most kind, and I am sure my wife would be glad to see you."

Anne turned to go upstairs. As she went, she said in a reflective manner: "These are indeed strange times. I passed poor Mad Meg on the street on my way here. Even she did seem different."

"In what way did she seem different?" Master Durand spoke sharply.

Surprised, Anne turned to face the reeve. "Your pardon,

sir," she said. "I did not realize that my words would cause such concern."

"No, Mistress," said Durand. "I would beg your pardon. I did not mean to speak so harshly."

Anne inclined her head in acknowledgement of the apology.

"It is simply that I needs must find Mad Meg to speak with her. You surprised me when you said you had seen her not many minutes since."

"It is rare that I am away from my home at this hour on the Sabbath," said Anne. "It may be that the poor woman roams the streets at all hours of every day, but I have had no thought of it." Anne paused. "Mayhap I should give more thought to the plight of such as Mad Meg in this cold weather. I am glad that some other has done so."

"Why would you say some other has had thought of Mad Meg?" asked the reeve.

Anne laughed. "I am not the wife of a trader in cloth for no good reason," she said. "It was clear to me that Mad Meg was wearing a cloak of much finer cloth than could be expected of a beggar woman. Some kind person must have gifted it to her to keep her warm during cold times such as we are having now."

Durand looked at Aileen and Robert. "I know not whether to thank you or chide you for interfering in my business," he said. "Yet once again I must follow the trail you have set for me."

With these words, Durand offered his farewells to the assembled company and left.

Anne looked at her daughter.

"Aileen," she said. "What did Master Durand mean by those words?"

"Mother," said Aileen. "It is not what it does seem."

She could tell from her mother's expression that Anne was not convinced.

"Mistress Arundel," said Robert, coming to Aileen's aid. "I spoke with Mad Meg some

days ago and had only this morning told Master Durand that I believed she was wearing the cloak owned by the murdered steward."

"What?" exclaimed Guy.

"Truly?" said Anne.

"Yes, mother," said Aileen. "That is why Master Durand wants to talk to her."

"He believes that that poor, old beggar woman murdered the steward?" said Anne.

"It may be so," said Robert.

"I cannot believe it," Aileen's mother said.

"We told Master Durand we did not think it to be so either," Aileen said. "Mayhap she just chanced upon the body after the murder was done and took the cloak to keep warm."

"I can believe that," said Guy. "Murder is another thing."

"Let us pray that, whatever be the truth, the reeve will discover it," said Anne.

So pray we all, thought Aileen.

Durand hurried through the empty streets of St. Edmundsbury, peering into alleyways and looking under discarded barrels and standing wagons. The afternoon of the Sabbath day is no time to be looking for murder suspects, he thought to himself. Better be beside my warm fire with a mug of mulled ale in my hand, just like so many of my fellow townsfolk. Still, there is little time left in which to solve this crime. If that madwoman knows aught of what has happened I must find her and discover it.

Finally, Durand spied the old woman hunkered down between the side wall of a tavern and a barrel. She had piled some old straw on top of her for warmth, and her cloak was wrapped tight around her with only the top of her head showing.

At the reeve's approach, Mad Meg drew the cloak up even further, covering her head as though to disappear from the view of the lawman. Durand stopped in front of her and waited.

Two eyes peeked out of the cloak, and the woman began to wail. "I ain't done nothing. Don't you go and throw me in the dark and leave me to rot. I ain't done nothing."

"Stop your crying, woman," said the reeve. "There's time enough to talk about throwing you in dark cells. For now, I just want to ask you some questions."

If Durand thought that this would stop Mad Meg's cries, he was sadly mistaken. The wailing intensified, and the old woman curled herself up into as small a ball as she could manage.

That's gone and torn it, thought Durand. How am I ever going to get anything out of her now.

"Meg," he heard a voice behind him. Turning, he saw Robert coming toward him, bread and cheese in his hand.

Durand began to ask Robert what he was doing there, but Robert put a finger to his lips and the reeve held his peace.

Robert knelt down by the old woman and gently bid her hush. "Meg," he said, "it's Robert. We talked a few days ago, and it did seem to me that we became friends. I thought to bring you some more victuals on this Sabbath day."

The wailing grew less intense. Once again, two eyes appeared out of the bundle of cloth, eyeing the two men suspiciously.

"Do you see?" Robert said, holding out the bread and cheese. "It is soft bread and good cheese. I know you did enjoy it before. Will you not take it now?"

Sniffles replaced the wailing, and a little more of the old woman appeared out of the cloak. Almost she reached out a hand to take the bread, but the sight of the big, severe man looming over her made her draw away once again.

"Master Durand," said Robert. "Do you think you could step a little further back? You are scaring Meg."

"I'm scaring her?" Durand exclaimed, and Meg instantly retreated into her cloak again.

Robert frowned. "Please," he said.

Muttering under his breath, Durand backed a few feet further away.

"Mistress Meg," Robert said, turning back to the old woman. "Please take my gift and talk to me a little."

It had been many years since anyone had addressed Meg in such a manner. The sniffling stopped altogether, and the old woman raised her head out of the cloak completely. She eyed Durand warily, and then turned to look at the young man who had been so kind to her.

Mayhap she does trust me after all, thought Robert. Fast upon that reflection came another: Mayhap she is just hungry.

"Friends is as friends does," she said.

Robert smiled and held out the victuals to her. Unlike last time, Meg reached out and took the bread and cheese from him without snatching, and she only put a small amount into her mouth upon which to chew.

"Methinks you want something yet from me," she said. "But few there are who are willing to give and not just to take from a poor, old woman like me."

"I am glad you know I would never hurt you," said Robert.

"Not like some I could name," she said with a malicious glance at the reeve.

Almost Durand responded, but, deciding that Robert was doing better than he could for the moment, he held back the words that leapt upon his tongue.

"Mistress Meg, I do have something I have to ask you," Robert continued. "It is about the cloak you are wearing."

Meg said nothing, only gathering it closer around her.

"When I talked to you the other day, I noticed the

brooch that clasps the cloak," said Robert. "It seemed old, but it was a pretty piece."

Meg looked alarmed but did not move.

"Was it from your mother?" asked Robert.

Silence.

"I ask only because most people who have to live as you do would have sold such a treasure for food long ago," Robert said. "Surely it must have much value to you if you have kept it all this time."

"It was not from my mother," Meg said grudgingly.

He is good at this, thought Durand. Already he has gained more than I could were I to have spent hours pressing the matter with the mad, old woman.

"It was not?" said Robert.

"No," confirmed Meg. "It was a gift the archangel did not take. It was a gift from Abel. Never would I part with his gift."

Abel, thought Robert. Who is Abel?

"I do not understand," said Robert. "I know no Abel. Who is he?"

"I did tell you of the archangel and his great struggle before," Meg said sternly.

Yes, and I could not make head nor tail of it then either, thought Robert ruefully.

"I do remember, Mistress Meg," Robert said. "You told me you saw the archangel Michael."

"Yes," said Meg eagerly. "Abel tried to reach the archangel's sword to save the world from the darkness, but he could not."

Light crowded into Robert's brain. She saw it, he thought. Meg saw the murder!

Taking a quick look at Durand, Robert saw understanding in the reeve's eyes as well.

"Meg," Robert said. "This is important. Few have ever seen the archangel Michael. Could you tell what he looked like?"

"When I were young," said Meg inconsequentially, "my mother did tell me that you could tell angels by the brilliance of their eyes."

"I have never heard that before," said Robert. "Is that how you could tell that you were seeing an archangel?"

"Aye," said Meg. "It cannot have been any other than the archangel Michael. It is Michael who stands with a sword. And if angels have brilliant eyes, then the eyes of archangels must be even more rare."

"The archangel's eyes were so different from any others then?" asked Robert, trying to contain his excitement.

"Aye," the old woman responded calmly. "One brown and one blue. Who else but the archangel Michael could that be?"

Stunned, Robert had only one more question for Meg. "Meg, was Abel wearing this cloak when he met the archangel Michael?"

"Did I not just tell you that," Meg said as though she was talking to a child of two. "Abel had no more need of his cloak, so he gave it to me."

Looking from man to man, Meg said, "Meg is an honest woman. Meg does not steal."

With this, the old woman rearranged the cloak around her shoulders and returned to her unexpected supper.

Robert rose and bid the woman farewell. Receiving no reply, he walked over to Durand.

"She saw Aylwin killed," said Durand.

"Yes," agreed Robert. "I did not understand when first I spoke to her. She seems to have confused archangels with Bible stories."

Durand suddenly smiled. "She is confusing plays with real life," he said.

"Now I am confused," Robert said, wrinkling his brow.

"Do you not remember the mysterious players from earlier this year?" asked Durand. "They did travel all the way from London to perform for us stories from the first book of the Bible."

"Cain and Abel!" Robert exclaimed. "How could I have forgotten? The players told the story of the first murder."

"Yes," said Durand. "I am certain sure that Meg must have seen some of the play. No one within the town can have failed to notice the gaudy stage and the men in costume."

"And now I remember that at the time I thought I had not heard the priest talk of angels when recounting the tale," said Robert. "The players added to the story."

"I agree," the reeve said. "Yet all their words and deeds were meant to point out the moral of the tale: Thou shalt not kill."

The two men were silent for a moment. Then Durand straightened his shoulders and made to leave.

"I had thought to find the rag and bone man to see what he may know about this murder," said Durand. "I think now that he may simply have been trying to find someone who could be gulled into buying him a drink."

Robert flushed, embarrassed that the reeve might think him a fool.

Durand smiled and laid a hand on Robert's shoulder momentarily. "Master Robert," he said. "Always it is best to bring any possible information about a crime to me. It is my job to sort through what is truth and what is false. Hadric is skilled in the art of begging. You did right to come to me with his story."

"Thank you, Master Durand," said Robert. "I would never wish to waste your time."

"You did not," said the reeve. "Indeed, you and Mistress Aileen have done much to aid me in this search for the killer." The reeve's face took on a grim expression. "I needs must talk with Sir Walter de Nantes," he said. "Then I must seek audience with the abbot and mayhap even Sir Gilbert de Cley."

Bidding Robert farewell, the reeve walked heavily toward the abbey. Robert looked after him and then, in much the same manner, walked back to the house of the blacksmith to pass on the news that the crime was solved.

24. Chapter Twenty-Four

*And ye shall chase your enemies, and they shall fall before you
by the sword.*

Leviticus 26:7

"I still believe there is another part to this tale," said Aileen. When Robert had returned to the Short's home with his account of Meg's revelations, she had quietly drawn him outside to talk while everyone inside exclaimed over the news.

"Aileen, it seems so clear," Robert said. "What is it that is troubling you?"

"Your pardon, Robert," said his friend. "I know it seems as though Sir Walter de Nantes must have murdered the poor steward. It is only that…"

"It is only that what?" Robert was a little exasperated. "I do not understand."

"Why did he kill him?" Aileen said. "Why would this knight follow the steward all the way to our town just to murder him.? It is as we said the other night. He could so easily have done so any time he had wanted. Why wait until he is surrounded by other people and risk capture?"

"I do not know," said Robert. "Yet all that we have learned seems to point in that direction. What other answer can there be?"

"I do not know," Aileen said. "Yet there is some thread in this pattern that is awry."

"Do you want to talk through what we know?" asked Robert. "I know you too well to doubt the strength of your belief."

Aileen smiled. "Robert," she said. "You are the most true friend anyone could have. Even as you offer everything to your friends, you never ask for anything in return. Thank you." She reached out her hand to touch his.

Robert blushed and stammered that he was merely doing what was right. Clearing his throat, Robert continued, "We may not have much time before your mother takes her leave of the blacksmith and his wife, and you will have to leave."

"That is true," said Aileen, leading Robert to a bench close by the wall of the house.

"Let us list what we know," Aileen said.

"We know that Master Aylwin was afraid almost from the time he arrived in St. Edmundsbury," said Robert.

"Yes," agreed Aileen. "It would appear that the arrival of Sir Walter de Nantes and Sir Edward Strode did cause the steward concern."

"That would support the theory that Sir Walter is the killer," said Robert.

"I doubt not that these two knights have some part in this tale," said Aileen. "Yet in my mind, I am not sure they have the whole part."

Robert nodded. "Very well," he said. "What is the next item on the list?"

"We know that a tale of this sword has spread around town," Aileen said. "Many think it is the sword of the Emperor Constantine, and yet Hugh's father does doubt it is that old."

"If the story is false, then mayhap the sword is not the reason for the killing," said Robert.

"That is not necessarily so," said Aileen. "We know that the sword is unlikely to be that of the great Constantine, but not all within the walls of our burgh know that. Even a hope of the power or money such a trophy could bring would be enough to cause some men to commit such a crime."

"Truth," said Robert. "So where does that leave us?"

"Let us leave aside the question of the sword itself," said Aileen. "What else do we know?"

"We have heard much of the household of Sir Gilbert," Robert said. "We know that Sir Gilbert de Cley is a kindly master and was a friend to Master Aylwin. We know that one of his sons is good and the other ill-tempered. We also know the marshal is feared by all and we know that the two knights who arrived the day after Master Aylwin are filled with pride."

"Yes," said Aileen. "We have heard tell of the moods of Roger de Cley and Sir Thomas Warren as well as the deeds and loose talk of Sir Walter de Nantes and Sir Edward Strode. We have even confirmed those accounts by reason of our own experience."

Aileen fell silent. She had what Robert called "that look" on her face. A look that usually means she is putting together something in her mind, thought Robert. Best not to disturb her, but I certainly hope she tells me what it is soon. It cannot be much longer before her mother comes out.

Aileen raised her head. "Robert, what else do we know about these men?"

Robert was confused. "What else?" he asked. "I am not sure what you mean. We know that Sir Walter de Nantes had a cut on his finger that could easily have come from a thrust of a knife. We know that Mad Meg saw a man trying to fend off a blow, and it seems likely that what she was describing was the attack on the steward.

"Is that what you mean by 'what else'?" he asked.

"Not exactly," said Aileen. "All that we know, of course, but have we not also heard much of the conversations between these men?"

"Yes," said Robert. "Yet I am not sure what help that is to us in solving this riddle."

"It may be of great help," said Aileen, turning eagerly to her friend. "Robert," she said. "Think of our friendship and our relationship with our other friends."

"Yes," Robert said, still uncertain what she could be thinking of.

"Do we not tell each other things we would not wish others to know," Aileen went on. "Do we not tell each other our hopes and dreams? Do we not show each other when we have found something exciting or have made something new?"

"Yes, Aileen, we do," said Robert. "But I still do not see what that has to do with the murder of the steward."

"Hope can become bitterness," she said. "New ambitions can destroy old friendships. Is this not so?"

"I suppose so," said Robert.

"I am sure I am right," said Aileen. "And Robert, it was you who gave me the key."

"What key? What are you talking about?"

"Never mind," said Aileen. "I have to find Master Durand."

"Now?" said Robert. "It is almost twilight, and your mother will expect you to walk home with her."

"Let me just go in and tell her I will be home in a little while," said Aileen. "Then come with me, Robert, and I will tell you all on the way."

Suiting her actions to her words, Aileen disappeared into the blacksmith's home. In only a few minutes, she came back out and started running toward the reeve's house. There seems little option but to follow her, thought Robert, as he hurried to catch up with his friend. Aileen is rarely wrong, and I can sense that we are near the solution to the whole puzzle.

25. Chapter Twenty-Five

Put up again thy sword into his place; for all they that take the sword shall perish with the sword.

Matthew 26:52

It was a cold Monday morning in St. Edmundsbury. Frost covered the stones of the abbey courtyard, and the snorts of breath from the horses being led out of the stables appeared as short-lived fog in the air.

The courtyard was bustling with the usual throng of monks, merchants and servants, all going about their daily tasks. Perhaps there was a little more hustle and bustle, it being the start of a new week. Yet some there were who seemed still in the midst of the action.

Durand stood quietly near the stables. Aileen and Robert too were not about their business. They stood together a little way off, saying nothing. As they watched,

Abbot Samson walked through the courtyard and stood next to the reeve. The two men acknowledged each other with a nod of the head and then stood silent, waiting.

It was not long before Sir Gilbert de Cley and his party exited the guest hall. Sir Gilbert's face was grim, but he strode toward the abbot with purpose in his step. Behind him came his sons, Roger wearing his usual expression of ill-humor, and Stephen watching his father with a slightly puzzled expression.

Several other members of Sir Gilbert's household exited the guest hall, including Sir Walter de Nantes and Sir Edward Strode. Edward's face almost seemed to show relief, but Walter's face was expressionless.

Sir Thomas Warren came out of the door next, still shouting orders to the servants who straggled out behind him. "Be careful, you fool," to one and, "Make haste, you clodpoll," to another. Striding up to stand beside Sir Gilbert, the marshal glared at the reeve.

"Master Reeve, you have come to bid us farewell," the marshal said loudly. "Would that you had come before this to bring my lord the comfort of knowing who did murder the steward."

"Sir Thomas," said Gilbert sharply. "Do you not have words of greeting to offer Father Abbot and the reeve, or must you speak only words of anger?"

The marshal looked at his lord in surprise. "Your pardon, my lord," he said

"And yours as well, Father," he said to the abbot. To Durand he said nothing.

To Aileen and Robert, it seemed as though the air crackled with tension. How can they not feel it? thought

Robert. Looking around at the gathered party, Aileen thought that Stephen de Cley was the only one who seemed uncomfortable. It is as though he feels there is something strange in the air, she thought, but he cannot quite decide what it is.

"Sir Gilbert, you have graced us with your presence," Abbot Samson said. "That such a terrible event should have been the cause of your visit to our great abbey is to my sorrow."

"I thank you, Father Abbot," said Sir Gilbert. "I too would rather have been a guest in your hall by reason of pilgrimage and not death."

At this, Durand stepped forward and took out from under his cloak a bundle wrapped in fine cloth.

"My lord," he said to the knight, "I have kept this sword in safekeeping this last week. It is now time to place it back into your care. I am grieved that I have not until this day presented you with the truth surrounding the death of your steward."

Sir Gilbert took the bundle and carefully unwound the cloth until the hilt of the old sword was visible. Looking thoughtfully upon the weapon, he wrapped it in the cloth once more and held it out to the abbot.

"Father Abbot," he said. "I present to the abbey of St. Edmundsbury this sword of renown. I can no longer bear to look upon it, for it will be forever stained with the blood of my friend. May the blessed Saint Edmund wipe from it the mark of murder."

As Abbot Samson reached out to take the sword from the knight, Sir Thomas Warren and Roger de Cley both stepped forward as though to snatch the blade out of the hands of the monk.

"My lord," said the marshal. "Surely it is not fitting to give a gift that is tainted by the blood of a murdered man. Let us not act hastily in deciding upon the fate of this revered blade."

"Father," said Roger. "Sir Thomas speaks truly. Think you not that we should discuss this first?"

Sir Gilbert looked at his son and the marshal, his eyes boring into them as if to see into their very souls. For a moment, Roger hesitated, but the urgency of his plea was too great.

"If you do not wish to keep the sword within our walls," he went on, "mayhap you would give me permission to take it as a gift to the king in London. Such a great gift would surely show the strength of our oath of fealty and be certain to gain the king's favor."

To Aileen and Robert, the scene unfolding before them almost seemed like a tableau from a mystery play. The actors stood in dramatic poses, the audience holding its breath, waiting to see what happened next.

For a moment, Sir Gilbert slumped over, but then he drew his shoulders back and stood tall and proud. "Sir Thomas," he said to the marshal. "The decision as to what to do with this sword is mine alone. You forget yourself if you think to stand on level ground with me in making decisions of importance."

The marshal's face darkened, and his fists clenched. "It is as you say, my lord," he said, though the tone did not match the words.

The knight looked hard at his marshal and then turned

to Roger. "Roger," said his father, "It has always saddened me that my older son and I share so little in temperament and ambition. Your mother has often had to play the role of mediator between us. Yet in spite of all, you are my son, and I have always loved you."

Roger's jaw stuck out. "I have seen little sign of that, father," he said. "I am your heir, yet you treat me as a spoiled child."

"Too often you have behaved so," said Sir Gilbert sharply. Then he sighed. "Enough, for now we must come to the truth," he said.

"What do you mean?" Roger stood face to face with his father, anger written in every line of his body.

"When the abbot and Master Durand came to me last night," said his father, "I was loathe to believe what they had to tell me."

All eyes turned upon the two men standing in front of the knight. Monk and reeve said nothing.

"They talked of knights and greed, of betrayal and murder," Sir Gilbert continued, almost as though no one was present but he and his son.

It was hard to identify from whence it came, but Aileen and Robert clearly heard the sound of indrawn breaths. The slight movement of shuffling feet followed upon the sound, and now they could see Sir Walter de Nantes and Sir Edward Strode moving uneasily.

"What are you saying, my lord?" asked Sir Thomas Warren. He gestured toward the reeve.

"Did this man accuse any of your household of this deed?" The marshal had the appearance of a man maligned by one of little consequence. "What bumbling dolt would make such an accusation? No one of our party could have done this thing, for we were all in Sussex when the steward was killed."

"Not all were in Sussex," said his master.

Now all eyes were turned upon the two young knights.

Panic stared out of the eyes of the younger of the two men, but Sir Walter de Nantes was made of sterner stuff.

"Why would we want to see Aylwin dead?" he said. "Sir Edward and I were here on pilgrimage. It was mere chance that we were within these walls when the steward met his fate. We had no reason to wish him ill."

Durand stepped forward and faced the knight. "That is a question I must ask," he said. "Why did you choose this time to come on pilgrimage to the site of our blessed saint?"

"Why should we not?" responded Walter.

"You must have known that the steward had been sent here by Sir Gilbert," the reeve said. "Yet you chose not to travel with him, That too seems curious."

"I cannot help what may seem out of place to your mind," said Sir Walter. "We asked permission to attend upon the saint in St. Edmundsbury and, once it was granted, we made the journey."

"I did not give you permission to ride to St. Edmunds-bury," said Sir Gilbert. "Had you made clear to me your desire to come to the shrine of St. Edmund, I would gladly have given you permission, but I would have suggested you accompany my friend along the way."

"My lord," responded Sir Walter. "We would not disturb you with such minor matters. We asked permission of the marshal, for it is he who guides our daily lives."

"Is this true, Sir Thomas?" asked Durand.

"It is truth," answered the marshal. "Sir Walter and Sir Edward made sincere request that they be permitted to make a pilgrimage to the blessed shrine. Had they made the request a day earlier, they could have ridden out with the steward. As it was, I suggested they leave immediately so that they might perhaps meet up with the Saxon on the road to St. Edmundsbury."

The marshal looked confident in his explanation, and some of the tension went out of the bodies of the two young knights.

"Sir Walter, I would have you remove your gloves and show me your hands," Durand said softly.

Sir Edward Strode gasped, and the look of panic returned to his eyes.

Sir Walter gave him a frowning glance and then turned back to the reeve. "Why should I do that?" he asked. "You have no power of command over me."

"But I do," said Sir Gilbert, stepping up to the young man. "You will do as the reeve has asked, or you will feel my anger."

Shrugging, Sir Walter slowly took off his left glove and stretched out his hand.

"The other glove as well," said Durand.

Hesitating for a moment, Sir Walter slowly took off his glove and extended his hand.

Durand took the knight's hand in his and turned it over.

"How did you come by this cut, sir knight?" he asked.

"It was a careless accident," said Sir Walter. "I was peeling an apple and the knife slipped."

Durand reached into a barrel close by him and picked

out an apple. Taking out his knife, he made as if to begin peeling the fruit, but then threw it at Sir Walter de Nantes. Surprised, the knight caught it with his right hand and angrily threw it down on the ground.

"It does seem passing strange," the reeve said easily, "that a right-handed man should cut himself so while peeling an apple. Rather the wound seems to be more that would result from a knife slipping while it was being thrust into some prey."

The silence that followed this statement was broken by a high-pitched cry. Sir Edward Strode looked all around him, seeking a way of escape, and then took off running toward the abbey gate.

Durand made to go after him, but he had no need. Stephen de Cley, who was standing closest to the fleeing knight's route, casually stuck out a foot. Sir Edward tripped and fell to the courtyard stones in an untidy pile.

"It did seem to me that something needed to be done to prevent Sir Edward from escaping," he said. "Master Aylwin was a good man and a friend. I would have justice for him."

Having had his say, Stephen de Cley stood back to allow Durand and one of his men to haul Sir Edward to his feet. Two others held the arms of Sir Walter de Nantes, who looked at his companion with contempt on his face.

Sir Gilbert looked at the two young men, distress and anger writ large upon his face.

"Why?" he asked. "Why would you do such a foul deed. Aylwin never did anything to cause you harm. I do not understand."

"It was not us that desired his death," cried Sir Edward.

"We would never plot such a thing. It was not us; it was not our plan." He was sobbing, and once his mouth was opened, it could not be stopped.

"Speak plainly," said Sir Gilbert. "What do you mean that it was not you that desired my friend's death?"

"We were ordered to do it," said Sir Edward. "We were promised a reward, yes, but we were ordered."

"Be quiet, you fool!" The harsh voice of Sir Thomas Warren broke into the man's babbling. "For your life, be quiet!"

It was too late. Edward Strode was completely undone and nothing could stop him now.

"It was him," he cried out, breaking free one arm from Durand's grip. "It was the marshal who told us to kill the steward!"

26. Chapter Twenty-Six

*If I whet my glittering sword, and mine hand take hold on
judgment; I will render vengeance to mine enemies.*

Deuteronomy 32.41

"The man is mad with fear." Sir Thomas Warren
withstood the looks of all present and, turning
to Sir Gilbert, repeated his words as though to
give them emphasis. "Sir Edward is mad with fear. He seeks
any way out of what is certain death. Placing the blame on
his master is his only hope."

Almost I can believe him, thought Aileen. He is so
confident, so persuasive.

What an arrogant man, thought Robert. He thinks to
talk himself out of guilt simply by asserting his authority.

"I have always known you to be an ambitious man, even
a ruthless man," said Sir Gilbert. "Yet you have been, to my

knowledge, a loyal man. I gave you command of my fighting men, and I even gave you charge of training my son to be an upright and loyal man."

A look passed between Sir Gilbert and Roger de Cley. The men looked away as quickly as they had exchanged glances, but Sir Gilbert did not miss the smirk on the face of his son or the involuntary curl of the lip of his marshal.

Slowly, he turned to his son. "My son," he said almost gently, putting his arm on Roger's shoulder. "Tell me now. Did you have any part in this foul murder?"

Roger pulled away from his father's grip. "You would ask me that," he said angrily. "No son should have to hear such a question from his father." But he would not look at his father. Rather, he looked down at the ground.

"Face me like a man," Sir Gilbert said. "I have raised no cowards. If you have any part in this, I must know it. If you, like these two foolish knights, have been persuaded by Sir Thomas, then tell me now. I can do nothing to help if the truth be not known."

"You do not see the truth when it is in front of your eyes," said Roger, his face turning red and his fists clenching as though to hold in the violence of his temper. "When I tell you I believe your villeins are keeping too much of their crops, you say they are loyal servants and keep only what is needful. When I ask to be placed in the household of your great ally, the Lord de Warenne, so that I can seek greater preferment, you say only that I am not yet ready."

"You were not ready, Roger," said Sir Gilbert. "I have not yet seen in you the interest in truth and in managing your land and people that I desire in my heir, and that is equally as important to my Lord de Warenne."

Tears of anger loomed in the eyes of his son. "I hate you, I hate you!" he said. "My whole life, the only man who has cared anything about me is Sir Thomas. From him have I learned all that I know about fighting and wooing and gaining authority and power. I hate you!"

"Then it is true. You joined with Sir Thomas and these two base knights to murder my loyal steward and friend." Sir Gilbert spoke quietly.

Roger suddenly seemed to realize his position. Like the other two knights, there was only one punishment for murder, and he was not ready to accept such a fate.

"No, father," he said, dropping to his knee and grasping his father's hand. "I did speak out of anger, but I could never plot such a thing against Aylwin. He was a good man, as all have said, and I would not do anything to harm him."

Gilbert looked at his son with pity in his eyes. "Do not make of yourself a lesser man," he said to Roger. He tried to pull his son up, but Roger clung on to his hand and would not rise.

"Father," he said. "It is as I said. I have believed Sir Thomas to be my true friend all my life. I did not take part in any plan to do harm to Aylwin. Only afterward did I find out that these two young knights had carried out the murder and that Sir Thomas knew of it."

Rising, he grasped his father's shoulder as though to push into him belief in his son's story. "When I found out what had happened, I was torn. How could I tell what I knew when the result was certain death for them all, even for the man who has been my tutor and friend since I was but a child."

Sir Gilbert wants to believe his son, thought Aileen as she watched. Yet I see in his eyes that he cannot.

It is a tale that might persuade many, thought Durand. Mayhap there is some truth in it.

But they had all reckoned without the marshal.

With a look of fury on his face, he strode over to Roger. "Foul liar and traitor that you are. It was not only for my ambition that we did this deed. It was for yours as well. When men do perilous deeds for great gain, there is also great risk. Now you seek to snivel your way out of the punishment that comes to those who throw the dice and lose. It shall not be!"

Turning, Sir Thomas walked over to the reeve. "I shall tell you all," he said. "The noose shall take all four of us, but I shall go to it as a man, not a coward."

The reeve turned to Abbot Samson. "Father Abbot," he said. "Might we make use of your chambers? It is not fitting that this sad play be brought to its conclusion in public."

"I agree with you, Master Reeve," said the abbot.

Turning to Sir Gilbert, the abbot laid a gentle hand on his arm. "Sir, will you come with me and take a glass of wine? It may ease the chill in your heart a little."

Sir Gilbert nodded his head. Walking over to Stephen, he put a hand on his shoulder and said, "Come with me to the abbot's chambers, my son. We shall hear what there is to be told, however hard it may be."

Together the knight and his younger son followed Abbot Samson.

Aileen and Robert came forward to meet Durand as he directed his men to take the two young knights to the cells and then bring Roger de Cley and Sir Thomas to the abbot's rooms.

The reeve looked at the two young people in front of him, eyes alight with hope.

"Very well," he said. "In truth, I cannot deny you the right to hear this sorry tale. Were it not for you, we might not have solved this riddle before the murderers had long since left our Liberty."

"Thank you, Master Durand," said Aileen meekly. She and Robert fell in behind Durand as he walked toward Abbot Samson's chambers.

"I think I mentioned to you, Father Abbot, that I had been sent to train as a knight in the household of Sir Gilbert," Sir Thomas Warren began.

The abbot's receiving room was large enough for most situations, but it seemed small when all those involved were settled within and the door was closed. Sir Gilbert was seated across from the abbot, in front of the fire. Stephen de Cley stood behind his chair, his hand resting almost protectively upon the back of it. Roger, guarded by one of Durand's men, was standing not far off, alternately glaring at his father and pleading with his eyes.

Durand sat at the table across from the marshal, while Aileen and Robert stood quietly in a corner where they would be little observed.

"Yes," Abbot Samson said. "You did tell me that your

family was close to that of the Earl of Surrey, just as is that of Sir Gilbert."

Sir Thomas laughed, though there was little humor in it. "Yes, we are very close," he said. "I grew up on the estates of the Lord de Warenne," he continued. "It was my belief that I was kin to him by way of one of his many cousins. Some there were who said that I was sired by the Earl himself."

The abbot's brows rose. "So this is why you carry a name that bears such a strong resemblance to that of the Earl of Surrey?"

"It was perhaps not the one my mother bore," said the knight. "Yet when I adopted the name of Warren, none in the Earl's household objected."

"Pray continue," said the abbot.

"I played with the sons of the Lord de Warenne," Sir Thomas said. "We took our lessons together, and we learned to fight and tussle just as do any siblings in any house." The knight's face darkened. "Then, one day, I was told that I would no longer remain in my place. The Earl had decided that we were too old to stay longer in the schoolroom and that it was time for his sons to be trained for knighthood."

"Is this not normal for the sons of great lords?" asked Robert, unable to contain himself any longer. Durand and the abbot frowned at him, and Aileen pinched his arm.

I had better remember I am here only on sufferance, he thought, subsiding into the shadow of the wall behind him.

"It is normal practice," said Sir Thomas. "But while the lord's sons were to be trained in royal households I had hoped that I might remain with the Earl and learn my craft there. After all, as one of his blood, there was still prefer-ment I might attain. It was my greatest desire to remain within the Earl's household so that he might see that I was worthy of the rewards that come with power and authority."

"Did you make request of him that you might stay?" asked the abbot.

"He would not hear me," said Sir Thomas bitterly. "He sent word that I was to leave the next day and ride to the estate of Sir Gilbert's father for my initiation as a squire there."

"It would not appear that the change in situation has harmed you in any way," said Abbot Samson. "You have risen far in the household in which you were placed. There are few more powerful than the marshal on any estate. You have command over the fighting men and are responsible for the safety of your lord."

"There is one more powerful than the marshal in any lord's household," said Sir Thomas.

"The steward," Durand said.

"Yes," said the marshal.

"You have never said anything to me that would indi-cate you were dissatisfied with your role in my household," said Sir Gilbert. "To rise to marshal is a great honor. Yet it was not enough for you?"

"Since I was a child I desired to serve the Earl of Surrey," said Sir Thomas. "I sent word when I was made marshal to let him know that I was a man worthy of further prefer-ment, but he sent back no word."

"It seems to me that you desired not to serve the Earl of Surrey," said Sir Gilbert, beginning to lose his patience with this tale. "It seems to me that your desire was for the power that close association with the Lord de Warenne could bring."

"Without power, you have nothing," snapped Sir Thomas. "Look at all that you can do, simply because you are a friend to a powerful man. As a marshal, I thought to receive more regard, but I was disappointed in that."

"Power in and of itself is nothing," said Sir Gilbert. "It is as I said to my son, a man must show himself to be a just and honorable man in order to receive the esteem of others."

"You can say that, but I do not believe it," the marshal said.

"Sir Thomas," Durand said. "We need you to continue with your account. How did the murder of Master Aylwin come about?"

"When the steward's father died, I had hoped that Sir Gilbert would make me steward," the marshal said.

Durand frowned, thinking that this was no answer to his question.

Sir Gilbert looked surprised. "I had not thought of that," he said. "You have always been far more suited to training and controlling fighting men than you are to farms and rents."

"Howsoever that may be," said Sir Thomas. "The Saxon was made steward. As the years went by, he grew in respect and love. Few complained of his treatment, and most did his bidding willingly."

He was jealous of the steward, thought Aileen.

"You were jealous," said the reeve. Aileen tried not to smile at the parallel their thoughts had taken.

"The steward was favored. I was not," said Sir Thomas.

Sir Gilbert opened his mouth to say something but thought better of it. There was little that could change the hardened heart of the man before him.

The marshal picked up his tale once again. "Thus it was for many years. The steward gained favor, but I was invisible, even though I served my lord faithfully."

Resentment burned deep within him, thought the abbot. It was that, I believe, that I sensed in him when we spoke. Yet there was something more.

"Sir Thomas, I would ask you something," Abbot Samson said.

"Father abbot, if I know it, I will answer," said Sir Thomas.

"When we spoke, you told me you had not taken the road of the pilgrims to Rome," said the abbot. "It did seem to me that you wanted to test my memories of that journey."

The marshal said nothing, but the tension in his body became marked.

"We talked of the camaraderie of those who walked the Chemin des Anglois," said Abbot Samson. "It was only after you left me that evening that I realized for certain why there was something in you that seemed familiar."

Sir Thomas sighed. "I did fear that my teasing your memory would be a mistake. Yet I had to know whether you would remember me at all."

"What is this?" asked Sir Gilbert. "Father Abbot, are you saying that you have met the marshal before?"

"I have," said the monk. "It was many years ago, but I

have been reminded several times within the last few days of an encounter I had when I made my pilgrimage to Rome."

Turning to the reeve, the abbot continued. "Master Durand, do you remember my telling you about the conversation I had with three others around the fire one cold night on that road?"

"Yes, father," said the reeve. "You mentioned the merchant and a Cistercian monk and, I think, one other."

"Yes," said Abbot Samson. "There was one other. A Norman knight who held his peace and spoke only when asked a direct question." As he spoke the abbot turned to look at the marshal. "That man was you, was it not, Sir Thomas?"

The marshal sighed. "Yes, I was that man," said Sir Thomas.

"Why did you not say so?" the abbot asked.

"Because I did not want you to make any connection between the merchant Brenier and myself," said the knight. "That is why I had to know if your memory be sufficient to identify a Norman knight on the road to Rome."

Durand was growing impatient. This man, this killer, is taking far too long to get to the point, he thought.

"You have still not explained how it came about that you ordered the murder of the steward in our town," Durand said firmly.

Sir Thomas looked at the reeve with scorn but continued with his tale.

"When Brenier arrived in England, I recognized him at once," said the knight. "He did not recognize me."

The marshal paused for a moment, his eyes looking inward as if to see that day when the idea of murder first formed in his mind. "I found that he had brought with him the sword that he swore was a sword of power, possibly even the sword of the Emperor Constantine."

Sir Thomas Warren's voice was filled with awe. "I desired that sword with a passion," he said. "In the years since you met me, Father Abbot, my resentment of the powerful lords around me has grown. Can you imagine the power that a man who wields the sword of Constantine could attain?" The marshal's voice rose, and his fist pumped the air in front of him.

Durand was not to be distracted from his purpose. "But still I do not see how that ambition should lead to the death of the steward."

"At first, I thought to wait for the right opportunity to take hold of the sword," Sir Thomas said. He turned his head slightly and looked at Roger de Cley. The young man gave a slight shake of his head, but the marshal smiled at him grimly.

"Were you not such a coward, I would have carried the day," he said. "But you are weak, like your father. You have not the mettle to fight and win. Now you will bear the cost of he who tries and fails. I doubt not you will make a sorry sight as they drag you to the gallows."

Roger cowed at the venom in the marshal's words. But desperate men will snatch at any chance. "Father," he said, "I beg of you not to listen to this man's lies. You can see the hatred in him. He will do anything to cause you grief, even deny you the love of your son."

Sir Gilbert looked at his son, his face expressing both hope and sorrow.

"I know we have often fought," said his son. "We are of

a like nature, and thus sometimes we do clash. Please, father, please know I would never do anything to harm you. This man lies!"

"'Of a like nature'," said Roger's father. "We clash because we are of such different natures. Yet my heart longs to believe your words."

A moment longer the father considered the son. Then, raising his hand in a gesture of resignation, he turned back to the marshal. "Continue your tale," he said grimly. "I cannot know whether my heart betrays me until I know all."

"Your heart has oft made of you a fool, but you shall hear all," he said. "My ambition is great, but that of your son is no less powerful. Impatience to wield power is a quality Roger and I share. I wished to own the sword to raise myself in the eyes of mighty lords. Your son was willing to cede to me the weapon in exchange for my help in slaying you so that he might inherit."

Aileen gasped, but none reproved her. Shock was written on the faces of those who heard the words of the disgraced knight.

Sir Thomas looked around the room with contempt, smiling.

"The plan was to waylay you when you rode out to visit your outlying estates," said the knight. "I knew there was a risk that Roger would not have the courage to kill you looking into your eyes as he plunged his dagger into your heart, so I arranged for Walter de Nantes and Edward Strode to do the deed."

The marshal could not complain of the reaction his narrative received. All those within the abbot's chambers were transfixed. The only sound was that of wood spitting as the fire burned low.

"It was not hard to persuade them, for they are greedy and simple-minded," Sir Thomas said. "A promise of preferment when Roger became the Lord de Cley and I became chief among the knights of the Lord de Warenne was all that it took.

"Then you decided to offer the mighty weapon at the shrine of St. Edmund," the marshal said. "At first, I was furious that our plans would have to be changed. Then you announced that you would be sending the Saxon to St. Edmundsbury with the sword. It was at that moment that I knew that at last all my humiliation and rejection had not been in vain."

The marshal's face shone with pride at his own cleverness. "In one glorious stroke, I could gain possession of the sword and rid myself of the troublesome steward. Truly, the plan was divinely inspired!"

He cannot be sane, thought Aileen. No man could claim foul murder to be of God. Why, last Sunday's sermon was on the fifth Commandment: Honour thy father and thy mother.

Sir Thomas was almost finished. "When your rider came to Sussex to tell us of the success of our plot," he continued, "I told Roger we would deal with his father upon our return from St. Edmundsbury. And so we would, had the boy not proven himself a weak-kneed coward and unworthy of the position he so ardently sought."

The marshal fell silent. Looking around the room, Aileen saw a stricken father whose younger son now laid his hand upon his father's shoulder. She saw Roger, white-faced and broken, who made no further outcry. She saw that Abbot Samson had his head bowed in prayer, but Durand stood solidly in front of the fallen marshal, face set in an expression of outrage.

Turning to Robert, she quietly took his hand in hers. Robert smiled at her and whispered, "Well done."

27. Chapter Twenty-Seven

And I will give peace in the land, and ye shall lie down, and none shall make you afraid; and I will rid evil beasts out of the land, neither shall the sword go through your land.

Leviticus 26:6

"So it really was about the dead man's sword," said Hugh.

Aileen and Robert sat beside Hugh at the river's edge. The sound of the water gently lapping at the bank beside them had provided a backdrop to the cruel tale Aileen and Robert had narrated to their young friend.

"I suppose you could say that," said Aileen. "From everything we have learned, the sword itself was not what all these men thought it to be, but it certainly was behind all their actions."

"I am glad it was not the sword of Constantine," said Robert.

Aileen was surprised at the intensity of her friend's voice. "Why are you glad?" she asked.

"The Emperor Constantine was a great man," said Robert. "He was a powerful warrior, and it was he who brought Christianity to Rome. I do not think he would like it if his sword influenced greedy and cowardly men to commit murder."

"That is well said," Aileen said. "I believe you are right."

"I believe so as well," said Hugh.

For a minute, the three sat still, each contemplating the history of the sword and the terrible events of the past week.

"I believe Master Aylwin led me to you," said Hugh. "He knew you could solve his murder and make things right."

Startled, Aileen and Robert looked at their friend.

"Hugh, that is a strange thing to say," Aileen said.

"Perhaps," said Hugh. "Yet I do not believe this riddle would ever have been solved had not you and Robert listened to me and offered to help."

"But why would you say the steward influenced you to ask for that help?" said Robert.

"From all that you have told me, it does seem that this man was a good and wise man," Hugh said. "Even in the few days that he spent in St. Edmundsbury, he struck all those with whom he spoke as being kind and generous. Why, practically the whole town attended his funeral. When was the last time that happened upon the death of a stranger?"

Hugh was right. Outsiders had died within the walls of

St. Edmundsbury in the past, but their funerals had not been attended by more than a few monks of the abbey.

Hugh was warming to his theory. "Even in death, Master Aylwin continued to give. Mad Meg was certain sure that he had gifted her his cloak, and who can say that she was wrong?"

Not quite sure what to say, Robert cleared his throat. Aileen smiled encouragingly at Hugh and said, "I know not how it came about, Hugh, but Robert and I are grateful that you would trust us enough to seek out our help."

"You are my friends," said Hugh simply. "I knew no others to whom I could turn."

This is getting a little uncomfortable, thought Robert. It is time to change the subject.

"Aileen is always very good at solving riddles," he said. "I remember a time when we were little and I forgot where I had left the basket of herbs my mother had told me to put inside the house."

Aileen was smiling at the memory, but Hugh was confused.

"How could you forget where you placed the basket?" he asked. "It is not as though your house is large."

"The basket never made it inside the house," said Robert. "I got distracted by the sight of a swarm of bees at the other end of the garden and put the basket down on the ground behind a barrel. It was not until my mother asked me about it that I remembered what it was I had been told to do."

"What happened?" said Hugh.

"Aileen came over while I was searching for the basket," Robert said. "She asked me to go through everything that had occurred, and then, when I had done so, she looked around the garden for a minute and then went straight to the barrel and picked up the basket."

"Truly?" Hugh was agog at the tale.

"Really, it was not that difficult," said Aileen. "As soon as Robert told me what had happened, it was clear to me that he had never taken the basket into the house. If that was the case, then the basket had to still be outside. I merely looked around and saw that there were few places it could be hidden from sight. The water barrel was the obvious place to look."

"However simple the explanation," said Robert, "it is still impressive."

"I agree," said Hugh. "And that is how you solved this riddle, is it not? You looked around and went straight to the solution."

Aileen laughed. "It was not that simple this time," she said. "I was not the only one seeking the solution to this riddle. I am sure Master Durand would have found the murderer in the end."

"Mayhap he would," said Robert. "But I think the culprits would have been long gone before he arrived at the solution. I am glad that he thanked you for your help, for without you, Sir Gilbert de Cley may have met a dreadful end, and two greedy and wicked men might have achieved their ambitions."

"That would have been terrible," said Aileen. "But you give me too much credit. It is only a question of being observant and fitting together a lot of different facts, rather like weaving together threads in a tapestry."

Robert and Hugh clearly thought Aileen was giving

herself too little credit but chose to drop the subject. Aileen was getting a little pink in the face, and they did not want to embarrass her further.

Robert thought of a question he could ask to break the silence that seemed to go on for a little too long. "Aileen," he said. "Right before you ran to tell Durand what you believed to have happened, you told me I had given you the key to the solution. What did you mean?"

"It was not really just one thing," said Aileen. "Of course you had provided us with the information about the brooch, and you were the one who helped Meg make plain her story. But, as we sat there talking about my questioning Walter de Nantes' role in the murder, we talked about friendship."

"Yes?" Robert questioned. "Go on."

"Well, it came to me that friendship can be a good thing, but also a bad thing. If you cling too tightly to friends who lead you astray, then it is bad. For Sir Walter de Nantes and Sir Edward Strode, while they were not exactly friends of Sir Thomas Warren, their arrogance and desire for wealth and power allowed them to be greatly influenced by him. I have to wonder if they would ever have committed such a great crime as murder had they not been so close to the marshal."

"That is a good point," said Robert. "Mayhap the same is true for Roger de Cley."

"That may be so," said Aileen. "We will never know."

Aileen smiled. "It has just occurred to me that this adventure began with our bond of friendship," she said, looking at the other two. "It would seem that it has ended in the same way."

"I never thought of it that way," said Robert. "But you are right. It seems somehow fitting that it be so."

Once again, the trio sat still and quiet, but this time it was Hugh who broke the silence. "So the rag and bone man had nothing to do with the murder?" he asked.

"No," said Aileen. "His behavior seemed suspicious, but his reputation may have led to us making it seem more significant than it actually was. In the end, though, we were able to set aside the false threads and come up with the right solution."

Hugh picked up a blade of grass and rubbed it between his fingers. "One blade of grass is so insignificant," he said. "Yet when you put thousands of blades of grass together, they form something that is so strong and yet sweet-smelling."

"That is true," said Aileen. "Well observed, Hugh."

The three of them laughed. But Robert's face turned serious almost immediately. "Men, great and small, may take please in the smallest things," he said. "Grass, church bells, peace, good ale."

Aileen smiled at Robert's list but said nothing.

"But the actions of these same men may impact the daily lives of thousands of men," Robert went on. "Those actions may even affect history going forward and for all time."

"I see what you mean," said Aileen. "The Emperor Constantine was a great emperor. His exploits have given rise to many tales. The legend about his sword cost a good man his life hundreds of years after he himself was placed in the tomb."

With this sobering thought, a moment of quiet lay

between the trio. Then, sighing, Robert stood up and gave his hand to Aileen to help her rise. The three young people said their farewells and set out for their homes, each considering what had taken place in their town and what it might mean for the future.

Also by Anne-Marie Amiel

The St. Edmundsbury Mysteries Series

Crusaders Way (Book 1)

Penitent's Sword (Book 2)

Bishop's Pride (Winter 2022)

Coming Soon

Road Trip Trivia: High Middle Ages

About the Author

Anne-Marie Amiel joined the Royal Navy straight from high school, after which she attended law school. In addition to her career in England she has worked in France and as an attorney in several U.S. States.

In the course of her career Ms. Amiel has won short story competitions, been featured in several legal publications and has written for *Cobblestone* magazine and *Devotions for the Public Servant.* In her spare time, Ms. Amiel writes music and practices martial arts. Just like any self-respecting English woman, she also loves to drink hot tea and knit!